WAITING FOR SUNRISE

BAYTOWN BOYS SERIES

MARYANN JORDAN

Cover Design by: Graphics by Stacy

Cover and model photography: Eric McKinney

ISBN ebook: 978-1-947214-22-4

ISBN print: 978-1-947214-23-1

❀ Created with Vellum

AUTHOR INFORMATION

USA TODAY BESTSELLING AND AWARD WINNING AUTHOR

I am an avid reader of romance novels, often joking that I cut my teeth on the historical romances. I have been reading and reviewing for years. In 2013, I finally gave into the characters in my head, screaming for their story to be told. From these musings, my first novel, Emma's Home, The Fairfield Series was born.

I was a high school counselor having worked in education for thirty years. I live in Virginia, having also lived in four states and two foreign countries. I have been married to a wonderfully patient man for thirty-seven years. When writing, my dog or one of my four cats can generally be found in the same room if not on my lap.

Please take the time to leave a review of this book.

Feel free to contact me, especially if you enjoyed my book. I love to hear from readers!

Facebook

Email

Website

When I was counseling in a high school, I had a young woman whose story was similar to the one in this novel. It broke my heart and I was determined to do what I could to assist. I am pleased to say that for my student, like the young Brittany in this book, there was a happy ending. So, for all the young people who need to know that it is okay to dream, this is for you.

Head down, eyes scanning the nursing notes in her hand, Belle Gunn rushed around a corner in Careway Nursing Home where she worked. Her body slammed into something hard and she screamed, her arms flung wide, windmilling in an attempt to keep her balance. Unsuccessful, she flailed to the side, hitting her head against the wall. Landing awkwardly, the brunt of her fall was taken on her left wrist, causing a sharp pain. Shattered glass fell in a shower, covering the tile all around her.

"Aughh, shit," she cried out, lying awkwardly on the floor, shock reverberating through her.

"Fuck!" a deep voice sounded from above.

Lights flickered behind her tightly squeezed eyes. Pain radiated from her hand up to her shoulder and her forehead felt as though she had been hit with a hammer. Unable to process what had happened, she instinctively used her other hand to push herself upward.

The clattering of heavy boots on metal, followed by

the sound of crunching glass, met her ears. "Don't move!"

She did not need to open her eyes to see who bellowed the order. Him. *Oh, no. I can't believe it's him.*

One Month Earlier

Belle tossed back the covers and climbed from her bed. Grabbing a light blue robe from the bedpost, she wrapped it around her and tied it at the waist. Walking over to the window, her bare toes digging into the soft carpet, she pulled open the blinds and settled on the strategically placed padded bench. She had found the bench at a yard sale, seeing the possibilities in the sturdy but worn piece of furniture. Sanding, then staining, she brought out the beauty of the wood, finally topping it with a thick, green cushion bought at a second-hand store. It fit perfectly under the east-facing window in her bedroom.

Leaning back against the yellow toss pillow placed next to the wall, she yawned as she stretched her arms above her head. Twisting, she placed her elbows on the narrow windowsill and stared out into the dark.

Within a few minutes, the sky began to turn a lighter blue over the trees. She watched as the sky morphed from night to daylight, the sunrise kissing the day. Her view was not the best so, sometimes, on a day off from work, she would get in her old car and drive to the coast to watch the sun rise over the ocean. But, for most days, watching the dawn from her little house in the mobile home park had to suffice.

"Another day started, Grandma," she whispered, lifting her eyes to the heavens as a slight smile curved her lips.

Standing, she stretched again before walking over to make the bed. The dark green comforter with little yellow flowers was tugged over the sheets and she fluffed the yellow toss pillows before placing them at the headboard.

Looking at the clock on the nightstand, she knew she needed to hurry if she wanted to have time to study before leaving for the party. Heading into the bathroom, she showered, pulled her hair back with a ribbon, and with only a tinted moisturizer, a swipe of mascara, and lips gloss, she was ready for her day.

Several minutes later, with a cup of coffee and bowl of oatmeal, she settled at the table, her nursing books and notes spread out before her.

She had been working for years at Careway Nursing Home, a place she absolutely loved to be, first, as a teen volunteer, and then, once earning her CNA, as a nursing assistant. Working full time, she attended the Eastern Shore Community College at night, and had already earned her Associates Degree with an LPN. Continuing her studies, both online and at the Community College, she was close to earning her RN.

Dream...then work as hard as you can to make that

dream come true. The words from her grandmother came back to her as a smile slid across her lips.

She had friends in Baytown, but as her studies increased—on top of her work—her chance to socialize decreased. Glad that there was a beach party to attend today, she was looking forward to the chance to be with all her friends again.

Taking another bite of oatmeal, she looked back down at her notes. *This...this is leading to my dream.* From the first moment she had stepped foot in Careway and had watched the nurses as they went about their duties, she had decided that was her goal. And each step led to wanting more, so, the studying continued.

Steady work, steady school. Not overly exciting, but steady.

Recently, someone had encroached upon her simple life, throwing her focus off kilter, and he did not even know her name. She knew his though...Hunter Simmons. He was the newcomer to town and, getting a job with the nursing home as a handyman, meant she saw him every day.

The first day she had seen him at work, her feet had stumbled as she walked down the hall. He was bending over, repainting the baseboards along the main hall where the walkers and wheelchairs often bumped and scuffed the paint. Unable to see his face at first, she noted his dark hair, closely cropped on the sides and the long hair on top pulled back in a ponytail. His upper body muscles strained against the navy blue T-shirt he wore, the edge of a tattoo peeking from the sleeve.

Nearing him, she was unable to drag her eyes away

4

as he stood to his full height. He towered over her as he stretched his back, moving his head from side to side to remove the kinks. His jaw was square and, with his eyes closed, she took the opportunity to drop her eyes lower, observing his trim waist and thick thighs encased in the blue jeans he was allowed to wear.

As though they had a will of their own, her feet moved slower and her eyes dragged back up his body, landing on his face. Scruffy beard. Firm jaw. And piercing, blue eyes. Eyes that were staring back at her.

A slight gasp escaped her and she staggered for a step before righting herself, hurrying on down the hall. Feeling foolish, she felt the burn of his stare on her back. She darted into one of the rooms, quickly ducking out of his sight.

It did not take long to hear the gossip about the new hire. No one knew much about him, but the other nurses and aides, regardless of their age, smiled and winked as they passed him in the hall. At least, all the single ones did... *hell, half the married ones did as well.*

For Belle, he may have made her heart race and her feet trip, but she knew he would never be interested in her. And, she reminded herself that her life goal had no room for a distraction. Especially a tall, muscular, handsome, blue-eyed, mysterious man.

For a month, she had ducked out of his way, passing him in the hall with nothing more than a polite nod in his direction, and had managed to skirt around him whenever possible. Of course, considering they had the same group of friends since he came to Baytown, it made avoiding him more difficult. But, usually, he immersed himself in conversations with the guys, giving her the opportunity to stare at him from a distance.

Looking back at her watch, she closed her books and took her long-finished oatmeal bowl to the sink. Running back into the bedroom, she slid out of her robe and into a floral sundress. She smiled, twirling in front of the mirror, loving the way the material swished around her thighs. Sucking in her stomach slightly, she knew the day would be full of good food, as well as good friends. *Oh, well, I'll eat light tomorrow.*

Belle walked through the tiny kitchen of the beach house belonging to Mitch and Tori Evans, two of her close friends. The old fishing cabin had been willed to Mitch by his grandfather and, now, it hosted many gatherings near the Chesapeake Bay. Mitch, the Police Chief, and Tori, owner of The Sea Glass Inn, were outside near the grill.

Darting into the bathroom, she washed her hands at the small sink, hearing the party in full swing through the tiny, open window. The blinds moved slightly with the breeze and her ears perked up as she heard a man call out. Leaning closer, she peeked through the blinds, ignoring the little voice in her head reminding her that eavesdropping was rude.

"Glad you could make it, man!" Zac Hamilton called.

She watched as Hunter walked over to Zac, nodding his thanks as he accepted the proffered beer in Zac's hand. Looking around the crowd of people milling about, he took a long swig before turning back to Zac.

Zac grinned, clapping him on the shoulder and said, "Just take a load off and enjoy the sunshine, Hunter. Baytown Boys don't bite...or force conversation."

Chuckling, Hunter grinned. As she continued to peek through the blinds she was struck by the sheer beauty of his rare smile.

She knew he and Zac had become friends in the Navy, both assigned to the same ship. They appeared to be opposite in personalities though—Zac never met a stranger he could not call a friend, while Hunter rarely spoke. She also knew Hunter had been born in Tennessee but she never heard anyone mention his family. He walked to the side of the deck and she leaned forward, keeping him in her sight as he spoke.

"Still can't get used to hearing the words Baytown Boys. I expect to see a little league logo on the back of your shirts."

Zac threw his head back in laughter. "You wouldn't be too far wrong with that. The title was given to us when we were kids and always played together. Once we hit middle school and played ball, it stuck all the way through graduation."

Nodding, he took another swig of beer. Indicating the group with a swirl of the bottle in his hand, he asked, "All y'all join up?"

"Yeah," Zac said. "Mitch and Grant joined the Army and met Lance when they were with the military police. Brogan and Aiden joined the Marines. Callan is still in the Coast Guard, now stationed here. Gareth came later...he was in the Air Force. Ginny moved here a couple of years ago...she was also Army MP. You know Jason, of course."

Hearing a noise, Belle observed Madelyn, Zac's wife, walk up to them, her arm slipping around Zac's waist as she smiled her greeting to Hunter. He nodded in return and then moved further down the deck, out of her sight.

Just then, a knock on the bathroom door jolted her, and she realized how long she had been in the room. It was the only toilet in the cabin and she threw open the door and breezed out, smiling at Katelyn as though she had only been in there a moment. Feeling her face heat with blush, she hurried through the kitchen, chastising herself for eavesdropping. *What the hell is wrong with me?* Standing at the door leading outside, she sucked in a fortifying breath and walked outside.

───

Hunter had listened carefully to Zac reciting the residents' military service, causing him to think back on their own unlikely friendship as he headed towards the grill, giving Zac and Madelyn a moment of privacy. Zac, always smiling, had taken to his taciturn personality and the two clicked. How? He could never figure that out, but he was glad for Zac's friendship. He and Jason made a little more sense, since they were both mechanics.

"Hunter," Mitch called out. "Good to see you."

He watched as Mitch expertly flipped the hamburgers, while also keeping an eye on his wife, Tori, holding their baby son, and carrying on a conversation with his co-workers. Grant Wilder, Lance Greene, and Ginny MacFarlane, three other police officers for Baytown, stood with him, drinking beer and shooting the shit as their boss manned the grill.

Hearing a cheer from the beach, his gaze drifted over, seeing Brogan and Aiden MacFarlane with a group playing beach volleyball. Several women played as well or lounged against the log seats around a fire pit. He recognized some of their wives, Jillian Wilder and Tori Evans, who was bouncing her son on her lap. Katelyn and Gareth Harrison walked out onto the deck, she carrying napkins and utensils while his hands were full of platters to set on the groaning picnic table.

"You settled in yet?" Grant asked, drawing his attention back to the people at the grill.

Nodding, he replied, "Yep. Got my camper. It's all I need right now."

"You at a campground?" Lance asked. "I've got a little piece of land, beachfront, south of town, and you're more than welcome to park it there."

"Brogan and I also have room on our land," Ginny offered, smiling at him. "We're building a house, but still have room for your camper if you want." Her dark brown hair, usually pulled back in a regulation bun, was hanging around her shoulders and, he had to admit, the look was striking with her all-American vibe. Finding out she had been military police in Afghanistan only added to her allure and he knew her husband, Brogan, a former Marine, knew just how lucky he was.

"Thanks, but I'm good. Right now, the manager of

the mobile home park has let me have a small plot. I got electricity and water, so it's all good." He did not mention that it also happened to be down the street from the woman he secretly stared at every chance he got.

"Don't forget the American Legion meeting next week," Grant reminded. "It'll be the first one since you moved here."

He had left the Navy before Zac was discharged, but his own small town in the rural hills of Tennessee had not been a good place to return to. Few jobs. Everyone expecting him to go off on a bender—get drunk and start a fight like his old man. A loner, he still felt constrained so, after only a couple of weeks, he moved to Norfolk, where he had last been stationed with the Navy. At least there, he could start something new. And one job led to a career change he had not been expecting.

Zac had emailed numerous times once he, too, was discharged, eventually telling him about Baytown and the American Legion that he and his buddies had formed, but with a new job, the timing was not right. It took another year before he finally decided to take Zac up on his offer. Once in Baytown, he was glad he had made the move. *But, for how long?* He wondered if he was just a wanderer or would ever feel like settling down.

He listened quietly as the others talked about the upcoming American Legion meeting, impressed that Baytown had opened their arms wide for the veterans that came back and also welcomed so many newcomers.

His mind on the upcoming meeting, he had not realized uncertainty showed on his face until Ginny leaned
over and placed her hand on his arm.

"It'll be good, I promise. A chance to meet more
people, but no one gets in your face."

He was not sure he believed her, but he nodded
silently nonetheless. The game on the beach ended and
Brogan headed straight to Ginny, tucking her into his
embrace. As the gathering closed in on the food table,
he stepped off the porch and walked slightly to the side,
giving the others a chance to get to the food and giving
himself a chance to enjoy the view without so many
people around.

His eyes scanned the beach by the bay and he took
another swig, letting the warm sunshine ease the
tension from his shoulders.

A dark-haired woman walked toward the shore, a
pastel floral sundress swinging about her hips, modestly
hanging to just above her knees. Her sandals were
dangling in her hand and as she turned slightly to the
side, her generous breasts were showcased in a tight,
but also modest, bodice. Keeping his eyes toward the
water, he followed her progress in his peripheral vision.
Isabelle Gunn...*Belle.* The bottle halted on its way to his
lips as he sucked in a breath. Long, sleek hair that hung
down her back, with a light blue ribbon holding it away
from her face. A cross between an old-fashioned pinup
model and an innocent girl, his breath caught in his
throat before he let it out in a long, slow hiss. He did not
have a specific type of woman, but Belle...well, her
curves captured—and held—his attention.

Heart pounding a steady beat, he continued to observe her as she walked to the shore, barely sticking her toes into the water. Alone, she stared out over the bay, the breeze tossing her hair. *Fuckin' hell.* He not only had to endure seeing her as he integrated into Baytown, but also every day at work and in the mobile home park where he lived. It was agony...*pure, fuckin' agony to keep his distance.*

2

PRESENT DAY

The knock on the door in the early morning had Belle rushing to answer it. She was not surprised to see the young, teenage girl standing on her front stoop. Her gaze took in the thin girl, her dark blonde hair pulled back into a ponytail, her makeup-free face smiling up at her. She wore a pair of slightly large, worn jeans and a T-shirt. Typical for a teenager, but they were old and ill fitting.

She noted her pale complexion as she greeted, "Brittany, come on in. I'm still getting ready for work, but you can have some oatmeal or cereal if you like."

She had no idea where Brittany's dad was, but her mom, Trudy, was not a great influence. Their mobile home was toward the back of the park, in the section that was not well maintained.

She often wondered why the park was divided into two sections. The homes near the front were well maintained and the owner had more stringent rules and regulations for keeping the small lots beautiful. The few streets near the back of the park looked very much like the entire place had when she was growing up—trash cans overflowing, homes with paint peeling, late night parties.

Brittany had been coming by ever since she was a child and had seen Belle in her yard planting flowers.

"Whatcha doin'?"

I looked over my shoulder to see a young girl, her dress two sizes too big and no shoes on her dirty feet. Her hair needed combing and her knees were skinned, but it was her eyes that captured my attention. Bright blue.

Standing, I wiped my hands on my apron and said, "I'm planting flowers."

"How come?"

Chuckling, I said, "Because they're pretty and I like pretty things."

The girl said nothing but scrunched her face in thought.

"Do you want to help?" I was sure the child would scamper away but, instead, she darted next to me, a grin on her face and nodded.

We planted flowers along the front of my home for a few minutes. She watched what I did and, a quick learner, soon was planting without any instructions.

"How old are you?" I asked, assuming her to be about five.

"I'm eight," came the reply.

"Oh," I mumbled but she must have anticipated my thoughts when she wiped her cheek with a dirty hand and told

me that she was little for her age. I noted her thin arms and legs. She did not talk much, but I found out that she lived with her mom in one of the run-down trailers. As we finished, I invited her in and she readily accepted.

Stepping into my house, she stared, wide-eyed, as though in a castle. Taking her into the bathroom to wash her hands, I managed to wash her face and legs as well. She even let me put antiseptic cream on her skinned knees.

With her clean face, I grinned and said, "I knew there was a beauty underneath that dirt."

Her eyes held mine and she said, "Ain't no one ever called me a beauty before."

"Well, I told you I like pretty things and you are certainly pretty." I watched her face break into a smile and offered her a hug.

As we walked into the kitchen, I made sandwiches and served her. Watching her eat, I realized how hungry she was when she put away two of them, plus chips and apple slices, two glasses of milk, and four cookies.

Grinning, she looked up at me with those blue eyes and said, "Can I come back sometime?"

"Of course, if your mom says it's okay."

Her face scrunched again, and she shook her head. "She won't care...she never cares where I am."

As much as it broke my heart to hear her words, they resonated with me in a deep place that I rarely let anyone see. Sucking in a shuttering breath, I smiled and said, "Then come anytime."

.   .   .

Brittany did not come by every morning before school, but Belle knew that she would be there when the young girl wanted to get away from her house.

A few minutes later, Belle walked back into the kitchen, wearing light pink scrubs, and smiled, seeing Brittany shoveling down a microwaved bowl of oatmeal with cinnamon sugar sprinkled on top.

"Are you doing okay, sweetie?"

Brittany smiled up at her, and nodded. "Mama wasn't up yet...she kinda had a late night. We didn't have anything for breakfast, so I figured I'd stop by your place on the way to school."

She was not surprised that Brittany's mom was not up yet, considering it was only seven a.m. Her mother seemed to have a constant parade of company that liked to party late and Brittany had confessed how much she hated that. Setting those thoughts aside, she patted her shoulder as she walked by. "Well, you know you're welcome anytime."

"You gonna to be at the next game?"

Brittany was one of the children and teens playing on the sports teams the American Legion sponsored and organized. For many of the children in the area, whose parents were unable to afford the cost of uniforms, equipment and fees, the AL sports program was a godsend. "Of course I'll be there," she replied.

Brittany finished her oatmeal, taking her bowl and spoon to the sink to wash them out. A shy glance shot over her shoulder, she remarked, "You been studying more? It's like you study all the time."

Glancing at the open textbooks on the table, she

nodded, "Gotta work hard to get where you want to go." Cocking her head to the side, she asked, "How's school going for you?"

Lifting her thin shoulders, Brittany replied, "I get all A's."

"I'm not surprised, as smart as you are."

"There's not much else to do but study," she said. "I stay at school extra to study in the library 'cause it's quiet."

She nodded, understanding, since she had spent a lot of her study time in the same library as a teen.

Brittany suddenly changed the subject, commenting, "Seems like all your friends are hooking up."

"What?" Surprised at the unexpected turn, she tilted her head.

Shrugging, Brittany said, "I see 'em after the games. All your friends...you know, like Miss Ginny is with Mr. Brogan, Miss Jillian is with Mr. Wilder, Miss Tori is with Chief Evans, and Miss Jade is with Mr. Green. Even Chief Hamilton is with that new lady, Miss Maddie."

Narrowing her eyes playfully, she placed her hand on her hip and asked, "And your point would be?"

"Nothin'. I just kinda thought maybe it was your turn." Brittany dropped her eyes and sighed. "You're awful nice and real pretty. I know some of the single men in town would be a good catch. I just thought you might be looking to get hooked up with someone."

A flippant reply died on her lips as she stared intently at the young teen in front of her. Too thin, because her mom did not always have enough food in

17

the house. Too tired, because her mom often had parties late into the night. Starved for attention because her mother gave her little. And, as she continued to stare, she saw something else in Brittany's countenance...fear.

Walking the few steps over to her, she placed her hands on Brittany's shoulders, drawing her gaze back up to her eyes. "Yes, one day I'd love to find someone that I can have a relationship with. And, yes, one day I'd love to get married. But, so far I haven' t found anyone special that I want to spend my life with."

Brittany sighed and Belle added, "I promise, when that happens, I won't forget about you. We can have breakfast any time."

Brittany's face transformed into one of young beauty as she smiled widely, radiating relief.

Offering her a quick hug, she said, "Grab your backpack and I'll drop you off at the bus stop."

Belle was standing next to the driver's door as Brittany climbed into her old car, when the roar of a motorcycle engine grabbed her attention. Twisting her head to follow its path, she watched as the driver headed down the road. Sucking in a quick breath, she bit her lip as her eyes traced the brawny man, his thick thighs hugging the powerful engine underneath him as he leaned to the side, turning out of the mobile home park and onto the main road.

Thinking about the party this past weekend, that had her scoping him out from the bathroom window, she sighed. She saw him all the time since they worked in the same building and her heartbeat raced every time their paths crossed. But, other than a barely-there nod sent her way, he appeared to not know she was alive.

Giving her head a quick shake, she pulled herself from her musings. Stopping at the bus stop, she called out, "Have a good day, Brittany," as the young woman alighted from her car with a little wave. Driving away, she looked into the rearview mirror and noticed Brittany hung back slightly from some of the other, tougher-looking teenagers waiting for the bus, and had a flashback to herself years ago.

Hours later, her white, rubber-soled shoes padded softly down the hall as she hurried along. *Only fifteen more minutes.* Feeling the effects of studying late last night and finishing a full shift, she had glanced at the clock on the wall and sighed. Running through the list of what she needed to remember for the upcoming test, she hoped she could leave on time. One more night of heavy studying and she was sure she would ace her class.

"Isabelle!"

Skidding to a stop, she backtracked two steps, peering into one of the rooms. "Mr. Rasky? What can I do for you?"

"Is it time for dinner yet?"

Walking into his room, she smiled at the white-haired, wizened man whose bright blue eyes were staring up at her from his wheelchair. "Well, now that you mention it, I do believe it is almost time. Would you like some help?"

"Hell, no, Missy. I just can't read the clock on the TV anymore but my stomach is growling."

"Then, let's take care of that growling stomach," she said cheerily, side-stepping out of his way as he wheeled erratically out of his room. Walking next to him, she escorted him into the dining room, smiling and calling out greetings to the other patients along the way.

Once she had him settled, she hurried back into the hall. She had a few more tasks to cross off her list for the day before she could leave. With the residents mostly in the dining hall, she picked up her pace, knowing the path was clear of walkers and wheelchairs.

Pulling a small notebook from her pocket, she looked down at the notes she had taken while studying last night. The test was still two days away, but she believed in being as prepared as possible.

Suddenly slamming into a hard object, she screamed briefly before quickly finding herself on the floor, sprawled out and in pain amongst broken glass.

"Auggh, shit." Not one to typically curse in public, this occasion warranted the slip.

"Fuck."

She cringed. *Oh, no. Of course Hunter would witness this.*

Gaining her bearings, she peeked open her eyes and found Hunter staring at her. *Maybe if I lie here long enough, he'll just disappear.*

Hunter stared down, horrified at the scene below him. Changing the long, thin, fluorescent light fixtures in the back hallway, he had been standing on the stepladder close to the wall. With the residents at dinner, he had determined it would be a good time and a quiet place to get the job completed. Never hearing anyone approach, he had been shocked when the ladder suddenly jolted violently underneath him, causing the light to fly from his hand, shattering to the floor.

Hearing a yelp of surprise before it turned into a cry of pain, he grabbed the ladder, forcing it to steady. Twisting his body, he looked down, seeing the crumpled form of the woman he had been surreptitiously staring at for two months.

Belle. As beautiful as her name indicated, his eyes always found her no matter where she was. She was not particularly short, but at six feet, three inches, he towered over her. It was hard not to stare when she approached him in the hall, her nursing scrubs pulled slightly over her full breasts. Watching her walk away had been equally pleasurable, as her hips swayed underneath the light cotton material.

Whenever he had chanced a look at her face, he found himself turning away, her beauty impressed on his mind. Lustrous, thick, shiny dark hair, always pulled back away from her face, either in a ponytail or a bun when she was at work. And the ever-present ribbon. Usually the color matching her scrubs, or sundress, the strip of cloth gave her an innocent air that caused his heart to beat harder every time he saw her.

Her face, highlighted with the lightest makeup, fresh and unblemished. A smattering of freckles crossed her cheeks, causing his fingers to twitch, wanting to trace

21

each one. Her eyes, deep brown, would meet his before jerking away as she hurried along.

When they were at the same gatherings, he noticed she did not lack for male attention, but from all appearances, she did not date anyone. When their eyes met there, too, she blushed and looked away. He did not blame her for hustling by, knowing his rough looks were more suited to a biker bar, but had often wished for a chance to talk to her.

He had driven by her house in the mobile home park and it always made his day when she was outside working in her little postage-stamp yard or talking with a neighbor.

He had watched her with the patients as she cared for them, her soft voice and quiet manner soothing even the grumpiest ones. Unlike some of the other nurses and aides, she eschewed the employee lounge that was often filled with gossip or complaints. More than once, he saw her eating on the patio, often with a textbook open in her lap and a pen furiously scribbling what he assumed were notes.

As his feet came unstuck, he clambered down the ladder, his heavy boots crunching the broken glass on the floor next to her. Seeing her attempt to push up to a sitting position, he yelled, "Don't move!"

She twisted her head upward, her pain-filled eyes meeting his and her mouth opening slightly. Uncertain of her injuries, he knelt down placing one arm under her knees and the other one under her arms. Standing, he lifted her and carried her away from the glass.

Belle, stunned to find herself in Hunter's arms, yelped again as she threw her good arm around his neck.

"It's okay. I've got you."

His deep voice soothed over her but, unable to relax, she stiffened in his embrace. As soon as he moved her past the broken glass, he knelt again, setting her gently onto the floor. He grimaced as she winced in pain. "I'm so sorry. So fuckin' sorry, Belle."

Even in her pain, she was surprised he knew her name, having only ever greeted her with "Ms. Gunn."

"No, no. I wasn't looking where I was going. It's all my fault." Even as tears threatened to fall, she glanced down the hall at the shattered glass light fixture. "Please, I'm fine, we need to get the glass cleaned up before anyone gets hurt."

"Don't worry about it. I'll take care of it. All the residents are at dinner, so we need to check you out first."

"Oh, my goodness! What happened?" The owner of Careway, Tobias Weldon, came rushing down the hall, skidding to a stop right behind Hunter. His salt and pepper hair was neatly brushed back and his ever-present suit, spotless and pressed. He made everything about Careway his business, desiring to operate the finest nursing home in the area. His care and dedication to the residents, as well as the staff, were evident.

"I'm fine. I'm fine," she insisted, still sitting on the floor cradling her injured wrist.

"No, she's not," Hunter interrupted, lifting his hand to gently touch the rising lump on her forehead.

"Oh, dear!" Tobias exclaimed, his hands worrying together. "We must get you to a doctor."

"I'm sure it's just a sprain," she rushed, her mind filled with all that she needed to get done. Desperate for another night of studying, the idea of spending hours in an ER made her head hurt even more.

Hunter opened his mouth to contest her refusal, but Tobias jumped in first.

"Isabelle, no, no. I'm afraid it's policy. You have to be seen by a doctor, so that he can sign off on any workmen's compensation that might be needed. I'm afraid you have no choice."

She closed her eyes, battling nausea from the pain, and dropped her chin to her chest. Sighing heavily, she simply nodded.

Rusty, one of the other maintenance men, turned the corner and as his eyes landed on the mess, he volunteered, "I'll get the glass cleaned up."

Tobias agreed and, turning his attention back to her, said, "I need to get someone to take you to the—"

"I'll take her," Hunter interrupted.

Her eyes shot open and she looked up, first at Mr. Weldon and then down to Hunter. "But—"

Tobias was already nodding enthusiastically, looking down at Hunter. "Wonderful, wonderful. Mr. Simmons, you can take her to the ER."

She protested. "But you drive a motorcycle and I'm sure I can drive myself—"

"I'll take the maintenance truck. Don't worry...I've got you," Hunter repeated. Placing his hands under her arms, he stood, assisting her to her feet. "Can you walk?"

"Of course I can walk," she snapped, the pain overwhelming her good manners. Immediately contrite at the tone in her voice, she watched Hunter's eyes rove over her. Unable to discern his thoughts, she turned to walk down the hall, still cradling her wrist. Battling tears, she forced a smile on her face as several other nurses and aides came toward her, all clucking their concern. Assuring them that she was fine, she moved through them with Hunter's large presence parting the crowd.

"I'll bring the truck around," his voice rumbled. "Give me just a moment, and I'll meet you out front."

She felt a tingle as Hunter's fingers landed lightly on her shoulder before he moved down the hall.

A few minutes later, she stood at the front of the nursing home, her purse slung over her shoulder. The huge pickup truck, with the nursing home logo painted onto the side, pulled to a stop right next to her. Before she had a chance to fumble with the door, Hunter met her at the passenger side. After he opened it, she looked up, wondering how she would ever climb into the seat with her injured arm.

Before she could ask for help, he scooped her up once more, placing her gently into the seat. He leaned over to secure her buckle, his face inches from hers. Her breath caught in her throat as desire pooled in her core. The intense desire to kiss him was broken when he accidentally bumped her wrist, and she winced.

"Fuck!" he cursed, breaking the momentary spell.

Apologizing again, he closed her door before stomping around to the driver side.

The truck rumbled to life again and she leaned her head back against the headrest as he headed down the highway toward the hospital. Sighing, at both her clumsy accident and her ruined plans for her night of study, she glanced sideways at his hard, set jaw. *Great, just great. The man of my dreams just fell into my nightmare.*

3

Hunter scrubbed his hand over his face before sliding his fingers around to the back of his neck, kneading the tense muscles. Still unable to believe his placement of the ladder had caused an injury, he sighed, inwardly kicking himself. Knowing he would have felt this way no matter who had been injured, the fact that it was the woman he had obsessed over for months made it even worse.

He sat up straighter on the hard, plastic chair in the ER waiting room, his gaze pinned to the door through which Belle had been taken, as though staring at it would make someone come through with news about her.

Watching as the clock on the wall ticked another hour by, he startled when the receptionist called his name. Jumping up, he stalked over to the window, peering down at her sitting at the desk.

"You can go back now to see your girlfriend. She's

finished in x-ray and the doctor has been in to see her. She'll be ready to be discharged soon."

Nodding his thanks, he pushed past the door she had buzzed open for him. Not feeling guilty about identifying himself as Belle's boyfriend, he knew it was the only way he would be able to get information. Hating that she was back there by herself, he wanted to make sure he knew what she needed when they left the hospital.

Walking down the hall, he headed to the ER bay the receptionist had indicated. A nurse walked out of Belle's room and, catching sight of him, turned and called back into the room, "Your boyfriend is coming." He felt the heat of blush creep up his face as he entered her room, seeing the quizzical look upon her face.

Sitting on the edge of the bed, her wrist was wrapped and lying in her lap. She stared at him as he made his way over to the bed. Aware of the smallness of the room, he tried to figure out where to stand so that his large body did not bump into anything important. He decided to ignore the *boyfriend* issue, and asked, "How are you?"

Belle blinked slowly, the pain medicine causing her thoughts to feel jumbled in her head. Deciding that she must have misunderstood the nurse, she replied, "I'm okay. No broken bones, just a severely sprained wrist. My head hurts where I ran into the ladder, but no concussion."

"They give you something for pain?"

Nodding, she said, "Yeah. They gave me something

that makes me kind of woozy, and a prescription for more."

"We'll stop by the pharmacy when I take you home."

"No way, I'm loopy enough as it is," she claimed. "I've got work to do tonight and can't afford to not be able to concentrate." She slid off the edge of the bed, staggering as her feet touched the floor.

Hunter reached out and grabbed her, pulling her body close to his as he steadied her. He watched as she gave her head a little shake, blinking, in an attempt to clear her vision. Just as he was about to suggest he carry her out, the nurse walked back into the room pushing a wheelchair.

Grinning at the pair standing in a clinch, the nurse said, "I almost hate to insist you use the wheelchair with that handsome boyfriend of yours willing to hold you in his arms."

Opening her mouth to protest, Belle did not get a word out before he assisted her into the chair. Walking along as the nurse wheeled her down the hall, he said, "I'll bring the truck around."

Watching him walk away, Belle could not help but admire Hunter's body once more. Wondering how she managed to get herself into this situation, she slowly shook her head.

"Your boyfriend is gorgeous," the nurse said, grinning widely. "And, the whole time we had you back here, he kept asking the receptionist what was happening and how you were."

Shifting her gaze up to the nurse, she remained

quiet, her muddled mind having difficulty processing all the events of the past few hours.

The drive back to her house took almost forty minutes, most of which was spent in silence. Normally shy, she felt completely tongue-tied in Hunter's presence and knew it had nothing to do with the pain medication.

"Can't believe the hospital isn't closer," he grumbled.

She winced, assuming he hated the time it was taking to get her home. "I'm sorry. I could have called a friend—"

His head jerked to the side, his brows lowering as he pierced her with his gaze. "You got nothin' to be sorry for. I just hated that it took so long to get you from the nursing home to the hospital."

"Oh." Silence filled the truck cab again and she fiddled with the brace on her wrist. Trying to think of something to say, she finally settled on the topic he brought up. "North Heron County used to have the hospital closer to Baytown. You could get there in about twenty minutes."

With his brow still lowered, he asked, "They moved it?"

She started to nod but the motion made her head ache, so she said, "Yeah. Just about a year ago a new hospital in Accawmacke County was built, and they closed the one in North Heron. Actually, they kept it open, but it's mostly doctor's offices and labs. The ER went with the new hospital."

He grunted his disapproval of the ER's move and she wondered if she should try to keep a conversation going. "I really do appreciate you taking me so far. I feel bad that your evening was ruined."

He glanced her way again, before saying, "You don't gotta thank me, since it's my fault you got hurt. I shouldn't have put the ladder so close to the corner."

Twisting slightly in her seat toward him she argued, "You can't help where the light fixtures are. You had no choice but to have the ladder where it was. I was the one who didn't pay attention to where I was going."

Seeing him about to protest again, a giggle slipped out. "You know, it's kind of silly for us to argue about each one of us is taking the blame. It happened, it's over, no big deal. Nothing but a sprained wrist for me and a lost afternoon for you."

The heaviness in Hunter's chest began to ease as he watched the smile on her face beam toward him. He had spent two months watching her, thinking about her, even fantasizing about her. He never figured he would have a chance for a real conversation and here she was, in the truck with him. Turning onto the road leading to Baytown, he now wished they had longer.

"You said you wanted to study tonight. Are you taking classes?" he asked. Seeing her smile continue, he breathed a sigh of relief, glad that he had chosen a topic she was obviously happy with.

"I take nursing classes at the Eastern Shore Community College."

Shifting his eyes from the road again, he glanced at her. "I thought you already were a nurse."

"I am. I'm a Licensed Professional Nurse, but I've

almost finished my degree to become a Registered Nurse."

"Did you have a class tonight?"

"No, thank God," she breathed, before another sigh escaped. "But, I do have one tomorrow night and have an exam that I need to finish studying for."

Before he had a chance to speak further, they arrived at her neighborhood and he flipped on the blinker to turn into the mobile home park on the east side of town.

Looking out the window, she asked, "How did you know I live here?"

"Seen you here. I got a camper and the manager let me set up on one of the empty lots. We get off work about the same time, and I happened to be behind you one day. I saw you pull in and figured this is where you live." He did not add that he had been paying close attention, watching her every chance he got.

"Oh." Belle already knew that he lived there, having watched him going in and out of the park on his motor-cycle. Then, what he said made it through her foggy mind. "Camper? You live in a camper?"

"Yeah."

She twisted slightly so that she could face him in the cab of the truck. "Like a little camper or one of those great big motorhomes?"

Chuckling, he replied, "Can't see a man my size living in a little camper."

Shaking her head, she agreed silently.

"But then, I don't have a big motorhome, either. I got

a good deal on a mid-sized camper. It's just me, so I make do."

"But why?" She realized belatedly, the pain medicine was making her mouth run more than usual, but her curiosity won out. "Don't you want a real home...a place to put down roots?"

Shrugging, he said, "Never needed them before. Left home to join the Navy and it wasn't a place I wanted to stay when I got out."

"So...you came here?"

"Nah...moved to Norfolk. Had a couple of jobs...one thing led to another. Finally took Zac up on his offer and got a job at Careway."

"And the camper?"

"I take my home with me. Don't have to worry about finding an apartment, or rental agreements, or room-mates. Always got my stuff with me as long as I can find a place to park it."

She remained quiet, turning his words over in her mind. The way he explained his camper, it made sense. And yet, seemed so temporary. *Is he just here for a short time and will up and leave soon?* Yawning, she leaned her head back, too tired to ponder the mysteries of Hunter Simmons anymore.

Driving to her home, Hunter was pleased it was in the renovated section of the mobile home park. Each of the homes here was well maintained, lawn mown and flower beds planted. Turning onto her short driveway, it was easy to see the work she had put into maintaining her place. Flowers bloomed along the front walk from the gravel driveway to her steps. Her shutters and front door were painted blue against the pale, yellow siding.

"You've got a nice place here," he said. When she did not reply, he slid his gaze to the side and observed her looking out the window at her single-wide, mobile home, light pink staining her cheeks. He reached over and placed his large hand on her arm, and reiterated, "I mean that. It's a really nice place. I can tell you've done a lot to make it your home."

Belle's eyes landed on his hand resting on her arm, the warmth and tingle from them unfamiliar, but not unwelcome. Her lips curved ever so slightly, as she lifted her gaze to his. With a slight shrug, she said, "It's home. This neighborhood is the only home I've ever known. I grew up here...it wasn't so nice back then. But, I've worked hard, and I dream."

"Dream?"

"Dream that one day I'll have a real house, on my own piece of land. One with an upstairs and down-stairs. One with a front porch that'll hold a swing and a back deck, where the breeze off the bay can keep me cool."

His smile met hers, and he said, "Sounds like a real nice dream."

"One step at a time."

She reached to open the truck door, but his growl stopped her. "Don't touch that door, Belle," he warned. "Let me get it." He moved quickly around the front of the truck and opened her door, assisting her down with his large hands on her waist. Walking her to the front steps with his hand on her good arm, he slid her keys from her hand and opened the door, escorting her inside.

A quick view gave him the knowledge that she cared as much about the inside of her house as she did the outward appearance. The front door opened into a living room with a vaulted ceiling and cream carpet on the floor. A buttery yellow sofa, with blue throw pillows, sat on one wall underneath a window. Two matching blue chairs flanked the sofa. In the corner was an entertainment stand complete with a flat-screen TV. Framed paintings decorated the walls.

Off to the right, was the eat-in kitchen. A small oak table with four matching chairs sat next to another window, facing the L-shaped kitchen counters. Yellow and blue curtains fluttered over the window. Through the kitchen, he could see into a small bedroom. To the left of the living room was a hall, and he assumed it would lead to the master bedroom and bathroom.

Hearing a noise, he turned around and observed her moving into her kitchen. She reached into a cabinet and pulled down a bottle of ibuprofen with her good hand. Before she had a chance to struggle with the lid, he stalked over and gently took it from her hands, popping off the top. She shot him a smile as she filled a glass with water, taking two of the tablets.

"Are you sure you don't want the stronger painkillers?"

Shaking her head, she said, "No way. This will knock the edge off the pain and I really do need to get some studying in tonight."

"Are you going to take tomorrow off?"

"Oh, goodness gracious, no! I'll be fine... Remember, it's just a sprain."

He grimaced his disapproval, but said, "Listen, Belle. I'll come by tomorrow and pick you up to take you to work." Seeing her about to protest, he added, "Your car is still at the nursing home and so is my motorcycle. I'll get you there tomorrow, and then, if you feel okay, you'll have it to drive to your class tomorrow evening."

She nodded and stepped closer. Lifting her uninjured hand, she placed it on his arm, holding his gaze. "Hunter, thank you. You've been a really good friend today."

He liked hearing her call him a friend. Nodding his acknowledgment but unable to think of another reason to prolong his stay, he turned to leave. Stopping at the door, he twisted back around, his eyes pinned on her. "You got a really nice place here. And you keep taking classes to get more education. Sounds like you know exactly what you need to do to make your dreams come true." With that, he stepped through the door and gently closed it behind him.

Belle walked to the window near the table and peered at him as he climbed up into the truck. Sucking in a shuddering breath, she closed her eyes for a moment. So handsome, it almost hurt to look at him, she let the air hiss through her lips. It was true...she was working hard to check all of the goals off of her life-list, but there was one she had not found yet. And that was a man to share it with.

As she watched him drive away, she wondered if that dream would ever come true.

Hunter drove toward the middle of the mobile home park, his camper on a lot that was between the renovated section and the back lot that was still a run-down area. The owner had assured him that he was in the process of reclaiming all the lots from previous owners, instigating new rules concerning the landscaping and cleanliness of the mobile homes, but it was a slow process. Some of the residents had lived there for years and getting them on board with the new regulations had been difficult, especially since some of them owned their homes and did not just rent them.

Pulling the truck to the side of his camper, he climbed down, his sharp eyes scanning the area. Unlocking the door, he stepped inside, his large body taking up a lot of the space, in spite of the camper's size.

Entering the kitchen, he moved toward the back, into the small bathroom. Many campers had bathrooms so tiny the shower took up the whole space, raining water down on the sink and toilet. He had carefully chosen one that had a separate, if minuscule, shower. Scrubbing his hand over his face and hair, he washed the sweat off his body.

After toweling off, he stood and stared into the foggy mirror for a few minutes until his image became clearer. His mind traveled over the events of the day, focusing on the moment Belle ran into his ladder, falling at his feet. He wanted to purge the memory of her pain-filled face, but it remained. While he had done nothing to overtly hurt her, the image of his mother lying on the floor from one of his father's rages crept in.

Giving his head a shake, he stalked out of the small bathroom to the cabinet where he kept his clothes. Pulling on boxers and cut-off sweatpants, he rubbed at the ache in his thigh and moved to the stove to begin his dinner. Draining a can of tuna and a can of green peas, he stirred them into the pot where he had made boxed macaroni and cheese, dumping the simple meal into a bowl after it heated through. Sitting down at his table, with his food and a beer, he turned on the TV, found a sports channel and settled in for the evening.

Two hours later, with the dish and pot washed and drying in the sink, he double-checked his door to make sure it was locked. With his size and glower, he figured most people in the area would leave him alone, but he had seen enough drug deals in the neighborhood and knew that junkies could get desperate.

Climbing into bed, he lay on top of the sheet not wanting to run the air conditioner more than he needed to. A small fan on top of the nightstand kept the air moving over his body. He thought about his explanation to Belle concerning his living arrangements. He had been living in this camper for a couple of years, finding it to be as good a home as any. On a ship in the Navy, he never had any privacy. And going back farther than that, his childhood home certainly never gave him any peace. The camper was easy to take wherever he roamed and hoped to settle. Was that Baytown? Would he want to stay here?

Blowing out a breath, he thought of Belle's idea of

home...*One day I'll have a real house...one with an upstairs and a downstairs...one with a front porch that'll hold a swing and a back deck where the breeze off the bay can keep me cool.*

He placed his hand underneath his head as she continued to fill his mind. Clean, sweet, wholesome. He was surprised to learn that she had been raised in the mobile home park. Not that that was a bad thing, but her admission that it was not a good place to be when she was growing up made the person she was all the more admirable. He could imagine what the place had been like based on the back section of the current park.

Still hating what happened to her today, he could not deny how much he enjoyed spending time alone with her. *And tomorrow, I get to pick her up in the morning and take her to work.*

He stretched his long frame on his bed in his camper, lying at an angle so his feet did not hang over the edge. Flipping open the window near his head, he listened to the sounds of the residents nearby...a dog barking, a baby crying, a couple arguing. Sighing, he longed for the time when he could move his camper closer to the beach and let the sound of the waves gentle his thoughts. But, for now, he was where he needed to be.

4

Hunter pushed open the door to Jillian's Coffee House and Galleria, immediately assaulted with the comforting scent of freshly brewed coffee. His gaze passed over the few early morning customers sitting at the small tables enjoying their breakfast and landed on a tall woman dressed in a bright pink shirt paired with bright blue pants, standing near the counter. Her blonde hair was pulled into a long braid and, paired with her athletic beauty, it was easy to imagine her as the high school prom queen that had captured Grant's attention many years ago.

As he moved toward her, past dark walls with antique brass sconces, she looked up and her smile widened.

"Hunter? How nice to see you! I don't think you've ever stepped foot in my shop," she said, turning fully toward him.

"Fancy coffee's not usually my thing," he offered in explanation. Seeing her head tilt in question, he explained, "Wanted to get some coffee and breakfast stuff to take to Belle this morning."

If possible, her smile widened even more and he felt the heat of scrutiny passing over him. Feeling the need to continue his explanation, he said, "She had a little accident yesterday and I wanted to give her breakfast before taking her to work."

Before she had time to dig more information from him, the tinkling of the bell over the door rang again and two more women made their way toward the counter. Turning his head slightly, he observed Katelyn walking toward him, Tori right behind her pushing a stroller. Shoving his hands into his pockets, he sighed, knowing enough about these three to expect that they would not stop until they had all the information from him.

"Hunter was just telling me that Belle got hurt yesterday!" Jillian exclaimed.

Just as he suspected, both Tori and Katelyn rounded on him, immediately demanding the news.

"She fell at work and sprained her wrist. I took her to the ER, where they checked her out. I was just getting some breakfast to take to her—"

Katelyn, eyes wide, said, "We should take it and check on her. Let's get some—"

"No!" Tori all but shouted, shooting a pointed look at both Katelyn and Jillian, before glancing back into the stroller at her sleeping child. "Right now, she probably needs some peace and quiet and I think Hunter would be the perfect person to take her breakfast. After all, it was his idea. We can check in with her later."

Immediately agreeing, Jillian grinned as she prepared two large coffees to go while Katelyn moved behind the counter, scooping up several cheese and bacon biscuits and putting them in a bag. He fought the urge to roll his eyes heavenward. The women could not be more obvious. Not wanting to fight their assistance —he knew a lost cause when he saw one—he was glad that he was still the one who would be able to take the treats to Belle.

Jillian waved away his money, declaring it to be her treat for an injured friend, before saying, "Let her know that we'll be by later on to check on her."

He nodded and with a slight wave turned to walk out of the shop, ignoring the grins on the three women's faces.

"But, Mr. Weldon—"

"No, absolutely not. The note faxed from the ER doctor said that you were not to report into work until you had been off the narcotic pain medicine for forty-eight hours. That means today and tomorrow you are not to come in."

Huffing, Belle, still in her light green drawstring pajama bottoms and matching camisole top, leaned back against the kitchen chair, knowing that he was right. As they said their goodbyes and she laid her phone on the table, she had to admit that it felt nice to have a day off. Her wrist ached, but not unbearably so, as long as she did not move it much. *Well, at least I can get some studying done.*

A knock on the door startled her and she jumped up, hurrying to open it. Expecting Brittany, she stood in mute surprise when her eyes landed on Hunter, his Careway polo straining over his chest and arms. Dropping her gaze to his hands, she spied a cardboard tray with two coffees and a large paper bag with Jillian's logo printed on the side.

"Wh...what are you doing here?"

Hunter's heated gaze dropped from Belle's face downward, before jumping back to her eyes. Taking in her sleep-tousled hair and figure-hugging pajamas, her hard nipples clearly evident through the thin cotton, he decided to keep his eyes on her face, hoping the cock twitch in his jeans would not be noticeable. "Brought you breakfast so you wouldn't have to hurt your wrist in the kitchen."

Touched by his concern, Belle unlocked the screen door and exclaimed, "That's so sweet. Um...please come in." As his large body moved into her house, she instinctively sucked in her stomach to let him go by, but his chest slightly rubbed against her front and she tried to ignore the tingle. She nodded toward the kitchen table and said, "You can just put it there and have a seat. I'll be right back...I need to...uh..." Not wanting to draw more attention to her lack of clothes, she turned and hurried down the hall.

Closing her bedroom door, she whirled around in a circle trying to decide what to put on. *A thick housecoat?*

Too old and ratty. A nice shirt? No, that looks like I'm trying too hard. Glad to have a front-snap bra, she managed to get it on without too much difficulty. With her bra firmly harnessing her heavy breasts, she felt more decent. Finally deciding to go with ease since her wrist was wrapped, she pulled on a soft pair of yoga pants and paired it with a light blue, tunic top that settled gently over her hips. Turning toward the mirror, she was aghast that Hunter had seen her with her morning bed-head. Grabbing her brush, she pulled it through the long locks.

She struggled to pull her hair back, finally giving up and leaving it loose about her shoulders. Realizing that he was simply being neighborly and this was not a date, she gave up on the idea of makeup.

Stepping back into the living and kitchen area of her home, she observed that he had already placed the savory biscuits onto two saucers with forks nearby. With the lids off the steaming cups of coffee, she was greeted with the scent of Jillian's flavored brew. Her eyes moved to Hunter's face, seeing his slight smile directed at her. In her wildest dreams, she could never have imagined him standing in her kitchen smiling at her.

Forcing her legs to move forward, she met his smile with one of her own, and invited him to sit. She took a bite of Jillian's biscuit and, closing her eyes in food ecstasy, she moaned. "I can't believe you went to Jillian's shop for me."

Hunter felt her moan shoot straight to his cock, and shifted slightly in his chair. Forcing his eyes back to his breakfast, he tried to ignore the continued sounds of delight coming from her mouth.

"I feel guilty that you went to this much trouble. I just got off the phone with Mr. Weldon and he's not allowing me to go to work today. He says I have to be off the prescription pain medication for forty-eight hours before I'm allowed to be back with the patients."

Already taking a bite of the deliciously filled biscuits, he washed it down with a healthy sip of coffee. "I know," he said. "While you were getting dressed, Mr. Weldon called me, knowing that I was supposed to be your ride today. He told me to take a day off as well so that I could make sure you were taking care of yourself."

Her eyes jumped to his, wide in surprise. "You're taking a day off? You shouldn't waste a day off for me. I'm fine...honest I am."

He shrugged and said, "Don't worry about it. He told me it'd be a day off with pay."

"Oh," Belle said, unable to think of another response. The idea of having him around was exciting, but also distracting. Taking another bite and chewing it slowly, she finally swallowed, saying, "I was just going to stay in today. I really need to study for my test tonight."

He looked over at her. "I won't get in your way, but if you've got any odd jobs around your place that need to be done, I'd be glad to take care of them."

Her face scrunched as she tilted her head and considered his proposal. As much as she would love to have the eye candy around, she couldn't think of anything that needed to be done. Before she had a chance to answer, another knock sounded on the door.

"Belle?"

Jumping from her seat, she hurried to the door, throwing it open. "Good morning, Ms. Sanders. Can I help you with something?"

The older woman's eyes dropped to her wrist brace and she exclaimed, "What happened to you, girl?"

"Oh, just a little accident at work," she explained. "I'll be home today and maybe tomorrow. Come on in."

Once inside, Ms. Sanders shifted her gaze over to Hunter sitting at the table.

Coming to his feet, he nodded his greeting.

Ms. Sanders grinned widely. "Don't see a lot of young men with gentlemanly behaviors around here. Nice to see you got some, boy. Your parents must 'a raised you right."

Belle was smiling at him when she saw the dark cloud pass quickly through his eyes at Ms. Sanders' comment, before it shifted away. Turning back to the older woman, she said, "Is there anything I can help you with?"

Ms. Sanders' smile dropped from her face, replaced with a look of irritation. "I was just hoping to use your washer to wash out a few things. Seems like my washing machine pipes are clogged again."

"Of course you may—"

"Doesn't the management take care of those things?" Hunter asked.

"Hmph," Ms. Sanders groused.

Turning to him, Belle explained, "No, they only take care of the lawn maintenance and, if someone is renting a house, then they will do *some* work. But for those of us that own our mobile homes, all maintenance is up to us." As she patted Ms. Sanders' arm, she opened her mouth to extend the invitation for the older woman to use her washer again, when Hunter interrupted once more.

"I'll take care of it." As both women turned to stare at him, Hunter reiterated, "Probably nothing I can't handle, and I've got the day off anyway." Taking a last sip of coffee, he moved to the sink, placing his plate and cup in her sink after rinsing it out. Walking toward the two, he said to Belle, "I'll be back at lunch to check on you. Don't do anything more strenuous than studying."

As he held the door open for Ms. Sanders to proceed through, he reached out and trailed his fingers along Belle's shoulder, giving it a little squeeze.

Belle stood in the doorway, her breath caught in her throat, and watched as Hunter escorted the older woman back to her home across the street. Her shoulder tingled where his fingers had touched. Finally, giving her head a slight shake, she moved back to her kitchen table, spreading her nursing books and notebooks over the surface.

"I've seen you on that big, loud motorcycle."

Hunter shifted his large body, peering around from behind the washing machine, looking up at Ms. Sanders' face as she hovered nearby. The older woman was of indeterminate age, but clearly still spry. She had been chattering away ever since they entered her home.

The stacked washer and dryer were in a small closet, affording him little room to maneuver. Holding her gaze, he replied, "I hope I haven't disturbed you when riding." She had not given him the indication that she judged, but he knew that many people had a negative connotation of someone who rode.

"Oh, no," she exclaimed. "It don't bother me. My own boy, God rest his soul, used to ride his motorcycle every chance he got. At the time, it would drive me crazy worrying about him." She sighed, adding, "He died in the first Gulf War. Honest to God, I'd give anything to hear him ride up on his motorcycle again."

His face gentled as he observed the wistfulness in her expression. "I'm sorry to hear about your loss, ma'am."

She smiled, and said, "He'd be pleased to know another veteran, who also liked to ride, was here to see to his mom."

Nodding, he leaned back behind the washing machine, replacing the back panel. "I think that'll do the trick," he said, hauling his body up. Turning the knobs to the appliance, they listened as the water began filling the tub.

She clapped her hands in glee, thanking him profusely. As he maneuvered the washing machine back against the wall, she hustled into the kitchen and opened her small freezer. Taking out a container, she moved toward him, holding it out. "Got some home-made lasagna. Take it over to Belle, so the two of you'll have something to eat for lunch."

Hesitating, he said, "Not sure she's expecting me for lunch."

Ms. Sanders stepped closer, her head leaned back as she looked up into his face. "Son, I've lived in this mobile home park for many years. I've seen good people come and go and I've seen some people come that I wish would go, 'cause they ain't no good. I've known Belle since she was a little girl, and I'm telling you right now, they don't get no better than her. I also know, she hasn't had no one take her back. Lord knows, her waste of a momma never did. So if you've got any sense in you, boy, you'll take this food over to her and share it." Smiling, she added, "Nothing settles friendships like breaking bread together."

Hearing her words, they moved deep inside of him, and he nodded. "Obliged, ma'am," he said, taking the container and turning to walk away. Her voice captured him once more as he was leaving.

"She ain't always had the best, but she's worked hard to be the best."

With a chin lift, he left her house smiling, walking back across the street.

5

"I'm fine, I'm fine. Really, I'm spending the day studying because I have a test tonight."

Belle was on the phone, assuring Jillian that she did not need company. Jillian, Tori, Katelyn, Madelyn, and Jade had all wanted to come by and see her, but she told them that she had everything she needed.

"Okay, if you're sure," Jillian replied. "By the way, I just have to ask...how was breakfast?"

Knowing her friend was itching for details, she grinned. "Well, since the breakfast came from you, I'm sure you know it was delicious, as always."

"And..."

"I suppose you're asking about Hunter?"

"Of course, I am! Stop beating around the bush and give me something I can tell the others!"

Laughing, she gave in, saying, "Hunter is the one who took me to the ER yesterday and then brought me back home. I didn't think anything about it until he showed up this morning with breakfast, which was really sweet. But, don't read any more into it. I'm sure he's just being neighborly."

"Honey, I don't think there was anything just neighborly about bringing you breakfast! I'd say that was a man who's definitely interested."

Her eyes continued to watch out her front window near the table, wondering when Hunter would leave Ms. Sanders' place. She hated to admit that she had set up her study materials on her table at the angle to give her the most advantageous place to observe across the street. Sighing, she replied, "He felt really bad about the accident and perhaps breakfast was just out of guilt. Anyway, as busy as my life is right now, it would be hard to think of him as anything more than just a kind neighbor."

Before Jillian had a chance to reply, Hunter walked out of Ms. Sanders' front door, carrying what appeared to be a casserole dish. Biting her lip, she watched as he crossed the road toward her house. "Jillian, I hate to rush away, but I really need to get back to studying. Tell the others I'm fine, and I'll talk to everyone tomorrow." Disconnecting, she held her breath as he moved toward her house.

Walking to the front door, she opened it before he even had a chance to knock. He looked up in surprise, seeing her standing in the doorway, her smile wide on her face.

"I know you're trying to study, but Ms. Sanders sent you some lunch."

Stepping back, she motioned for him to come in.

"From the size of that container, I'd say she meant for both of us to share it."

"I didn't want to assume anything—"

"Please join me," she begged. "I've done nothing but study all morning while you were helping Ms. Sanders and I'd love the interruption."

As they sat down at her small table, digging into the heated lasagna, he said, "When's your class tonight?"

"It starts at seven. It normally goes until ten, but we can leave as soon as we're finished with the test." She cocked her head to the side, wondering why he asked.

Taking a sip of iced tea, he said, "I'll pick you up about thirty minutes earlier to take you there." He watched the confusion spread across her face and reminded, "Your car is still at the nursing home."

She blinked, before exclaiming, "Oh, no! I completely forgot!"

"No worries. I'll take you and then bring you home."

"Hunter, you can't do that—"

Staring at her wide eyes, he said, "Why the hell not?"

"It's too much to ask you to do that." She sucked in her lips as she pushed her food around her plate with her fork.

"Don't recall you asking me. I volunteered. Got nothing else more important to do this evening, so I can drive you in the truck, read while you're inside taking your test, and then I'll drive you home. That way, you get there safe, back home safe, and I don't have to be worried about you."

She lifted her gaze, staring at his sincere face, wanting to ask why he would worry about her. Too shy to ask and unable to think of a reason why he should not take her, she nodded. Her lips curved into a barely-there smile, as they finished their meal.

Hunter pushed the seat of the old truck back as far as it would go, comfortably settled, reading his book. The sun had set, but with the light on inside the truck, he was still able to read. His eyes occasionally drifted to the door of the community college building, where Belle had entered two hours earlier.

He wondered if it was a smart idea for him to become involved in her life, knowing the time might not be the best. *If she knew everything about me, would she still be interested?*

Unable to come up with an answer to that question, he closed his book with a slam and leaned back against the headrest. Heaving a sigh, his head bolted forward as he heard a few voices in the distance. Belle and two other women were exiting the building and as he watched her wave goodbye to them and approach his truck, he breathed a sigh of relief at the huge smile on her face.

He climbed down quickly and met her at the passenger door, opening it. The parking lot lights reflected brightly in her eyes.

"Looks like it was a good night," he said, offering his hand to assist her in, careful of her wrist brace.

She twisted in her seat to look at him after he settled back into the driver's seat, and exclaimed, "It was! The extra studying paid off... I'm sure I aced the final."

His smile met her exclamation and they drove home, conversation flowing easier between them than the previous evening when they left the ER. Arriving at her house, he escorted her inside, checking to make sure she was safe. Before he left, he turned and said, "Lock up behind me, Belle. I'll see you tomorrow."

Parking the truck by his camper, he was looking forward to going to work the next day and getting back on his motorcycle. The idea of not having a vehicle to haul Belle around hit him, but it was soon followed by the image of her holding tight to his back, her breasts pressed against him, as they roared down the road on his motorcycle. Climbing from the truck, his dick twitched at the thought before sighing as he realized that girls like Belle probably would not be interested in a ride.

Loud noises, a few houses down, caught his attention. He looked over and saw what appeared to be a party in full swing. Standing on the step to enter his camper, he trained his eyes to the neighbor's yard before moving inside and locking his door. An hour later the noise had lowered and it appeared the group had moved inside. He observed a police vehicle roll down the road and wondered if a neighbor had called the cops.

Lying in bed, he shifted around to find a comfortable position. Without thinking, his fingers dug into the scar tissue in his thigh, where the embedded metal had been removed. Just as sleep was about to claim him, he heard the sounds of the party breaking up. *Might be time to approach the neighbor who liked to party, see if he had anything worthwhile to sell.*

Mitch sat in the conference room of the police station going over the agenda items in his briefing with his officers. Most of the topics were quickly reviewed and they were just winding down when Sheriff Colt Hudson stalked into the room. As the Sheriff of North Heron County, he often collaborated with the smaller Baytown Police Department. He was followed by Hannah Freeman, Easton town Police Chief, Liam Sullivan, the Accawmacke County Sheriff, Wyatt Newman, the Manteague town Police Chief, and Dylan Hunt, the Seaside town Police Chief. The gathering represented the heads of the law enforcement for the Eastern Shore of Virginia.

"Glad you could make it." As they settled into chairs, Mitch turned to his team, and explained, "I talked to Colt this morning and we discussed a new problem that has crept into the area." Seeing he had everyone's rapt attention, he amended, "To be fair, it's a problem that has been around for a long time, but we're just now seeing more and more of it."

Colt, wearing the khaki uniform of the Sheriff's Department, settled his tall, muscular frame into one of the chairs around the table. With chin lifts directed at Officers Ginny, Grant, Lance, and Burt, he said, "I've been given a heads up from our State Police liaison, concerning the prescription drug problem in our area. I know that it seems like it might be easy for medical facilities to keep track of the prescription drugs that come in and then are prescribed out for patients, but a large number of drugs go missing every month, finding their way into the hands of those who'll use them recreationally, or sell them."

"Do they have a lock on where they're coming from?" Grant asked. As one of the original Baytown Boys, Grant and Mitch had been friends since childhood, both joining the Baytown police force after returning from the military.

Shaking his head, Colt said, "Other than telling us that they're cracking down on the problem, and trying to identify the perpetrators, they don't have any specifics. I will say that my office arrested a nineteen-year-old last night. He was stopped for a traffic violation, but my deputy noticed his eyes were glazed and dilated. He was high as a kite when he brought him in."

"Anything on him?" Dylann asked.

"Searched his car and came up with a small amount of Oxycodone. Not enough to charge him with intent to distribute, but at least got him on possession. We were hoping he'd lead us to his distributor, but he clammed up real quick. We'll see. When he realizes his options, we might get something out of him."

Hannah added, "I've got a medical officer watching him as he sits in our jail. As of this morning, he was still coming down from what he was on."

Ginny, intently observing Mitch, asked, "Chief, you

look like you've got something on your mind. Something specific?"

He sighed as he nodded, and replied, "We've got certain pockets in our town and in the County of North Heron that we know have problems. One of them is the back section of the mobile home park. The land that the property sits on is mostly in the town of Baytown, but the back section is over the town and county line, situated in North Heron County. I've spoken with the owner and he's as frustrated as we are."

Lance, the newest member on the police force, cocked his head to the side, and said, "Sorry, Chief. Maybe it's because I'm new to this area, but I don't understand the problem."

"Baytown has certain ordinances and policies regarding home properties, and that includes the mobile home park. Maintenance, curb appeal, lawn care, garbage disposal, and vehicles, all come under Baytown's ordinances. The County of North Heron does not have the same policies."

Burt leaned back in his chair and added, "In many places, cities and towns have more regulations than counties do, as far as housing, due to more rural farms areas."

"For example," Colt explained, "it's very common in rural counties for a house to have a non-running vehicle sitting in the driveway. But, in Baytown, all vehicles on the homeowner's property must be in running condition."

"So, in the case of the mobile home park, the large section that is in the town of Baytown has more regulations and is easier to maintain, while the section on the North Heron side is more of our problem area," Grant confirmed.

Mitch nodded, and said, "It's got nothing to do with the people who live there. Mobile home parks have often had negative connotations, but it's a great community— a playground for the kids, hardworking families that are able to afford the housing there. But, because it is also a lower rent area, it can attract people who want to prey on those less fortunate."

"What Mitch and I discussed this morning was a combined effort to keep a closer eye on the back section. There are a few owners and renters there that we suspect are some of our dealers," Colt added. "But, what we really want, are the people that are higher up so we can determine where they're getting their prescription drugs from."

Liam, looking at Colt, asked, "Did the State Police give you an idea of what they're doing about the problem?"

Shaking his head, he answered, "All I know, is that they're following leads from pharmaceutical companies and pharmaceutical deliveries. As to which medical facilities in our area they think might be involved, they did not say."

"We've got doctor offices, pharmacies, home health services, nursing homes...hell, the rural health center has drugs on the property, with deliveries every day," Mitch said.

"Not to mention pharmaceutical delivery companies and salesmen," Ginny threw out.

The others shook their heads at the wide scope they faced in attempting a crackdown in a large area with a small police and deputy force.

"So, that's it for our meeting today. You've got your patrol schedules, but you'll notice that we have added increased visibility in the back of the mobile home park." As the Baytown officers filed out of the room, leaving Mitch, Colt, Wyatt, Dylan, and Hannah alone, he asked Colt, "You got nothing else to go on?"

Colt shook his head. "Nothing specific, but I've got a bad feeling about this. Don't know what, just something in my gut isn't sitting right."

The others nodded silently as Mitch sighed heavily.

6

Hunter looked around at the eclectic gathering in the basement of the building holding the American Legion meeting. From what he had gathered, they had held the new officer elections a few months ago and Grant was now the commander.

He had never been to an AL meeting and was uncertain of the procedures. Grant stood on the platform at the front and rapped the gavel on the podium. The new Sergeant at Arms, Ginny, closed the doors in the back before walking with her husband, Brogan, the Color Bearer. He carried the flagpole in his hand, the American flag billowing before he set it in the floor stand.

Hunter bowed his head as the chaplain offered the prayer, but as soon as it was over he looked around in curiosity. The crowd, mostly men but sprinkled with women, ranged in age from early twenties to well into their nineties. Many had lapel pins, stuck in their shirts or jackets, with the various military insignias from which branch they served under. Strangely self-conscious that he had few articles with US Navy on them, other than a pair of old sweatpants and a couple of T-shirts, he thought he would ask Zac where he might purchase a pin.

Before considering that further, Grant called for the POW/MIA Empty Chair Ceremony. Intrigued, he watched as a chair was designated as a symbol of the thousands of American POW/MIAs still unaccounted for from all wars and conflicts involving the United States of America. The POW/MIA flag was placed on the Empty Chair. He noticed all faces turned toward the chair and he did the same. He had only known a few servicemen who had died and was ashamed to admit, he had not thought about them in a while.

Brogan talked for a moment about the baseball teams and coaching positions that were needed for the American Legion youth program.

Zac nudged him in the arm, and whispered, "I gotta get you out there with the kids. You'd be great."

After the financial report was given, Zac, as the Post Service Officer, approached the podium and spoke about the Eastern Shore Mental Health Group, and the services they provided specifically for veterans. His attention was captured when Zac talked about one of the new medical groups on the Eastern Shore that included physical therapy.

"The Pain Management Center has two doctors that specialize in veterans' injuries, and they wanted me to make sure our group knew that they not only treat pain with certain drugs, but more importantly with ongoing physical therapy."

His fingers moved to his thigh, once more slightly massaging the injured area, his mind riveted on the Medical Center Zac had just described.

When the meeting came to a close, he found himself in the middle of a large group heading down Main Street toward Finn's Pub. The original owner, Finn McFarlane, had given the pub to his three grandchildren, Aiden, Brogan, and Katelyn. A town fixture, the pub was the gathering place after every American Legion and AL Auxiliary meeting.

Walking through the bright red door, he remembered meeting Zac and Jason here on his first night in town. Zac and Madelyn had just been married that day, and all their loved ones were gathered to celebrate. It made for a bit of an awkward introduction, but everyone welcomed him with open arms. Still, he only stayed a few minutes before heading out, not wanting to crash the party.

A long bar lined the right wall, the old, wood surface highly polished. Mismatched barstools sat in a row next to the bar. A large mirror, flanked by shelves filled with alcohol bottles of every shape and size, lined the wall behind the bar. Brogan had explained that the original building housed a bank, and the old vault now functioned as a seating area. Toward the back were larger tables and booths, where their friends were waiting.

As he moved along with the crowd of friends, he observed Katelyn and another server bringing out platters of wings. As soon as her brothers and her husband, Gareth, saw her, they rushed to take the platters from her hands. His gaze dropped to her protruding stomach and he understood the action—the men did not want her to carry anything heavy.

He cast his eyes about the room, seeing many of the couples cozying up to each other. Not seeing Belle, he missed her presence, but assumed she was home nursing her injury.

"Here's the crab dip, everyone."

Jerking around, he recognized Belle's voice, and his eyes narrowed when he observed her, in another cute, floral, sundress walking from the back, a large tray in her hands. Seeing it balanced awkwardly on her injured wrist, he stalked over, plucking it from her hands.

Bending, so that his voice would only be for her, he asked, "What the hell are you doing? You're supposed to be taking it easy on your hand."

Belle blinked as she watched Hunter twist his upper body to place the platter on the table behind him. Before she could speak, he turned back and placed his hands on her shoulders, a muscle ticking in his jaw.

"What is your problem?" she hissed in a whisper, leaning forward and up on her toes. "I was perfectly fine and only helping Katelyn."

"She's pregnant and you're injured. I don't know what either of you were thinking," he replied, his voice just as soft but still filled with irritation.

Placing her hands on her hips, she said, "That's a patronizing attitude. She's pregnant, not infirm, and I went back to work today, as you well know. Other than needing to be careful, my wrist is fine."

Clearly done with the conversation, Belle whirled and walked away, going to the far end of the bar where a dart game had ensued. Scrubbing his hand over his face before dragging it through his hair, Hunter sighed heavily.

"That could have gone better," Zac said, coming up beside him.

He scowled at his friend, but swung his eyes back to the front of the bar, keeping them on the swish of her skirt. He observed Jason and Callan smiling at her before they resumed throwing darts at the board on the wall. "She doesn't lack for attention," he said, hating the peevish tone of his comment.

"Belle's great. She's kind of like everyone's little sister," Zac said.

At this, he swung his gaze back to his friend, his eyebrows arched. "Little sister? That's it?"

Understanding dawned in Zac's expression and a slow smile spread across his face. "You interested? Cause I gotta tell you, you'd be getting a prize if you captured her attention. She's sweet, pretty, smart, and about as nice a person as you could ever want to meet."

Sighing, he returned his attention to her. Watching her stand silently on the game's sideline, his fists landed on his hips. "Yeah, I see her at work and know you're right." Turning back to Zac, he asked, "I suppose she was part of the original Baytown gang of friends?"

Shaking his head, Zac said, "Nah. She was a couple years behind us in school and super shy. I know it sounds like we were self-absorbed dicks looking for girls who put out but, then, we were teenagers so I guess that pretty much describes most of us. By the time us guys had gotten back from the military and started hanging out again, she was already part of Tori, Jillian, and Katelyn's tribe. She's still really quiet, but not as shy as she used to be."

Listening raptly, his gaze nonetheless kept drifting to Belle. She was everything Zac said she was, and so much more. And he...well, one thing had led to another and now it felt like his life was not exactly in his own hands anymore. He felt Zac's eyes on him and looked back at him, seeing his friend's grin. Dropping his chin to his chest, he slowly shook his head.

"What's wrong? It's obvious you're into her—"

"Timing sucks," was his only reply.

Zac continued to observe him for a moment, then, said, "Speaking of timing, I'd been asking you for over a year to come check out Baytown. What made you finally decide to come?"

Silent for a moment, he lifted his head, his eyes still on Belle, watching as she threw her head back in laughter at something Callan had said. "Still timing, I suppose. The timing was just right to come here."

Just as Zac was getting ready to turn away to join his wife, Hunter halted him with a hand on his arm. "Sorry to keep you, man, but I wanted to ask about the Pain Management Center."

Zac's eyes opened wide, and he nodded enthusiastically. "Shit, Hunter, I forgot about that equipment explosion that sent some metal into your leg. That still bother you?"

Lips pinched, he offered a silent nod.

"Absolutely, I'll get that information to you. In fact, you can check their website tonight and I'll get the info to you tomorrow. We've already had a couple of members try them out, and they say they're really good."

With a final nod, Hunter said, "Obliged." Watching Zac return to the group near the back where Madelyn greeted him with a hug, he swung around, keeping an eye on the beautiful Belle.

As though called up by a wish, she turned, catching his eye. He watched the color rise over her face before her shoulders slumped. She moved through the crowd toward him, stopping when her tiny shoes stood directly in front of his large size twelve boots. He opened his mouth, but she got there first.

"I'm sorry, Hunter," she said, her guileless gaze holding his. "You were just looking out for me and I took offense."

Shaking his head, he admitted, "No, you have nothing to apologize for. It was all me...me being overbearing."

She sucked in her lips, attempting, and failing, to hide her smile. "Why do I get the feeling that apologies don't come easily to you?"

A chuckle erupted from deep within his chest and his eyes twinkled. "Damn, girl, for a shy one, you know how to hit."

As soon as the word *shy* left his mouth, he watched a flash of unease move through her eyes. "Hey...you okay? I didn't mean—"

A self-deprecating grimace pulled her lips down and she shook her head. "No, it's fine. Actually, you're right. I've always been shy...but, I'm working on it."

He stepped closer, lifting her chin with his knuckle,

not speaking until he held her gaze. "You don't gotta be anybody but who you are. Nothing wrong with being shy." Just then, loud laughter rang from the back of the bar where their friends were still gathered. He jerked his head toward them and added, "In fact, I kind of like the quiet type."

A slight blush crept from her chest to her hairline as her lips curved upward again. Dropping his hand reluctantly, he asked, "Are you still interested in the game or can I take you home?"

She looked over her shoulder in the direction he was glancing and shook her head. "No, I was just hanging with them for a little while. Sometimes it's easier."

"Easier?"

Sucking in her lips again, she gave a little shake. "Oh, nothing...uh, I'm ready to go home if you'd like to take me. Katelyn brought me, so I don't have my car here. I was just going to walk home."

At that piece of information, he felt his jaw tick again and growled, "You shouldn't walk by yourself. I don't care how safe Baytown is...no woman should be out alone at night." Seeing her about to protest, he rushed, "Don't care if that sounds patronizing...I'm just cautious."

"Fair enough," she agreed. "In fact, it was only a year ago that we had a problem with women being attacked—"

A growl rose from his chest and she raised her hand, resting it on his bicep. "The police caught him."

Lifting his hand to cover hers, he said, "Just because they caught one doesn't mean there aren't others."

Keeping hold of her hand, he lowered his slowly and, with a little tug, pulled her closer to his side as they walked toward the door.

Belle looked to the back of the Pub and waved toward Katelyn, who had a huge smile on her face. As they moved through the door, Hunter continued to keep her hand tucked into his as he led her to his motorcycle.

Her feet stumbled as they neared and she jerked on his hand as she halted. "Uh...I've never ridden a motor-cycle before."

"Never?"

She shook her head and watched as he let go of her hand and grabbed the extra helmet from the back. He chuckled as he slid it over her head. "It's kind of big, isn't it?" she asked, feeling it wobble.

He bent and adjusted the straps, making it snug. "Yeah, it's not a perfect fit, but it'll do for now." He stood and stared into her wide eyes. "Scared?"

"Kinda," she admitted, but her lips curved slightly. "But, also kinda excited. I like trying new things."

"Well, alright then," he grinned, pulling his helmet on. Instructing her how to mount behind him, she hesi-tated again.

"Oh, dear. I'm in a dress."

Hunter's gaze slid slowly down her body, noting her curves for the hundredth time since he had seen her the first time. "Don't worry. You'll be pressed tightly to me and no one'll see anything."

Sucking in a deep breath, Belle placed her hand on his shoulders and swung her left leg over the seat, glad for the cover of darkness to hide any possible panty-flashing she might have given. Once on, she placed her feet on the rests and grabbed him around the waist.

"Tighter," Hunter ordered, pulling her hands to his front, carefully handling her injured wrist, and feeling her breasts press tightly to his back. "Ready?"

Belle nodded against his shoulder, but could feel her insides quaking with fear. He started the engine and her heart pounded, threatening to drown out the sound of the bike. Before she could change her mind, they roared off, heading down Main Street toward the beach.

Taking a roundabout way to get to the mobile home park, he heard her squeal and hoped it was in delight and not terror.

"You okay?"

"I love it!" she yelled over the roar of the engine.

He was tempted to head out of town and take her for a long ride, but did not want to push his luck. As it was, he had to focus on the road because the feel of her lush body pressed to his was stealing his concentration, the blood rushing from his brain.

Pulling up to her house, he cut the engine and kicked down the stand. Her hands did not unclasp and he called out, "Hate to have you move, babe, but I can't get off until you do."

"Oh!" she exclaimed, swinging her leg over, clutching his shoulder until her legs were steady underneath her. Her fingers fumbled with the helmet strap, but after he dismounted, he gently moved her hands out of the way and unfastened it effortlessly. Hanging it on the handlebars, he quickly added his there as well.

Missing the warmth of his body, Belle rubbed her palms over her skirt, forcing her eyes to his face. "Do you want to come in?"

Emotions warred within and, giving in to the loudest one, Hunter stepped closer and placed his hands on either side of her face. Using his thumbs to gently lift her chin, he bent, lowering his mouth until it was a whisper away. Searching her expression for signs that she did not want this, all he saw was desire matching his.

He took her lips, soft at first but as she moaned, the kiss morphed into white-hot passion. Thrusting his tongue into her warm mouth, he caressed the crevices, tasting the essence of her.

Her body fit perfectly to his, her mouth, everything he could have imagined. Pure sweetness. She lifted on her toes, pressing in closer, her hands clinging to his shoulders. Loving the feel of her desire, he angled his head slightly, taking advantage of the easier access. The kiss bloomed wild and hot, and the desire to take it further shot through his body, threatening to obliterate his good intentions.

Pulling back, he held her close to his body as she swayed toward him. Her eyes opened slowly, blinking several times as though she was unaware of her surroundings. Finally answering the question that she had asked minutes earlier, he replied, "I'd love to come in, but I'm not going to." Seeing the confusion wash across her face, he hastened to explain, "Nothing more I'd like to do than to keep kissing you, but Belle, I wanna do this right. You deserve nothing but the best and I don't think I can give that to you right now."

Her head tilted and with her hands still holding tightly to his shoulders, she asked, "Why not?"

He looked upward toward the stars for a moment before dropping his head, the words groaning from deep inside. "Got some shit I'm working through."

"Oh," she said, but her voice betrayed her confusion.

"Soon, I promise. As soon as I get a handle on some things." Cupping her face once more, he kissed her lightly. "Belle, when I can come to you, and I will come to you, I want all of you to have all of me."

Kissing her once more, he linked fingers with her and walked her up to her house. "I'll stay until you're locked in."

She stepped through the door and he heard the lock flip. Regret moved through his heart as he replaced his helmet and threw his large leg over his bike. Roaring the engine, he pulled out of her short drive and turned to head to his camper, his mind on what he needed to take care of before he could claim her. Necessity flooded his thoughts, staying with him long into the night.

Belle lay in bed, her sighs long and loud as sleep evaded her. She finally arose and padded into the bathroom, taking some ibuprofen to dull the ache in her wrist, recognizing that going to work and carrying trays at

Finn's might have been just as Hunter had said...too much too soon.

Hunter. If she were honest, she knew why she could not sleep and it was not just her wrist. More like the handsome man with the kiss that could alter her universe. *What was he talking about? What does he need to take care of?* Sighing, she lay back down, trying to get her mind back on her career goals and not the man who had invaded all her thoughts.

An hour later she finally fell asleep, but he invaded her dreams.

7

Belle walked to the top of the stairs and smiled, seeing the other women already sitting around the two tables that had been pushed together. The second floor of Jillian's Coffee Shop was her galleria, where she displayed artwork from various local artists. The floor to ceiling windows allowed natural light to pour into the space and overlooked Main Street. It was also where she had a few glass-topped, wrought-iron tables with matching chairs. Lacy tablecloths and floral napkins covered the tables, coffee cups filled with aromatic brew all ready for the gathering of friends.

"Hey," she greeted.

Madelyn, Tori, Jillian, Jade, and Katelyn called out their greetings in return as she took a seat. "It's nice to have a day off so I can have coffee with you all," she said.

"Did you get your errands run?" Tori asked.

"Yep. Cleaned the house, ran to the grocery, and paid some bills. And now this," she waved her hand out, "is my reward." Looking at Tori, she asked, "Where's Eddie?"

Laughing, Tori replied, "Mitch's parents are having a morning playing Gramma and Papa."

"I love your dress," Jade gushed, staring at her white sundress covered in light blue flowers.

"Thanks," she said, reaching for her coffee mug. "I found it at the Goodwill store in Easton. I couldn't believe that it fit."

"Well, you're just in time for our wedding planning," Jade announced.

Grinning, she looked at the others and said, "Remember when we had wedding planning meetings for Tori and then Jillian and then Katelyn...all involved lots of drinking and dancing."

"Oh, God, that was fun," Jillian laughed. She smiled at Katelyn, nearly bursting as she neared the end of her pregnancy, and added, "Those days are long gone!"

After only a few minutes of planning, Jade closed her notebook and sighed. "This is all we need to do for now. Lance and I are trying to keep it small, but both our parents are wanting a much bigger event."

"Will you give in?" Katelyn asked.

A smile slid over Jade's face as she shook her head. "Nope...small, here in Baytown. Just what we want."

Ginny rounded the top of the stairs, wearing her BPD polo and khaki pants. "Sorry, only have a few minutes to pop in and say hello."

"We were just talking about weddings," Madelyn said.

Chuckling, Ginny reminded them of her and Brogan's wedding by the beach. "Only had friends there...it was perfect." She sucked in her lips for a moment and said, "I also wanted to pop by with some news."

Everyone's eyes grew wide as they stared at the pretty policewoman, strangely nervous.

"Well, Brogan and I are expecting—"

"Oh, my God!" they cried in jubilation. Hugs abounded, as Ginny accepted their congratulations.

Katelyn grinned at her sister-in-law. "We'll have cousins near the same age. Now, if we can just find someone for Aiden, then we can all have babies that can be the next generation of Baytown kids."

"Good luck with that," Jillian quipped.

As their mirth ebbed, Madelyn looked at Belle and said, "So...we were just talking before you came in..."

Belle halted her cup on its way to her lips at everyone's guilty expressions. "I guess that's why my ears were burning as I came in." Completing her sip, she asked, "And do I want to know what you all were talking about?"

Tori began, "You went off with Hunter the other night—"

"On the back of his motorcycle," Katelyn finished, lifting her eyebrow.

"Well, I...uh..." she blinked, uncertain what to say.

"Zac is really glad he moved here," Madelyn threw out.

"He lives near you, doesn't he?" Jade asked, her wide green eyes turned toward her.

Jillian looked around the table at the gathering and said, "Hey, let's not overwhelm her all at once."

Katelyn shot Jillian a pointed look, saying, "You're just a curious as the rest of us."

Grimacing, Jillian nodded, then, said to her, "She's right. I am, but I don't want you to feel ambushed. We're all just curious."

"Why?" She took another sip, fully aware that a blush was rising from her chest to her forehead. "It's nothing...really. We're just friends, that's all."

"Nothing? Honey, you've been friends with all the guys, but never rode off with one before."

"It's not like I knew we were going on his motorcycle. He asked if he could take me home and when we got outside, there it was. I was actually afraid at first." As her mind roamed back to the vibrations underneath her ass, her body pressed from breast to crotch against his hard, muscular frame, a slow smile curved her lips.

"I knew it!"

Jolting, she blinked, looking at Katelyn smiling like a Cheshire cat.

"I knew you liked him. That smile says it all. You've gotten rides home from Aiden, Callan, even Jason, but I've never seen you with a smile like that!" she crowed.

Opening and closing her mouth several times, she finally hid behind the coffee cup once more, taking a large swallow.

Tori leaned over and placed her hand on her arm, saying, "You okay?"

Sucking in a deep breath, she looked at the concerned faces of her friends and nodded. "Yeah, I'm fine. Really. It's just that...I..." blowing out a breath, she admitted, "This is really hard." The others remained quiet, giving her a chance to pull her thoughts together.

"I was never...you know...the girl that anyone was interested in." Seeing them about to protest, she threw her hand up. "I'm not looking for sympathy...it's just the way it was."

Jade asked, "Why do you say that? My God, you're beautiful. Any man would be honored to be with you."

Hating to be the center of attention, she pushed through the uncomfortable emotions, wanting to share with them. "You didn't know me growing up, Jade. You weren't here. Jillian and Katelyn were, but I was a year behind them in school, so it was different."

"Different?" Madelyn asked.

Nodding, she said, "Home life wasn't so great. We were poor and lived in the mobile home park, which wasn't as nice then as it is now. Back then, it was run-down. Some of the people who lived there were just down on their luck or living on a fixed income, but a lot were pretty scary. I used to be afraid when walking from the school bus stop. I learned quickly to keep to myself and not talk too much to anyone."

"Hoping to be invisible," Tori said softly, her fingers squeezing Belle's arm.

"Exactly!" she replied, her eyes wide as she looked at the others. "Your guys were a couple of years older, so they never knew me, but the ones around me...they were only interested in me for one thing and I was terrified of them." Taking another sip, she gathered her strength and admitted, "At school, the hardest thing was dealing with the stigma of the park. I was called trash more times than I can remember. I was always the kid who was afraid of her own shadow, and as I got older I got braver, but I was just as shy. Being shy...it's just me, and I accept that. But growing up the way I did...we.., it was hard."

"Oh, Belle," Jillian breathed, her eyes filling with tears. "I feel so bad that I had no idea."

She smiled and shook her head. "Don't take that on, Jillian. You had a smile for everyone in high school...we just were in different grades and ran in different circles."

"Cliques, you mean," Katelyn said, regret evident in her voice.

"Hey, all that's important is that I found the desire, somewhere deep inside, inspired by my grandmother, to be more than the life that had been handed to me by my mom." Shrugging, she said, "Hence, my desire to keep up my education."

"Good for you—" Jade pronounced, but Madelyn quickly interrupted.

"Yes, good for you, but honestly...please tell us about Hunter and how he fits into all this."

"I like him." As soon as the words left her lips, she wished she could pull them back. Even with her closest friends, saying the words aloud made her feel vulnerable. Looking at their faces, she observed no shock or censure, but she sucked in her lips, trying to figure out what to say next. Grateful when Madelyn stepped in, she listened with interest.

"Zac met Hunter when they served on the same ship.

Jason and Hunter were both mechanics, but he and Hunter had different jobs. Still, they clicked as friends. Zac always liked him and knew he didn't have the best of home situations to go back to, so he wanted to keep in touch. But, they lost contact for a couple of years. When they finally reconnected, Zac invited him to come here to live, just like he had with Jason. It took a while, but he finally accepted Zac's invitation."

Her voice, soft, she said, "I noticed him the first day he showed up at Careway. It's hard to miss him, he's so big."

"I met him when he dropped in at our wedding reception," Madelyn continued. "His hair was longer then, but I remember thinking that he was huge."

Giggling, she nodded. "Mr. Weldon has strict rules about his employees' appearance. Hunter shaved the sides but had the top long and kept it pulled back in a bun. Eventually he cut it shorter as well, but still long enough to tie back if he wanted. All part of Mr. Weldon's rules...uniforms and trimmed hair." Sighing, she added, "Hunter never acted like he knew I was alive, but I was always tongue-tied around him so I guess that makes sense. It wasn't until I ran into his ladder and hurt my wrist that we had a real conversation."

"And now?" Tori prodded.

"He confuses me," she answered, putting all her feelings into three words. Seeing the lifted eyebrows, she tried to think of how else to describe her relationship with Hunter. "He...seems to want to know me better, but then pulls back."

Rolling her eyes, Jillian moaned, "Oh God, save us from relationship-phobic men!"

Belle had watched as Grant held Jillian at arm's length when he returned from the military, only to have her give up on them before he realized he wanted a relationship with his former girlfriend. Now, happily married, it was hard to imagine that he had ever been that pig-headed.

"I don't think it's that," she said. "He said that he had things he needed to work on before he felt like he could be the man that he felt I deserved

Nodding, Madelyn said, "Zac did mention that Hunter was somewhat of a mystery. They're friends, but he said that since Hunter has come to Baytown, he feels like he keeps more to himself."

"Ooh, a secretive man," Jade said, a smile curving her lips. "Sounds a lot like Lance."

She thought about the comparison, but shook her head. "Lance was more of a recluse that you had to pull out of his shell. Hunter isn't like that. There's just something he keeps close to the vest." Suddenly, looking around, she said, "Hey, I don't want all the conversation to be about me today."

The others slid into various conversations about what was happening in their lives, their jobs, and their relationships. She listened attentively, but could not keep her mind from wondering about the secrets Hunter kept deep inside...*and if he'll ever let me in.*

8

Pain Management Center. *Here we go.* Hunter entered the facility and spoke to the receptionist. Filling out the pages of initial paperwork, including medical history and recent symptoms, he handed them to her along with his insurance card.

"I see you had an injury due to active military duty," she said, scanning the papers.

"Yes, ma'am. I wanted to get an appointment as soon as possible."

She nodded and consulted her appointment program. "I can get you in to see Dr. Harber next Tuesday."

Agreeing, he took the proffered card and nodded as he left the building. *It's only a few days away,* he reminded himself. As he moved toward his motorcycle, he observed a pharmaceutical van parked at the side entrance. He watched as the driver alighted from his vehicle. As he moved closer, seeing his face, recognition hit. Glancing around discretely, he approached the driver.

"Lionel?"

The man turned around and looked at him, a questioning smile on his face. "Yeah?"

He smiled and stepped forward, his hand extended. "I was told you might work around here." Hesitating a second, he added, "Seems we've got a mutual friend...Scott."

Lionel's eyes widened in understanding. Shaking his hand, he kept his sharp gaze on Hunter. "How do you know Scott?"

"Served together. Last tour I did."

"Yeah? You in the Army, too?" Lionel questioned, his smile no longer reaching his eyes. "And how is Scott?"

Holding Lionel's gaze, unwaveringly, he replied, "Scott wasn't in the Army. Navy...same as me. And *Scott* is fine, but maybe he was wrong about you being someone I should get to know. Sorry, man." Turning, he made it two steps away before Lionel called him back.

"No, no, I'm sorry. Didn't mean to be an asshole. Just gotta be careful, you know? What'd you say your name was?"

He rotated slowly back around, his smile no longer in place. "Didn't say."

"Yeah, yeah, right. Well, uh, it was nice meeting you. Uh...you wanna meet for drinks sometime? Good place not too far from here."

"No so much into socializing unless there's something I can get out of it," he replied, his eyes remaining on Lionel.

"Look, any friend of Scott's is a friend of mine. Honest."

The desperate look in Lionel's eyes had him standing firm. Nodding slowly, he said, "When do you get off work? I'm free and got some time."

"This is my last run, so I just gotta take the van back to the company and then I can meet you."

"Company?"

Lionel's eyes shot toward the side of the van where the company's logo was located and he waved his hand in that direction. "Matrix Pharmaceuticals. They supply the needs of some of the people around here."

Nodding slowly, he said, "Seen you delivering to Careway Nursing Home." Just as Lionel's eyes widened, fright moving in, he added, "I work there. When I talked to Scott, figured it was a good time to make a connection. You know, make things easier…"

A grin spread over Lionel's face as he nodded enthusiastically. "Yeah, absolutely. Listen, I'll meet you at Toby's Bar, over near the wharf in Melton. It's about ten miles from here. We can have a drink and share a few old stories about Scott."

A chuckle rumbled up from his chest as he agreed. "I'll be there." As the van pulled out of the parking lot, he stalked back to his motorcycle. Swinging his leg over the seat, he settled and fastened his helmet.

An image of sweet, innocent Belle filled his thoughts again. Digging his fingers in to massage his thigh, he pushed thoughts of her to the recesses of his mind. Looking back up at the Pain Management Center he winced. He hoped they could do the job while simultaneously thinking of Lionel. Blowing out a breath, he started the engine and roared out of the parking lot.

The inside of the bar was dark and the floor was sticky underneath his boots. Several people looked up as he walked toward the booth near the back, but with his size, it was no problem to shoot them a glare that had their eyes jerking down quickly. He used to hate using his size to intimidate, but it was the one thing his father taught him that he actually found useful.

Seeing Lionel lounge in the booth, he looked over and jerked his head up to the bartender in a silent order for a beer. Sliding into the opposite seat, he stared at the man sitting across from him. Tall, but thin. His dark hair was long and appeared to need washing. He was still in the company's uniform of dark pants and a blue shirt with the Matrix Pharmaceutical logo on the pocket.

"So, what'd Scott tell you about me?" Lionel asked, taking a sip of beer while keeping his eyes on Hunter.

"You already call him? Checking?"

Lionel chuckled and nodded. "Yeah, you got me. He said you're okay. We can discuss business."

"Not interested in your business...just what I might get."

"Personal?"

Nodding, he lifted his beer and took a long drink, the cool liquid a welcome distraction from the distaste in his mouth from what he was doing.

"I can set you up. Percocet. Oxycodone. Fentanyl. That'll take care of what you need. But, I'm wondering why you're not tapping your own resources."

Lifting an eyebrow, he cocked his head, keeping silent.

"You work at a nursing home, man. That place is crawling with drugs. And I'm not just talking about the old folk's blood pressure medicine. Hell, they got high powered pain killers, mood-altering shit, narcotics... hell, it's a drug smorgasbord."

"I'm maintenance, asshole. It's not like I can get my hands on anything there."

Sniggering, Lionel leaned back. "All you gotta do is find a nurse who doesn't mind being compromised...or probably already is." He narrowed his eyes at Hunter. "I've got someone there who helps me out occasionally. But, I'm under strict orders to not mess with her. She's a sweet piece who has no idea she's part of a much bigger chain. She just makes it easy for me, that's all."

He buried his face into his mug of beer, taking a long swig, hoping to hide the surprise on his face. *Who the fuck is he talking about? Not Belle...he knew that for sure. Jesus, fuck.* Rolling his mind back over the nurses he knew worked at Careway, there were a few who could be called a sweet piece. Sucking in a deep breath at the thought of Belle, he stayed cool. *I've got to get myself straight first before I've got anything to offer her.*

Lionel interrupted his warring thoughts. "I gotta go, man. I'll fix you up until you see what you can do for me at Careway. Don't mind having another person to work with, that's for sure. Meet me back here in two days, same time, and I'll have some good shit for you." Standing, he tossed a few bills onto the table and chuckled, "It'll take your pain away for sure."

Hunter watched the other man walk out of the bar and gave him a few minutes before he headed out as well. What he had was enough for now. *But I'm gonna need more. Fuck!* Chest tight, he grimaced at the mess he found himself in. Roaring back down the road toward Baytown, he inwardly cursed the entire way home, caught between what he needed and Belle.

Hunter had to drive past Belle's mobile home to get to his camper. He intended to keep on driving, but seeing her in her front yard, bent over with her lovely, heart-shaped ass up in the air, his hands turned his motorcycle into her short drive before his brain had a chance to ignore the impulse.

She twisted her head around at the sound and when she saw him pull into her drive, her face lit with a smile. Standing, she wiped her good hand off on a little apron that was tied about her waist. She cocked her head to the side, waiting for him to cut his engine. A simple, unadorned T-shirt drew his eye until his gaze dropped to her cut-off jeans showcasing her legs. Her feet were bare and he wondered why he never noticed how dainty her pink-painted toenails were.

He glanced at her wrist, seeing it still wrapped. Her gaze followed his and she held it up, wiggling her fingers.

"It's fine. I'm just using my good hand to pull some weeds before they take over my flower beds."

He nodded as he pulled off his helmet. His eyes moved from her fresh face to the ground nearby. "Looks good. You keep a real pretty yard."

Her smile, which had sparkled, now beamed brighter. "Thank you! I try to keep it nice. I like having pretty things around me."

Neither one of them spoke for a moment and she shifted, looking at her feet. "Uh, would you like some iced tea? I was just about to get some for myself."

Nodding, he silently followed her as she turned and walked into her house. Once again, his eyes roamed over the cozy interior. "I know I said this the other night, but you've got a nice place here."

She smiled, moving into the kitchen to pull down two glasses. "It's a lot different from what I grew up in."

He remained silent and she continued as she poured the drinks. "My mama had a small trailer, and that was back when the whole place was run-down. Lots of people didn't cut their grass or plant flowers." She walked to the table and set the two glasses down, nodding toward the chairs.

He took her invitation to sit and settled in next to her. After a few minutes of chatting, he said, "Went to the Pain Management Center today to make an appointment."

"Oh," Belle replied, her head cocked and compassion lines creasing her face. She opened her mouth, then, closed it again.

Answering her silent question, he said, "I was injured while in the Navy."

Leaning forward, she placed her hand on his arm, her eyes holding his gaze. "Oh, Hunter. What happened?" Blinking, she rushed, "But only if you want to talk about it. I know some people don't want to talk and that's just fine if you—"

He chuckled, the sound rumbling from his chest. "Nah, it's okay. I wouldn't have brought it up if it was some big secret."

"Oh, right."

"I did maintenance on the ship...not on the engines. Just a Machinery Repairman on an aircraft carrier."

"The same ship as Zac?"

Nodding, he said, "Yeah, and Jason, actually. Jason was a mechanic, like me, but Zac worked as a Fireman on board. We met over a few small machinery fires. Couldn't be more different in personalities but, somehow, we became friends."

Smiling, she patted his arm. "Zac's a friendly guy."

"We bonded over bad coffee and discovered both our dads were drunks." Seeing her eyes widen, he inwardly cursed at his indiscretion, but before he could backtrack, she spoke softly.

"I can see how that would be. It's hard to talk about your parents to others when you don't know if they would understand."

He remained quiet and she looked down at the table, her fingers absently twitching on his arm. Lifting her gaze, she shrugged and simply said, "My mom."

Understanding crossed his features and he nodded. "Sorry, Belle."

Blinking, she sat up straighter and said, "Goodness, this was supposed to be about your injury. Please continue."

Shrugging, he said, "Not a lot to tell. Had an explosion when a small engine got too hot and I was unfortunately too close at the time. Some metal pieces flew out and into my thigh. Zac got there quickly, got the fire put out and made sure to get the medics to me. Ended up having minor surgery to dig them out, but the docs said there were a few small pieces still embedded."

Her fingers clenched on his arm and her brow lowered as she leaned in closer. "Oh, Hunter, that must have been so painful...still painful."

"It bothers me sometimes..."

"It must bother you enough to seek out the Pain Management Center."

Shrugging again, he focused on her hand on his arm, loving the way she alternated between giving a little squeeze and gentle rubbing. The thought of her hand doing that to other parts of his body had him shifting uncomfortably in his chair. Clearing his throat, he deflected, "We'll see."

"I've heard good things about them," she continued. "I'm sure they can help you."

"I have, too. Worries me a little that they focus so much on physical therapy. Sometimes you just need a little extra, you know? The therapy helps over time, but at first it can be a real pain. I'm hoping they've got something they can give me to just take the edge off the pain when it hits." He lifted his gaze to her face, observing as she cocked her head to the side.

"You have to be careful, Hunter. Those types of drugs can be addictive. I think seeking out the Center, where they have alternative therapies to aid, is a good idea."

"What about Careway? I know some of those patients have to be on pain medication. Aren't you afraid of them using those drugs?"

She sucked her lips in, her face scrunching in thought. "Of course, and it can be hard. Not every patient has the same doctors, so some are prescribed stronger drugs than others." Her shoulders slumped as she added, "And, of course, some are prescribed the heavier doses when they are terminal and near the end."

Shaking his head, he said, "I don't see how you keep all the drugs straight for all the patients."

"Oh, we have to be so careful," she replied, her earnest face turned up toward him. "We keep each patient's prescription bottles in their own section of the cabinet. Linda Sobieski, the head nurse, is working with Mr. Weldon to have us move to a different pharmaceutical company...one that puts each patient's medicines in their own punch-out card. She seems to think that will work best, but he is a little reticent to change."

"He seems pretty progressive..."

"Yeah, but I think he's got some friends in the pharmaceutical company that we use, so that may be why he's held off."

"Does Careway ever have a problem with missing

drugs...or thefts? Seems like I read an article about that —not with them, but with nursing homes in general."

Her face scrunched again, and she replied, "Not that I know of but, then, I'm not involved in ordering. Linda does that." She thought for a moment and added, "I mean, I guess it wouldn't be too hard. All it would take is for someone who is doling out the medicine to leave out a pill or two. Some of our residents know exactly what pills they are due, but others just take the little cup and swallow them down." Shaking her head, she looked back at him, her eyes full of concern and said, "That'd be so horrible. To steal drugs from a defenseless person."

She stood to refill their drink glasses. Sure that she was not the Careway employee Lionel intimated was selling drugs, he sucked in a huge breath before letting it out slowly, his mind in turmoil.

9

Belle walked out of Mrs. Lappendale's room, her smile strained. A few of the residents were very demanding and she was usually extremely understanding. Sometimes their complaints stemmed from pain, loneliness, or frustration at not being able to do all of the things they used to be able to do. But, in Mrs. Lappendale's case, she had an imperial attitude from years of having servants and saw no difference between the nurses and the employees she was used to ordering about.

Rubbing her forehead, she walked down the hall, wishing she could see Hunter. After their talk the other day, he had been more removed at work. Hearing laughter, she glanced through the open door of the employee lounge and saw him standing close to one of the nursing aides. *Nola.* A strange jolt to her heart had her turn away sharply. *We're nothing but friends...he owes me nothing.* She continued down the hall, trying to purge the image of the two of them, his head bent as he closely listened to whatever Nola was saying. Her hand on his bicep as she smiled seductively up at him.

Finding an empty corner, she leaned her back against the wall, her chin dropped to her chest. *Why Nola?* Snorting, she knew the reason. Nola was known as a flirt...bragged about her sexual conquests. A sigh slipped from her lips as she realized the underserved reputation she had when a teen was what grown men seemed to gravitate toward.

Pushing off the wall, she continued down the hall, determined to force thoughts of Hunter back into the co-worker category and out of her heart.

Hunter forced his body to lean intimately toward Nola, hoping their conversation would not be overheard, but the odor of her foul smoker's breath had him fighting to keep from recoiling back.

"So, you've worked here for a year?" he asked.

"Yeah," she grinned up at him, her hand moving to squeeze his arm. "We've never had anyone as good-looking as you come through."

"I met a guy the other day, said he knew someone who worked here, but I forgot to get the name. He's Lionel."

Nola's brow crinkled. "Don't know a Lionel." Her face relaxed as a sly smile curved her lips. "But then, I don't always worry about their names, if you know what I mean. Sometimes a hookup needs no name, unless you plan on going back for seconds."

Chuckling, he inwardly grimaced. "This guy works for a drug company. Delivers here, I think."

Her eyes widened. "Dark hair...kind of scruffy? Yeah, him and me had a quick fuck once. Can't say I know him, though, if you know what I mean." She giggled, adding, "But, hell, we did it in the back of his delivery van."

"So, you don't see him regular?"

Shaking her head, she replied, "Nah. Just that once and it was enough, if you know what I mean."

Forcing interest in her limited, repetitive vocabulary, he said, "Well, Lionel didn't kiss and tell."

Slapping his arm, she slid closer, her bad breath hitting him in the face, and said, "Don't bother me none, if they talk."

Standing back to his full height, he stepped backward. "Well, I gotta get back to work."

Her mouth fell into a pout, and she said, "I'm available...for whatever you might have in mind."

"I don't think so," he said, with an easy grin. With that, he turned quickly and headed back out into the hall. Breathing easier with the clean air, he knew he needed to be careful. It was risky to try to find out who he might score drugs from at Careway without gaining attention. Scrubbing his hand over his face, he listened as his name was called on the radio to come to one of the residents' room. Glad to get back to work, he walked down the hall.

Entering Mr. Rasky's room, he heard the older man say, "'Bout time you got here. Told her this was a bad idea."

His feet came to a halt at the sight of Belle's sweet ass at eye level as she perched on top of the bed, reaching to hang a picture on the wall.

"What the fu—what are you doing?" he growled, hearing her yelp of surprise as his hands grasped her waist and plucked her from the bed. "You just broke all kinds of rules," he continued, anger lacing his voice.

"I told her that, but she insisted," Mr. Rasky tattled. "Told her to wait for you to come, but she was determined to do it herself, so I called for you instead."

Belle's face flamed bright red as she rubbed her hands over her thighs. "He wanted a different picture hung there. The nail was already in the wall..."

"Doesn't matter," Hunter said, his fingers itching to pull her close and spank her all at the same time. "You've already got one injured wrist and here you are, risking the rest of you. What the hell were you thinking?"

She spared a glance over at Mr. Rasky, pursing her lips, before shooting her gaze up to Hunter. "I thought maybe you were *busy* in the break room or something."

He narrowed his eyes at her but she twisted around quickly.

"Well, since you're here, you can finish the job. I'll see you later, Mr. Rasky."

He watched as she skirted around him and hustled out of the room. Standing with his hands on his hips, he still felt anger flowing through his veins, but the sight of her ass as she walked out had him dropping his head. "Fuck," he breathed.

"Well, that could have gone better," Mr. Rasky cackled.

The same words had spilled from Zac's mouth when they were last at the pub and he wondered if he was destined to keep making mistakes around Belle. Swinging his head over to the older man, he nodded. "Yep."

"Wonder why she thought you were busy?"

Scrubbing his hand over his face, he chuckled ruefully. "Guess she must have seen something and made an assumption."

"Yeah...thing about assumptions," Mr. Rasky said. "You get an idea about someone and it's hard to let it go." He pinned him with his sharp stare and added, "I'm a good judge of character and I'd say you're just the type of man Belle needs in her life."

Glaring in return, he asked, "Did you call me in here, with her balancing up on your bed, knowing I'd have a fit?"

Leaning his head back, Mr. Rasky closed his eyes. "Kind of tired now, boy. Think I'll take a nap."

Staring at his boots, he shook his head. "Guess I better go make amends."

"You do that, Hunter. You do that."

Belle lifted Mr. Rosenberg's head enough that he was able to take a sip of water from the straw. Afterward, she gently lay his head back on the pillow and set the cup onto the bedside table. Taking a wet washcloth, she smoothed it over his face and neck.

She had managed to stay away from Hunter for the rest of the afternoon and now it was after hours, which meant he would already be gone. The day shift of employees had left, leaving only the minimum night staff, but she stayed to check on Mr. Rosenberg.

He did not acknowledge her presence, the pain medicine keeping him comfortable and allowing him to slip into a deep sleep. He was a long-term resident of Careway, having come to live there ten years ago when his wife died. She had met him when she was a teen volunteer and used to read to him. Their friendship continued as he encouraged her to pursue her nursing aide training, then her LPN degree, and recently as she approached graduation with her RN.

His encouragement was rivaled only by her grandmother's, but with Grannie's passing, Mr. Rosenberg had become a stand-in grandparent.

Linda stopped by on her way out, offering her words of comfort. "He's lucky to have you."

Shaking her head, she corrected, "I was lucky to have him."

Looking at him with a sympathetic gaze, Linda said, "It will probably be soon. I'll call hospice and have them come in first thing tomorrow morning."

She swallowed deeply. "I'll stay with him."

Patting her shoulder, Linda nodded her agreement. "Professionally, I should warn you against becoming so attached...but in this business, it only makes you a more caring nurse."

Offering a watery smile of thanks, she remained silent.

"Once you get your RN, will you stay with us?"

Her gaze shot to Linda's and her eyes widened. "I can't imagine working anywhere else."

Nodding, Linda simply responded, "Good," before walking out of the room.

The hours passed and she busied herself around his room. She cleaned a few things off his nightstand, throwing away old tissues and cups. Opening the top drawer, her gaze landed on his old, silver pocket watch. Picking it up reverently, she turned it over and traced the engraving on the back. "Your loving wife forever, Bea."

She sucked in her lips, pressing them tightly to keep the tears at bay, but it was to no avail. They flowed freely, knowing that soon he would be joining her. Swallowing past the lump in her throat, she replaced the watch carefully and shut the drawer.

Just when she thought she might take a break, his breathing became more labored. Following the hospice doctor's instructions, she increased his medication after having one of the night LPN's join her.

Alone once more, she sat by his bed, taking his hand in hers, and waited.

Lying in bed, sleep did not find Hunter. He had not run into Belle again that afternoon and when he left, he drove by her house several times but her car never showed up in her driveway. *She's probably out with the girls...trash-talking me.* As soon as that thought hit his mind, he dismissed it. It did not seem like Belle's style to trash-talk anyone, even if she thought the worst about them.

Kicking himself for not picking a more discreet time and place to question Nola, he heaved a sigh. *Maybe it's for the best...I'm in a fucked-up place in my life to try to start a relationship.* But, the idea of Belle made it hard to be noble. It had been a long time since he had anything so sweet in his life... *Actually, I've never had anything that sweet.*

Giving up on sleep, he headed out, determined to see if she were safe at home. A moment later, his heart pounded with fear as he noted her car was still not in her driveway. Roaring down the road in the middle of the night, he headed to Careway to see if anyone noticed when she left.

Pulling into the parking lot, he observed her car parked over to the side, not in her usual spot. *Was she parked there yesterday? Did I miss her when I left? Has she been here all this time?* Quickly securing his helmet, he stalked into the building. The night staff was on duty, and he watched as one of the aides walked quietly down the hall.

Heading directly to her, he asked, "Have you seen Belle? Her car's outside—"

"She's with Mr. Rosenberg. He's...he's..."

Understanding dawned and he started jogging toward the back hall. Slowing down as he neared the room, he willed his heart to calm. Sucking in a deep breath, he stepped inside, greeted by a sight that caused his heart to stutter.

Belle was sitting next to the dying man, her melodious voice speaking softly. He walked over and she looked up, her eyes widening as she saw him. Without saying a word, he moved into a chair on the other side of the bed and nodded toward her to indicate she should continue.

She licked her lips before turning back to the dying man. She continued to read from the book in her lap, a tale of lovers finding each other again after being separated for so long. As she came to the end of the story, she said, "I know you miss your Bea."

She looked over at him and explained, "Bea was his wife. They were married for over fifty years but she died ten years ago."

He offered a nod and she heaved a sigh. Pulling out his phone, he searched for a moment before turning the volume up. The sounds of beautiful, instrumental music filled the air, creating a peaceful backdrop to her readings. Reading another story, her eyes would stray up to his, a sad smile playing about her lips as he willed his strength into her.

Hours passed and they stayed with Mr. Rosenberg. Occasionally she would stand to stretch, and he would walk over to massage her shoulders. "I didn't get to do this with my mother," she said softly. Her words broke as she said, "She overdosed one night. That was it. She was there and then gone. No one to hold her hand…"

"Belle, don't. Your mother made choices that were her own…just like my dad did. But what you do here, is a choice. You give to those who are willing to receive."

Blowing out a long breath, she nodded before moving back to the bedside. Sitting on the edge of the bed, she rubbed Mr. Rosenberg's hands while Hunter told him stories of fishing off one of the Navy piers in Norfolk.

At one point, he laid his head back against the chair and drifted off to sleep for a few minutes. Waking in a jerk, he observed Belle, her head lying on her arm as her hand clasped Mr. Rosenberg's. The soft sound of crying met his ears and his gaze jumped to the machines hooked up to the dying man, noting the heartbeat had slowed dramatically.

He moved quickly and knelt on the other side of the bed from her, reaching over to place his large hand on hers. Together, they held Mr. Rosenberg's gnarled hands as he passed away. She lifted her head and stared, first at Mr. Rosenberg, and then at him. Their hands remained clasped, their breathing slight. The sunrise was just sending its rays through the window. Their eyes met and centuries of fresh grief passed between them.

"He's with Bea," he said, his voice raspy with emotion as he swallowed past the lump in his throat.

Nodding, a fresh tear slid down her cheek and he reached up to wipe it away. Before he had a chance to speak again, Linda hurried into the room and immediately moved to Belle. "Honey, it's time. You need to let him go."

Belle turned her tear-stained face up and nodded

silently. She allowed Linda to assist her up, accepting a hug from her supervisor.

"You've been here all night. Go home...take today off...rest."

Mr. Weldon walked into the room and said, "I'll call the funeral home. The only next-of-kin is a distant, great niece who said that she was told he would be cremated and his ashes were to be buried next to his wife. She said she won't be coming, and that the funeral home will handle everything."

He turned to Belle and Hunter and reiterated, "Go home, you two. You've done all you can for him." As she turned to walk toward the door, where he already stood, Mr. Weldon pulled her into a hug and patted her back. "You are what I always strive to have here at Careway."

Hunter watched as she walked toward him, still standing in the doorway, but she did not appear to see him. Her eyes were swollen and she moved robotically. Following, he watched as one of the aides brought her purse to her and she walked out the door.

He continued to follow at a distance, uncertain what he should do. He had wanted to talk to her, assure her he was only talking to Nola about work and nothing else but, now, he stood awkwardly watching as she stopped at her car door.

Suddenly, she slumped to the ground and his feet became unstuck as he raced to her. Dropping to her side, he scooped her into his arms, cradling her tightly to his chest.

"Belle," he whispered into her hair before leaning back to see her face. "When did you eat last?"

Her confused expression told him all he needed to know. Standing, he carried her to the passenger side and deposited her gently into the seat. Pushing the driver's seat back to accommodate his long legs, he started her car and pulled out of the parking lot.

"What are you doing?" she asked, her voice wan.

"Taking you home...feeding you...and then, tucking you into bed." He looked over as she started to protest, but he silenced her. "Nope, not a word. You need someone to look after you."

She remained silent for most of the drive home but, then, he heard her speak so softly, he had to strain to hear. "I've been taking care of myself most of my life."

His heart ached to hear the sadness in her voice, identifying with the words she said. "I know, Belle. But now...let me help. Please."

———

10

Belle woke slowly, her eyelids heavy. She lay in bed for a moment, trying to remember what day it was and why she was still in bed when the daylight poured in through the slats in the blinds. Piece by piece, her memory slid back into place. The long night, sitting vigil by Mr. Rosenberg's bed before he finally passed quietly in the early morning, just as the sun rose.

Hunter sharing that experience with her before she collapsed at her car and he drove her home. He had fixed her a bowl of oatmeal and made her drink a glass of milk.

She lifted the covers, checking her attire...a T-shirt and drawstring pajama bottoms. She did not remember changing out of her nursing scrubs, but refused to consider how else she might have gotten into her bedclothes.

Focusing her eyes on the clock on her nightstand, she saw it was almost three p.m. Tossing back the covers, she climbed from bed and walked to the bathroom. Taking care of business, she splashed water on her face, holding a cold compress on her eyes for a moment.

Walking down the short hall to her living area, she stopped short at the sight that greeted her. Hunter, lounging on her sofa, the remote in his hand as he watched a baseball game on TV with the sound muted. His eyes jerked up to hers and he turned the TV off, dropping the remote on the coffee table as he stood.

He met her in three steps, placing his hands on her shoulders. "You okay?"

"What…what are you doing here?"

"I brought you home."

"I know that…but what are you still doing here?"

He ignored her question and repeated his, "Are you okay?"

Blinking, she stared wordlessly. He gave her shoulders a tiny shake, drawing her eyes back to his. "Belle?"

As though waking from a dream, she nodded and replied, "Yeah. I slept."

"Good. You needed it."

"How did I get in my pajamas?" she blurted.

He licked his lips slowly before answering, "You did that…I just made sure you were still standing so you wouldn't fall on your face, but you did it all on your own."

She nodded again, her brain still too foggy to ponder his response. "Oh." Silence filled the space between them before she lifted her head and repeated, "Why are you still here? Aren't you tired too?"

"I slept on your sofa. I wanted to make sure you

were all right. I checked on you a couple of times and you seemed to be sleeping well, but I wanted to be nearby in case you needed me."

"Oh."

Grinning, he lifted her chin with his knuckle and said, "Sounds like you're still half asleep."

Pursing her lips, she grumbled, "No, I'm not. Just confused, that's all." Taking a deep breath before letting it out in a long sigh, she said, "I can't believe I slept the day away."

"You were up all night."

She nodded, her heart aching once more. "I needed to be with him. I know the drugs he was on kept him mostly unconscious but, just in case, I didn't want him to be alone when he went to be with Bea."

She lifted her gaze back to his and said, "He kept a pocket watch in his nightstand drawer for ten years that was from her with an engraving." Sighing, she added, "I know he's at peace now and out of pain. And with her."

Uncertain what to say, he pulled her forward, keeping one hand on the back of her head with her cheek pressed to his chest and she slid her arms around his waist. They stood in her living room for several minutes drawing strength from each other. He finally said, "You're a good person, Belle. You might be the best person I've ever met in my life."

She leaned back, keeping her eyes on his, but seeing only sincerity there. "Oh," she breathed.

Chuckling again, Hunter was getting used to her one-word answers when she seemed to not know what else to say. He walked her over to the sofa and gently pushed her down. "Hungry?"

Shaking her head, she answered, "Not really. Mostly thirsty."

He nodded and headed into the kitchen to open the refrigerator. As he poured a glass of iced tea, Belle watched, in awe, at the beauty of Hunter Simmons in her kitchen as though he belonged there. The memory of him standing closely with Nola came back and before she could hold back the words, she blurted, "So what's up with Nola?"

His gaze jerked to hers and she stopped breathing as she waited for his answer.

He moved his eyes over her face and said, "Breathe, babe."

Her breath left her in a whoosh. His lips curved as he walked back over and sat down on the coffee table, his long legs on either side of hers, effectively boxing her in. Handing her the glass, he said, "There's nothing going on with Nola. I thought we had a mutual friend and asked her about it. She didn't know him and the conversation ended. I came looking for you after I finished with Mr. Rasky, but you were nowhere to be found. I thought you'd left for the day."

He leaned forward and grasped her hands. "I wish I'd known where you were. I woulda never left you."

"But you came back...and stayed." She reached up and cupped his strong jaw with her hand. "I'm so thankful you came back. I'm so glad I had someone to share that with." She thought for a moment and amended, "I'm so glad it was you that I had to share it with."

"There's nowhere else I'd rather be than with you, Belle," he said, his hands squeezing hers.

She shook her head slightly from side to side and said, "You're giving me mixed signals, Hunter. First, you tell me that you can't be what I need, then, you seem to avoid me, and now, you're telling me you want to be with me. I don't understand. I've never played these games before...I don't understand the rules."

He took her face in both of his hands, cupping her jaw and pressing his fingers to the back of her head, pulling her close. "No games, Belle, I promise. I felt like the time wasn't right, and maybe it isn't, but, the fact of the matter is, I want to be with you." Closing the gap, he kissed her, far more lightly than he wanted but instinctively knowing what she needed.

His mouth moved over hers, not hungry, but caring. He angled her head as he licked the seam of her lips and as she opened, he slid his tongue inside. The barest touch sparked flames, but he was determined to give and not take. Pulling back, he could not help but grin at the tiny mewl of discontent she made.

Her eyes were still closed and her lips moist from the kiss. Fluttering her lids open, she stared into his face but said nothing.

Standing, regretfully, he said, "Gonna get you fed and then get you outta here for a little while to get some fresh air. Thought we could head down to the town pier."

She smiled, her shoulders relaxing. Nodding, she replied, "That sounds wonderful."

As he stood, he leaned over and kissed the top of her head before moving into the kitchen.

Belle looked down at their linked fingers and wondered what she was doing. As her gaze moved up to Hunter's strong profile, she stumbled at the realization that after years of guarding her heart, this man could be the one to finally break through...and possibly break it.

He glanced down at her and loosened his hand from hers before wrapping his arm around her shoulders, steadying her feet. "You okay?"

She nodded in response and looked away from his handsome visage and out toward the bay. The sun was lowering in the sky but the sunset was still over an hour away so they had plenty of daylight to enjoy the view.

The white clouds caused the water to appear more grey than blue but, with little wind, the quiet water barely rippled. As they made their way to the end of the wooden pier, she sucked in a deep breath of clear air, filling her lungs.

He lowered himself to the planks, gently tugging her down with him. She settled in the crook of his arm, her head leaning on his shoulder.

They sat silent for a while, watching the gulls dive into the surf and a few black pelicans fly low over the water.

"I've lived in Baytown my whole life," she said,

finally breaking the silence.

He barely moved his head but managed to snuggle closer. "It's a good place to live."

She snorted softly, replying, "I wouldn't have anything to compare it to. Sometimes I look at magazines or TV and imagine myself living in different places. Some people think of living in different lands, but I always just think about the different locations here in the United States. Each year, I'll buy a pretty calendar for myself and hang it in the kitchen. Whatever place is pictured for that month, is where I'll pretend to visit. Grand Canyon, the plains of Kansas, the Smokey Mountains, the desert in Arizona." She sighed and added, "But it's just a game I play. Pretend. The truth of the matter is that if I was given a choice of where to live in the world, it would be right here in Baytown." Another sigh followed. "I guess that's kind of sad, isn't it?"

Hunter twisted around, just enough to look into her face. The breeze had picked up and wisps of her dark, rich hair escaped her ponytail. Lifting a hand, he tucked the wayward strands behind her ear, drawing her gaze up to his. "Nothing sad about your life at all, Belle. I came from a place that I could not wait to escape."

She wanted to ask questions but also wanted him to talk to her when he was ready. He seemed to sense that and they settled back again, their eyes out toward the bay.

"Grew up in Tennessee...a little town, but not like this. More like a has-been place that time had forgotten. Coal mines and a factory used to produce jobs, but when both shut down, there were few jobs and too much alcohol to make for a good upbringing. My mom left when I was just a kid. I never knew exactly why, but I figure she had had enough of my pa. He was a drunk... and a mean one at that. He spent more nights in the county jail sobering up after a bar fight than at home and ma just got tired of it all."

Belle's breath caught in her throat as she listened to his story. "Oh, Hunter..."

Shrugging, he continued, "He'd get pissed at the world and then just go out and get stinking drunk. Used me as a punching bag, but by the time I was a teenager, I could punch back. Once I did that, he backed off."

Her body tightened with tension, but he continued. "I worked odd jobs while finishing high school. Spent time with the car mechanic down the street and he taught me how to fix engines. Spent summers working with a construction crew where I learned how to build and repair things." Shaking his head, he said, "Learned more from some of those men than I ever did from my pa."

Her body relaxed slightly and she leaned against him, the fatigue of the past twenty-four hours weighing on her. He took her weight and tightened his arm around her.

"Joined the Navy as soon as I got my high school diploma. Scored high on the technical parts of the ASVAB, and had a desire to work maintenance on the ships. Learned a lot there too. Met some good people... made a few friends...then, by the time I recovered from my injury, I was ready to get out."

"Did you go back to Tennessee?"

He did not answer for a few minutes and she wondered if he was going to.

"My pa died when I was in the Navy. Dumb fuck got drunk and behind the wheel of his car and ran off the road and into a tree. Thank God, he didn't hurt anyone other than himself. So, I went back, but it was as though the town was still stuck. No new jobs and everyone looking at me as though I was nothing more than Dan's boy—the next generation to get pissed and in a bar fight. I stayed for two weeks and left."

Fascinated with the idea of picking up and moving to someplace new, she asked, "Where did you go?" Twisting around to look at him, she said, "You could have gone anywhere!"

Chuckling, he held her gaze for a moment. "Yeah, I suppose. But, I still went somewhere I was familiar with instead of just anywhere. I moved to Norfolk...it was the last place I had been stationed when I wasn't on a ship overseas. I knew a little about the area...at least enough to know there were jobs there."

"Oh," she said, still curious, but settling back into his embrace. "Did you want to work on ships?"

"Nah. I was glad to have my feet firmly on the ground."

She grinned at that, but remained quiet, loving the feel of his warm, muscular chest moving underneath her cheek and his breath ruffling her hair as he talked.

"I found a job working maintenance. Liked what I was doing and who I was working for. A good man, someone I really looked up to, suggested I take some classes, further my education. I was never too bad in school, but also never applied myself when I was a teenager. Decided to take some night classes, see where it could go. Anyway, one job led to another and I kept busy. Zac had gotten in touch when he got out of the Navy...he was discharged about a year or two after me. He used to talk about Baytown all the time and, once out, began to tell me about the American Legion here. I wasn't in the right place in my life then, but eventually it worked out. I was ready for a change and the job at the nursing home came up, so the timing was right for a move."

"Did you leave behind any broken hearts when you moved?" she asked, attempting to sound disinterested.

Not fooled, he tightened his arm around her shoulders. "No...haven't been a monk, but no girlfriends."

"Oh," she said quietly, his answer pleasing her, but having no idea how to respond.

He shifted her around so that she sat straddling his lap, her knees tucked next to his hips. Cupping her face with his large hands, he pulled her in close. "Never been tempted to have a relationship with anyone before. Never met anyone that held my interest. And with my parents' example, wasn't sure that was in the cards for me." He held her gaze and added, "Until now."

Bringing her in, he planted his lips on hers, sealing his desire with a kiss. Grabbing on to his shoulders, digging her fingers in, she responded as the outside world faded away and the sun set, leaving only the two of them.

11

By the time they made it back to her house, Hunter began to have second thoughts. *Sex after an emotional night?* It did not feel right for him to take advantage of her raw state of mind. As soon as the door behind them clicked, he turned and opened his mouth, but she got there first.

Throwing herself at him, she jumped into his arms, wrapping her legs around his hips as she latched onto his mouth.

Taken by surprise, his eyes flew open but no words came forth, considering she now had her tongue tangled with his. With his back against the door, he held her easily. The feel of her in his arms and her body pressed tightly to his made rational thought impossible.

Angling his head, he took the kiss deeper as he explored her mouth. She ground her core against his swollen cock, the material between them an impediment to what he desired. She pulled back first and the cold shower of reality hit him. Attempting to lower her to the floor, she grabbed his face and pulled him close.

Nose to nose, she said, "Bedroom...now...please."

He held her gaze for a second before finalizing his decision, carrying her toward the master bedroom. Entering, he took in the space, seeing she had decorated it as nicely as the rest of the small house.

A cushioned wooden bench stood under the window. The seat was covered in green with a yellow pillow against the wall. A nightstand was squeezed between the full-sized bed and the wall. The bedspread was green with yellow flowers and more yellow pillows lay next to the headboard.

A small dresser was against another wall, the top covered with a few jars and tidbits. As he loosened her arms to let her body slide down his front, the rack of colored hair ribbons hanging on the wall met his eye. His gaze shot back to her, seeing her dark hair pulled back with a light blue ribbon.

As she stood in front of him, her fingers curled on his biceps, he lifted one hand and slowly drew the ribbon from her hair, letting the fullness fall down her back. His fingers continued to trail down through the silky tresses as he let the ribbon flutter to the floor. His breath caught in his throat as he stared at her beauty.

"Belle, I want to do the right thing here—"

"Then do it," she replied in a whisper.

"Are you sure? 'Cause I've never been in a relationship, and what I feel for you is no random fuck."

"I've never been in a relationship either and I'm not

one for random…uh…sex either. But, I want you…want this."

"This," he said, waving his hand between them, "means something. I can't do this with you and then just walk away or watch you walk away."

Her face softened as a slow smile curved her lips. "Then we agree. No walking away after this as long as we both want it."

His heart lighter, he grinned as he nodded. "No walking away until we've taken this as far as it can go." Bending to kiss her again, he added, "And, babe, I want it to go as far as it can for as long as it can."

As their mouths moved over each other eagerly, her hands found the bottom of his shirt and moved upward. When it reached to just under his arms, he leaned back and allowed her to pull it over his head. Her gaze landed on his body and she devoured him with her eyes. She knew he was big, but it struck her just how manly he was. Not just masculine, but *manly*.

His chest was wide and seeing the muscles of his pecs and abs was no surprise although, up close, she thought they were even more impressive than in her imagination. But as she trailed her fingers over his warm skin, she felt the real man over the defined muscles. A man who lived. A man who worked hard with his hands and did not starve himself to achieve a perfect body. He felt real. Her mind was processing this discovery, and she blinked as he pulled her T-shirt over her head and unclasped her bra, having missed his perusal of her as she was staring at him.

Hunter dropped her clothes to cup her breasts, his

gaze roaming over them hungrily. It would have taken a blind man not to know she was stacked, but seeing her filling his cupped hands had him realizing just how perfect they were. He flicked his thumbs over her distended nipples, feeling the hardened buds tighten even more. She sucked in a gasp and his gaze jumped to her face, seeing her eyes close as her mouth opened slightly.

Skimming his hand down her curves to her narrow waist, trailing a path to her hips, he snagged her pants, panties included, with his fingers and bent to draw them down her legs. She balanced herself with her hands on his shoulders, allowing him to strip her bare.

Suddenly self-conscious, Belle sucked in her lips, dropping her chin.

He lifted her chin with his knuckle, forcing her to meet his eyes. "We can stop, Belle. You just say the word and it stops here."

"No...that's not it." Seeing the question in his eyes, she confessed, "I'm...well, I'm...uh...not very svelte."

Hunter watched the blush start from her breasts and move upward over her face. As adorable as it was, he hated the reason for it. "Don't ever want to hear you put yourself down. You are so fuckin' beautiful, it takes my breath away. Your body is perfect...all soft and womanly...all curves. If I wanted something else, we wouldn't be where we are right now."

She cocked her head to the side and he continued. "It's no secret you had sexy curves underneath the scrubs I've seen you in for the past months. Add in the sundresses you like to wear when you're not at work,

and it's been damn hard to keep my hands to myself."
He held on to her hip with one hand and trailed a path
back up her body with the other. "And now...to have
you gift these curves to me...babe, you've just blessed
me with perfection."

Sucking in a deep breath, she let it out in a rush,
saying, "I think that's the nicest thing anyone has ever
said to me."

With his lips pressed to hers, he mumbled, "Then get
used to a lot of nice things being said to you, Belle."
Plunging his tongue into her mouth, he continued his
exploration of her taste, committing it to memory.

Their movement became a tangle of kissing mixed
with fumbling fingers as she tried to unzip his pants
over his cock. He took over, divesting himself of his
pants after kicking off his shoes and snagging a condom
from his wallet.

Bending past her, he jerked her covers down and
turned back to lift her underneath her arms. Laying her
on the mattress, he crawled over her body, his massive
one fitting perfectly with her curves. Holding himself
off to the side, he used his free hand to skim over her
body as his mouth assaulted hers again.

Belle's fingers decided to explore on their own as he
stole her breath with his kisses. Running her hands over
his shoulders and down his back, she discovered firm
muscles covered with warm skin. She had seen his
tattoos when his shirt was off, but now traced the
patterns slowly. His head moved down to her breasts
and she closed her eyes in ecstasy as he latched onto a
nipple, pulling it deeply into his mouth. She heard a

moan but was unable to tell if it rumbled from her chest or his.

Hunter slid his hand over her slightly rounded tummy and down between her legs. She was trimmed, but not shaven, and he loved running his fingers through her curly hair on the way to her sex, always preferring a natural woman. And to him, she was all woman.

He ran his forefinger through her slick folds, spreading the moisture to her clit, circling the nub. Her nails scratched over his back, clutching his shoulders as she arched upward. Inserting his digit, he moved it in and out as he continued to suck on her nipples, moving from one to the other.

Belle felt her body coil tighter, the unfamiliar electricity threatening to consume her. Suddenly, her body lurched, the coils deep inside loosening all at once and jolts of what felt like lightning shot throughout. His mouth moved from her nipple to her mouth, but she was afraid of not being able to breathe. As his finger continued to play with her sex, prolonging the orgasm, she no longer cared about oxygen.

Slowly, consciousness dawned and she opened her eyes to see him smiling down at her, bringing his finger dripping with her juices to his mouth and sucking. What breath was left in her lungs was expelled quickly.

"I...I...wow..."

A chuckled rumbled forth from him and he agreed, "Yeah."

With a deft move, he grabbed the condom and, after ripping it open with his teeth, he settled on his back just long enough to roll it over his cock. With another flip, he was back on top of her, his weight balanced on his forearms planted on either side of her shoulders and his hips settled between her legs.

"You ready, babe?"

Staring into his eyes, she answered, "I've waited my whole life to be ready for this moment with you."

Liking her answer without giving it much thought, he brought the tip of his eager cock to her entrance and plunged. Her eyes widened and a slight grunt passed her lips. Halting, he stared down at her, incredulous at how tightly her sex squeezed his cock. Fighting the urge to continue to plunge, he held his body over hers and realization slowly dawned on him. Glaring, he asked, "What the fuck, Belle? How the hell are you a virgin?"

Clamping her eyes shut as embarrassment flooded her, Belle tried to push against his weight with her hands on his shoulders. Her feeble attempt was unsuccessful and she swallowed deeply, concentrating on keeping the tears from falling.

Hunter's hand moved to cup her face, his thumbs stroking the heated, petal softness of her cheeks. "Oh, babe, why didn't you tell me?'

Belle opened her eyes and stared at the man above her, seeing concern, not anger, staring back at her. "I did...I said I've waited my whole life for you."

Now, it was Hunter's turn to close his eyes for a few seconds, the truth behind the meaning of her words soothing over him. Never...never had he been given such a gift.

"Is it bad?" she asked, her voice barely above a whisper.

Jerking his eyes open, he shook his head. "Oh, babe. You...you're the most beautiful thing I've ever held in my hands...and the most precious. I just wish I had understood so I could have taken more time with you... made it good for you...more romantic and sure as hell more comfortable."

Her lips curved slightly as her hands stopped pushing and instead moved to his back, pulling him in again. "There's nothing more special you could do right now...other than get moving!"

Grinning, he replied, "Yes, ma'am," and kissed her once more. Shifting his hips slowly, he moved in and out of her tight, slick channel, the physical sensations warring for dominance in his mind with the emotions coursing through him.

The sense of fullness had Belle gripping his shoulders, lifting her feet to press her heels against his muscular ass. The act caused her legs to open wider, allowing him to slide in deeper, his pelvis rubbing against her clit. Gasping, she clung to him, the friction building as he moved inside.

Her eyes never left his face, fascinated with the play of expressions crossing his features. His lips lowered to capture hers once more and he slid a hand from her cheek downward, skimming her breast, over her tummy, and between them, where he pressed her swollen nub. Sparks began to fly and she closed her eyes, allowing the fireworks to rocket through her.

Hunter looked down, observing her eyes closed and

prayed she was in the throes of pleasure, not regret. When her lips curved, his heart sang, viewing her response to her orgasm. Feeling her inner walls tighten over him, he gave in to the need and his orgasm rushed from his body. Powering through, he thrust harder and faster, all thoughts of any other woman fleeing from his mind, and he knew they would never return. For him, it was only her. Only this woman, who just gave the greatest gift she had to give to him. And, for an instant, he wondered if he would ever be worthy of such a gift.

As the cold air began to seep over them, he reluctantly rolled off and pulled the covers up over her. Climbing from the bed, he felt her hands reach for him.

"Are you coming back to bed?" she asked, her voice betraying her longing for his presence.

"Gotta take care of the condom and gotta take care of you, so yeah, I'll be right back."

Belle watched as he stalked to her bathroom and heard the toilet flush before the water in the sink began to run. Lying back on the pillow, she tried to memorize every moment of the evening, from their kisses to the walk and talk on the pier, culminating in their lovemaking. Before she knew it, he was walking toward her, a wet bath cloth in his hands.

Kneeling on the bed next to her, he gently wiped between her legs and then pressed the warm cloth to her folds. Searching her eyes, he asked, "You good?"

She blushed while nodding. "Never better."

He chuckled and moved back to the bathroom, rinsing the cloth in the sink before draping it over the shower bar. As he rejoined her in bed, he wrapped his arms around her, pulling her in tightly.

Tucked in, with her head on his shoulder, she closed her eyes. She wanted to whisper into the night, but the words were stuck in her throat. Deciding to talk to him with her body, she snuggled in tighter and fell asleep in his arms.

As Hunter lay there, his mind racing, he felt her body go still and knew sleep had claimed her while tucked into his embrace. It was the second greatest gift she had given that night.

12

Hunter opened his eyes slowly, noting two things instantly. One, he was in Belle's bed, in Belle's bedroom, in Belle's house, and that knowledge filled his heart. Two, she was no longer tucked in closely to him, and that had him bolting upright.

A slight sound came from the window and he saw her, wrapped in a blanket, sitting on the bench, peering outside.

"What's wrong?" he asked, his voice still gravelly with sleep.

She twisted her head around and gifted him with a beautiful smile. "Nothing," she whispered back.

Rubbing his hand over his face, he then settled it over his heart, gently massaging his chest. "Then whatcha doing over there?"

"I always watch the dawn...at least, every chance I get."

She turned toward the window again and he swore

her profile was as perfect as the frontal view of her face. "Sunrise?" he asked.

"My grandma taught me to rise early and wait for the sunrise. She said, no matter how bad life got, God always had the sun rise each morning to teach us that every new day dawning had the potential to be the best day we've ever had."

Stunned silent, he leaned back against the headboard, questions filling his mind but knowing Belle would let him in as she felt comfortable. *A lot like me*, he thought ruefully. His eyes moved from her profile to the exposed glass above her head and he saw the purple sky slowly turn to a lighter blue. He rubbed his chest again. There was a pang in his heart at the realization that he had not watched the dawn since leaving the Navy, even though that had been a particularly favorite time of day for him when he was on board a ship.

"My home life growing up wasn't very good," she said softly. "I never knew my dad. I'm surprised my parents were married, but it seems he only agreed to that because my mom was pregnant with me. By the time I was a year old, he was done with her and, I suppose, done with me. Mama was...well, she had problems. Addictions."

She turned away from the window and leaned back against one of the yellow pillows, drawing her legs up, wrapping her arms around them and resting her chin on her knees. Now holding his gaze, she continued. "Your dad drank...my mom used whatever drugs she could get her hands on. I don't think it was too bad when I was really young, but like with most addictions, it got worse with time. She took uppers to party and then downers to sleep. She had a job at a hardware store, but by the time I was about ten, she was fired for constantly showing up late, stoned, or not showing up at all."

He wanted to move to her, take her in her arms, kiss away the memories, but knew she needed to talk, so he gave her the only gift he could at the moment...his time and complete attention.

"We used to shop for clothes from the second-hand store...and that was fine. But, then when the money was running out, she started getting hand-me-downs from neighbors. They often didn't fit right." She held his gaze. "I never complained because she reminded me that there were kids in the world with nothing and I had clothes on my back and a roof over my head. She was right—"

"Baby, she was fucked," he growled.

Sucking in her lips, she nodded slowly. "Yeah...both right and fucked all at the same time." Sighing, she continued, "It was hard at school. I was the kid with the ill-fitting clothes. Mama wasn't the best at teaching me hygiene, so my hair was often greasy. It wasn't until the other kids taunted me that I realized I needed to wash my hair more often. Since we didn't usually have a lot of toiletries, laundry detergent worked as my shampoo."

His heart, now aching, had him ready to throw back the covers, but she stopped him.

"I need to get this out and it's easier if you're over there," she said, her eyes begging him to understand.

Not liking it, he continued to give her what she needed.

Blowing out her breath, she said, "Mama found ways to get money...I didn't know about what she was doing for a long time...too young...too naïve. I was twelve when I came home from school and heard her in the bedroom. I walked in, thinking she might be sick, and saw her with a man on top. I was scared but she looked over and yelled for me to get out. I knew about sex... just from sex education at school and hearing kids talk, but," she swallowed hard again, "this was different. I ran back into the kitchen and as the man left, he handed her some money and told her he'd see her next time. She turned to me and just said, 'Don't give me that sassy look, girl. I keep you in clothes and me what I need.' Then she walked back into the bedroom and I didn't see her again until the next day."

"Christ, babe," he groaned, his eyes seared by the sad expression on her face.

"I got a job the next year at the grocery store. The manager, Mr. Pullen, said he wasn't supposed to hire anyone until they were fifteen, but if I didn't tell anyone how old I was, he wouldn't either. Let's just say that by thirteen, I had boobs and looked a lot older, so I got away with it. I finally had some money, but Mama would take it and use it for drugs. So, I started having Mr. Pullen leave some out of my paycheck and he'd put it into the safe. I trusted him and he didn't disappoint. I only had a small portion that Mama could steal, since I bought food and better-fitting clothes and the rest I saved."

"Babe, this story sucks. Please, God, tell me it gets better."

A sad smile settled on her face as she replied, "Eventually. I told you the mobile home park back then was not like what we live in now. It was run-down, loud parties, drugs, drunk fights...I felt like I never had a moment's peace. And even at the store, it was full of customers all needing something. School was a respite, except for being called trailer trash. It was as though the boys thought that since I had boobs and lived here, then I was easy. When they discovered I wasn't, well, they lied anyway."

Anger continued to course through his veins as she confessed her childhood to him.

Belle looked over her shoulder, checking on the sunrise before turning back to face Hunter. The sight of him in her bed as the dawn began to streak the sky made her smile at the dream come true. "Mama became jealous as the men she...uh...serviced started looking at me. I began to hang out with my grandmother at the nursing home. It was the calmest, most serene place I had ever experienced. I'd catch the bus there on my days off and stay until one of the workers who lived here in town would give me a ride home. "Grannie knew how bad Mama was. Mama might have been her daughter, but Grannie didn't have blinders on when it came to Mama's addictions. She became my refuge."

"And the sunrise?"

A sweet smile spread over her face as she nodded. "Yeah. Every day dawning has the potential to be the best day we've ever had. I took that to heart and trained myself to wake every morning just before dawn, so I could look at it. Been doing that since I was a teenager. It's habit now...I don't even think about it."

Hunter's eyes never left her face but his heart pounded, both in anger for the young girl forced to live with an uncaring mother and awe, that she grew up to be the most caring person he had ever met.

"I started going to the nursing home as a teen volunteer and then worked there as soon as I got my CNA license. Mr. Weldon, like Mr. Pullen, gave me faith in good men again, 'cause he always encouraged me to keep getting more and more education. Mama died about that time and I inherited her little trailer. The new owner of the mobile home park was renovating it bit by bit, determined to weed out the ones who never paid rent or had loud parties. He put money into the place, hiring lawn care services...including some of the hard-working, but unemployed, residents. I got rid of Mama's house and managed to get one in the newly renovated section." She looked around her bedroom, a content expression on her face. "It's all mine and there is nothing of Mama's here."

She twisted on the bench again, her eyes staring out the window, a wide smile gracing her face as the sun painted the sky light blue in the distance. Looking back at him, she said, "Sunrise. A new day. And with what we shared last night and you in my bed this morning, it's the best sunrise I've ever had in my life."

Not willing to wait one more second, he threw back the covers with a growl and stalked to the bench, plucking her up in one swift movement. Peeling the blanket off her, he laid her back in bed, climbing over the top of her and curling his massive body around hers. The desire to protect was overwhelming, but without finding the words to express himself, he used his body, and prayed she felt his emotion.

Surrounded by all that was Hunter, Belle smiled as her arms reached around him. Burying her face into his neck, she breathed him in...spice, manly, all Hunter. Closing her eyes, she felt lighter than she had in years. The full story of her upbringing had been a secret to all, with just a few tidbits shared with her friends. Her grandmother knew much of the story, but not all. And now, her burden had been lifted with the simple gift of acceptance.

"Thank you," she whispered, her lips pressed against his skin.

He separated just enough to peer down at her, his brows lowered in question. "What for?"

"You heard the worst of me...and you're still here."

Leaning up on one elbow, he stared down. "Belle, I heard nothing bad about *you*. Yeah, about *your mom* and your *worthless dad* and the *dicks* that your mom didn't protect you from, instead of bringing you too close to them, and the *teenage assholes and bitches* who called you names and made assumptions about you...but not one thing in that story was worse about *you*. Babe, the fact that you are the kindest person I know, despite all that you've endured, solidifies you in my mind as a miracle. One that has been gifted to me, and I hold precious."

Her eyes searched his, finding only sincerity. Before she could speak, he continued.

"You heard my story yesterday. Do you blame me for the sins of my father?"

"God, no, Hunter!"

"Then, you have to separate yourself from all the actions from others as you grew up."

The dawn streaked the sky and the light flooded into the bedroom, illuminating them. He brushed her hair back from her face and nuzzled her cheek. "I love the ribbons you wear. For a couple of months, I would always look to see you at work, just to see what color you would be wearing that day."

"Back when I couldn't afford much, I would go to the Dollar Store and buy packs of ribbons." Shrugging, she said, "They made me feel pretty. Kind of like a princess wearing a tiara."

They lay quiet for a few more minutes, light kisses taking the place of words. Regretfully, she felt him lift off her and he pulled her up.

"I need to head to my camper to shower and get dressed. I'll be back and drive you to work," he said.

She nodded but her eyes drifted to the bed. He lifted her chin and asked, "What's going on in that beautiful head?"

"I just wanted you to know that no matter what, I don't regret a moment of last night."

Stepping closer, he said, "Belle, no regrets. I cherish the gift you gave me...both your body last night and your trust this morning. I told you, I wanted to wait because I have things I need to do to be the man you deserve, but I'm selfishly going to take what you're offering, because I don't want to wait anymore. My promise to you is that, I promise to work on myself."

Not understanding his cryptic comments, she said, "I just need honesty, Hunter. Please, don't lie. Not about me...not to me."

He bent to take her lips once more and they stood in the glow of the sunrise, silent promises made.

13

An hour later, Belle was showered, in her scrubs with a pink ribbon tying back her hair. Halfway through a bowl of oatmeal, she heard a knock on the door. She wondered if it was acceptable to give Hunter a key, but then decided that was too presumptuous and definitely too soon. Throwing open the door, she saw Brittany.

"Hey sweetie," she exclaimed. "Come on in."

"I haven't seen you this week," Brittany said, "and my mom doesn't have any food for breakfast." She stared at the bowl on the counter longingly.

"I'm having some oatmeal. Let's fix you some as well." She turned and walked back into the kitchen, grabbing a bowl.

Brittany poured the instant oatmeal, added water, and placed it in the microwave. Within a minute, she moved to the table with Belle and they finished their breakfast.

"How's school?"

"Same as always. Boys are jerks and girls are bitches."

She sat, thinking how similar Brittany's words were to her own that morning when she was talking to Hunter. Sucking in a quick breath, she wondered if she should step up her questions about Brittany's mother. "Um…do you feel safe at home? With your mom, I mean."

Shrugging, Brittany replied, "She's not too bad when she's sober and keeping a job. Sometimes, between jobs, money gets tight. Other than that, I only hate it when she parties, but I either stay in my room or go visit a friend." Shoveling the last of the oatmeal down, she said, "Thanks for breakfast, Belle."

Just then another knock sounded and Brittany's eyes widened as they jumped to the door. Belle hopped up and opened it up for Hunter. Her eyes raked over his body, now known intimately to her. Navy Careway polo, hugging his chest and biceps. Jeans, clean but deliciously worn. Boots that somehow, he made look sexy. His blue eyes had not left her, and his smile was wide. Meeting his smile, she invited, "Come on in. I've got company."

As he entered, his eyes landed on the young teen and she introduced them. "Pleased to meet you, Brittany," he said.

She blushed and blurted, "Damn, you're big."

Throwing his head back in laughter, he agreed.

"Hunter and I'll be at the next game, Brittany," Belle said. "He's going to start helping coach."

"That'd be good. Need another big guy to keep some

of those assholes in line." Grabbing her backpack, she walked over to Brittany and gave her a hug. "Thanks again."

"You want a ride to the bus stop?"

"Nah. I got it." With a wave toward Hunter, Brittany walked out the door stopping just as she was about to leave. Looking over her shoulder, she grinned at Brittany and said, "Looks like I was right...you are the next one." Her lips still curved upward, she tossed out her goodbye and headed through the door.

As it closed behind her, Hunter turned and cocked his head. Reading his silent question, she explained, "She lives near the back. Her mom is about as good a mom as mine was."

His head swiveled and he watched through the window as Brittany walked down the street. "Jesus, Belle." He looked back at her and asked, "Is there anything we can do?"

She walked closer, stopping just in front of him, resting her hands on his arms, a small smile playing about her lips. "I love that you want to help. But, so far, she seems okay...just needs another person to listen to her and understand. I keep an eye on her. It seems her mom parties hard but Brittany tells me she isn't afraid."

He wrapped his arms around her, pulling her in closely, kissing the top of her head. "You let me know if I'm needed. Got no problem putting the fear of God in some teenage boys or beating the shit out of another man."

Lifting up on her toes, she kissed the underside of

his jaw, loving the feel of his just-shaven skin under-neath her lips. "My hero."

Snorting, he replied "Hardly."

"Come on, let's get to work. I want to be there for the other residents as they grieve Mr. Rosenberg."

With Belle tucked underneath his arm, Hunter escorted her to her car, driving them back to Careway. Arriving, he hesitated as she alighted from the vehicle. Uncertain how much PDA she was comfortable with, he stood awkwardly next to the passenger door.

Looking up shyly, she grinned as she reached out her hand. Taking it gladly, he linked her fingers with his and they walked in together.

The day passed quickly and Hunter found that he barely saw Belle. He told her he had an appointment at the Pain Center after work but he would come by her house after it was over. Running into Mr. Weldon early in the afternoon, he stopped as the owner lifted a hand to call him over.

"Hunter, I wanted to ask you to be ready to paint Mr. Rosenberg's room tomorrow. That'll give the housekeepers a chance to finish cleaning it."

Nodding his acquiescence, he continued to stand in the hall, waiting on Mr. Weldon, who seemed to want to say more. The owner, neat and impeccably dressed as always, clasped his hands in front of him as he rocked slightly back on forth on his feet.

"I just wanted to thank you for staying here with Ms.

Gunn. It would have been hard for her to face losing a patient on her own."

"No thanks are needed."

"She's special. I've known Ms. Gunn since when she would come to visit her grandmother, almost ten years now. It didn't escape my attention, how she was with the elderly clientele."

"Belle's told me that you encouraged her each step of her education."

Eyes wide, Mr. Weldon smiled. "Well, I must say that's a surprise. She's normally very reticent to speak of herself." Continuing, he added, "If she's trusted you to share part of her life with, I hope you hold that trust in high regard."

"Yes, sir." He watched as Mr. Weldon walked on down the hall and sucked in a deep breath. Just then he observed Belle come out of Mr. Rosenberg's former room, walking with one of the housekeepers whose arms were full of linens. The sad expression on her face cut him to the quick, but when she looked up, he smiled at her, willing his strength onto her.

She answered back with a slight smile of her own before hustling down the hall to respond to another resident.

With the day almost over, he wanted to find her. The realization that they had slept together without him taking her on a proper date dug into him and he wanted to rectify that situation. Stepping into the employee lounge, he was glad to see that Nola was not hanging around. Moving to his locker, he opened it, surprised when a note fluttered to the ground. Bending to pick it up, he opened it, reading the typewritten words.

I'm a friend of Lionel's and he says you're interested in some shared business. If so, just leave a note in your locker and I'll get it. Hope we can help each other.

Scribbling on the bottom of the note, with a deep sigh, he left his affirmative reply in his locker. Scrubbing his hand over his face, he grimaced as he thought of Belle. *Fuck...I've got to work this out...for her...for us.*

"What have you got, Chief?"

Ginny walked into the BPD seeing Mitch, Colt, and Liam leaning over a laptop. Mitch looked up at her question and replied, "Colt's finished checking on the facilities in the area that have drugs in North Heron and Liam's been checking Accawmacke. Every doctor's office we talked to don't keep drugs on their premises, other than the samples given to them by pharmaceutical companies. In each case, the doctors have responded to our inquiries and have told us that the samples are kept locked up and the doctor is the only person who has access. Not even the nurses or office staff can access the sample drugs."

Colt added, "That's not to say we don't have a doctor that's selling drugs, but it cuts down on who has access."

Grant, already sitting at the table, asked, "What about the other facilities?"

"Nursing homes and pharmacies have ready access.

We checked with the two nursing homes in the county and they've reported that the CNAs are the ones who hand out the drugs to the residents, but that the LPNs are the ones who give the CNAs the drugs to distribute. There is only one RN per nursing home and they are the one in charge of ordering."

"What about the Pain Management Center?" she asked.

Nodding, Colt said, "Yeah, they have drugs and they're on my list to visit today."

The police and sheriffs meeting ended and Colt waved goodbye to Mitch and Liam, calling out, "I'll let you know what I find."

Thirty minutes later, Colt was ensconced in the Pain Management Center, waiting for Dr. Tom Caldwell to meet with him in the doctor's private office. He walked to the window and noted the pharmaceutical truck parked in the back. The driver was talking to another man, but he was unable to see who it was.

"Sheriff Hudson," Tom called out, walking in and extending his hand.

After the greetings were over, Colt nodded toward the window and asked, "Is that the usual pharmaceutical delivery truck and driver?"

Tom peered out of the second-floor window and looked down. "Yes, we use Matrix Pharmaceuticals. They are based out of Baltimore and I think they deliver up and down the Eastern Shore."

"Same driver?"

Tom's face scrunched in thought and he confessed, "Yes...Lionel...uh...something. I'm usually the one who sees him when he comes in, so that I can lock the drugs in our safe, but sometimes our head nurse locks them up as well."

"Her name?"

Grinning, he replied, "Rosalinda Caldwell. My wife."

Nodding, he met his grin, then, asked, "You didn't want to use a pharmaceutical company out of Virginia Beach?"

Shaking his head, Tom said, "Bad weather can shut down the Chesapeake Bridge. We want to be able to get what we need, and Matrix has been able to accommodate. They also supply to others in the area."

"Is it unusual that you have narcotics here on site instead of just going through a pharmacy?"

"On occasion, we use injectable drugs when working with patients, if and only if needed, so we do keep some locked up here."

"And who has access?"

"Only the doctors. Not the nurses or physical therapists. And we only use them after a group meeting has occurred where we, as a team, agree that the patient needs it. So, no one person, even the physician, uses the drugs without others knowing about it."

Nodding, Colt shook his hand and walked down the stairs and into the lobby. Seeing Hunter, he walked over. "Hey, man. I didn't know you came here."

Hunter forced a smile. On the one hand, it was not unusual to see a fellow American Legionnaire at the clinic, since it was talked about at the last meeting. But, even so, he hated to feel like his privacy was invaded. "Got some pain from my time in the service."

"Sorry to hear about that. Hope these people can help you out. I know Dr. Caldwell…heard good things about him and the clinic."

"Good."

Colt's eyes dropped to the shirt he was wearing, his eyes landing on the logo on the breast pocket. "I forgot you work at Careway Nursing Home."

"Yeah…maintenance."

Colt shook his hand and said, "Well, I gotta go. It was good to see you."

He watched the sheriff walk out of the building and breathed a sigh of relief. Hearing his name called, he turned to walk back to the examining room, his heart pounding. *That was a fuckin' close call.*

14

"Oh, I wish I had your boobs," Jillian moaned, looking at Belle's numerous, colorful sundresses hanging in her closet. Glancing down at her slender build, she said, "If we were the same size, I could share your clothes."

As soon as Hunter had asked Belle for a date, she had been excited about another motorcycle ride, but had no idea what to wear. This resulted in an impromptu girls' meeting at her house where Jillian, Tori, Katelyn, Madelyn, and Jade went through her outfits.

"They're overrated," she said, looking down at her chest.

"I agree," Katelyn nodded. Pregnancy had made her lush body even more voluptuous.

"Speak for yourself," Jade commented. "I'm happy with my body, but I'd love to have a little more to fill out the top of my bathing suit."

"I bet Lance is thrilled with your body," Madelyn said, her voice muffled as she went through her underwear drawer.

"I can't wear a sundress on his motorcycle," she said. "I did that once, but was afraid of giving everyone a peek show."

"I say just wear jeans and a cute top," Tori said, pulling several shirts from their hangers and laying them on the bed before she bent over the baby carrier and checked on a still-sleeping Eddie.

"This!" Madelyn cried, pulling out a dove grey matching satin bra and panty set.

Looking over, she eyed the lacy underwear with undisguised doubt. "I bought them on sale, but only tried to wear them once. They don't cover very much—"

"They're perfect," Jade said, enthusiastically agreeing.

She took the lingerie set and moved into the bathroom to slip them on. Poking her head out the door, she said, "I don't know about this."

Stepping back into the bedroom, she was met with silence and quickly turned to rush back into the bathroom.

"No!" they all shouted at once.

"You are absolutely gorgeous," Jillian said, her smile wide. Everyone else was equally effusive in their praise.

The women had her try each shirt Tori had picked out and they finally agreed on the light blue, jersey shirt with the little cap sleeves. Paired with a pair of form-fitting dark jeans, they declared her perfectly dressed for a night at a seafood restaurant and a ride into the sunset on the back of Hunter's motorcycle.

"But what about your shoes?" Katelyn asked.

"Oh," she replied. "Uh, what should I wear?"

"Can't go wrong with boots," Jillian said, backing out

of her small closet with a pair of leather, low-heeled boots in her hand.

Agreeing with their choices, she hugged the girls goodbye and bent to kiss Eddie's cheek. Their wishes for her to have a good time filled the air, and she waved as they drove down the lane. Hurrying back to her bathroom, she applied simple makeup, followed by braiding her hair and tying it with a light blue ribbon, before she stared into the mirror.

Hearing the roar of a motorcycle coming closer, she grinned at her reflection and ran to open the door.

The sight of Hunter in thigh-hugging jeans, well worn in all the right places, a midnight blue shirt with the sleeves rolled over his forearms, and boots on his feet had her standing in the doorway, speechless. She wondered if she would ever get used to someone as ruggedly handsome as him coming to call.

Before she had a chance to ponder that thought more, he stepped into her space and wrapped his arms around her. Taking her lips in a searing kiss, she melted in his embrace. Pulling back, she blinked several times, bringing his smiling face into focus.

"We gotta go, sweetheart, or I'm liable to skip dinner and head straight to dessert," his rough voice washed warm against her face.

Her lips curved as he stepped back and linked fingers, leading her outside. A few minutes later she wrapped her arms around his waist tightly and held on for the ride. With the motorcycle's engine rumbling underneath and his ass pressed against her crotch, she wondered if it were possible to orgasm just from the trip to the restaurant.

Hunter's steak almost filled his plate but his eyes were only for the beauty sitting across from him. The smile Belle had greeted him with at the door was still firmly on her face. The ribbon in her hair matched the shirt that managed to be both modest and seductive at the same time. Walking her into the restaurant, he had been proud to have her on his arm, while sending a few well-earned glares toward a couple of men at the bar whose eyes strayed to, and then stayed on, Belle. He knew his size could intimidate and was glad the men quickly turned back to their beers.

Now, his steak was almost finished, she was eating the last of her shrimp and sitting opposite of him...he felt like he had won the lottery. He heard her speak but was so engrossed in watching her he missed what she said. Blinking, he said, "Sorry?"

Wiping her mouth, she repeated, "I wondered if I had anything on my face. You're staring and I wasn't sure if—"

"You're beautiful," he blurted as his reply. Seeing the blush creep across her face, he continued, "And what's so fuckin' sexy is that you have no idea how beautiful you are."

She opened her mouth, then, snapped it closed as he kept talking.

"You walk into a room and men's eyes follow you...

you've got no idea. You dress like a sweet pin-up girl, covering every asset, and you've got plenty of them, and have no idea that you're sexier than if you were walking around half-naked. You show up to work each day with a ribbon that matches your scrubs and it puts a smile on the residents' faces just to see you walk into their rooms. You wear sweet dresses to the gatherings in town because, to you, it's worth the effort to show up somewhere and look nice. And again, you've got no idea how the appreciative stares follow you."

She blinked several times, but he was not finished, so she just stared, wide-eyed at him.

"You have a shy smile that lets people know you're not stuck on yourself, but you're willing to share it with others. And that is also sexy as fuck. And the reason I was staring at you was that I can't believe someone like you, someone any man in this room would lay down and die tomorrow if they had a chance at your beauty tonight...you are here with me."

Tears filled her eyes and she found her breath stuck in her throat.

"Breathe, baby," he whispered.

The breath rushed from her lungs and she blurted, "I want you to take me home and show me your camper."

Hunter blinked slowly, twice, then pulled out his wallet and tossed a huge wad of bills onto the table to cover their dinner and leave a generous tip. Grabbing her hand, he gently assisted her up and with one hand protectively on her lower back and the other in front, guiding her between people so she would not get bumped, he led her outside.

Snapping her helmet onto her head, he mumbled, "Got to get you a helmet of your own that'll fit better."

With no other words, he swung his long leg over his motorcycle and waited for her to do the same. She did not make him wait and in a moment, with her hands wrapped tightly around his waist, her front pressed to his back from breast to crotch, he roared out of the parking lot.

At the mobile home park, he parked outside his camper and, as soon as she had dismounted, jumped off and grabbed her hand. Stopping at the door, he turned, still holding her hand, and peered down at her. "You sore, sweetheart?"

Eye wide again, she repeated, "Sore?"

"From our first time."

"Oh," she breathed.

He waited for a beat then said, "Belle, *oh* is not an answer."

"Oh," she said again, then shook her head. "Sorry. I mean, uh…no…I was a little tender the next day, but it's okay now."

"Good," he said, bending down to take her lips. Fighting to keep the kiss chaste, he rose up and explained, "I always want it to be good for you. I'm hanging on by a thread, but I'll take it as slow as you need."

She nodded, saying, "I'm good." Smiling, she added, "With you…here in your camper…I'm great."

"Jesus, you're gonna make me come the first second I slide into you," he growled, fumbling with the key.

She jolted at his words and he grinned as she wiggled impatiently. Throwing open the camper door, he stepped in before twisting around and offering his hand to assist her up.

"Wow," Belle said, looking around at the compact area. Upon entering, they were standing in the space designated for the kitchen and living area. Directly in front of her was a counter, complete with small sink, stove, half-sized refrigerator, and upper and lower cabinets. A small microwave was built over the stove. To the left, across from the cabinets, was a table with opposing bench seats. She had seen pictures of campers and assumed the table could lower to the level of the benches and form an extra bed as needed.

To the right was a bench sofa and, again, she assumed it could also form a bed. A flat-screen TV was mounted on the wall opposite the sofa. The cushions were in a deep green plaid pattern matching valences on the windows.

To the left, beyond the cabinets and table, was a short hall, closets on either side. He led her further in, and she could see a bedroom at the end of the hall. Her eyes jumped to his and she smiled widely.

"This is so cool!" she enthused.

Meeting her grin with a smirk, he replied, "Don't know how *cool* it is, babe, but it serves as home for now." A flash of uncertainty moved through his eyes and he asked, "You want something to drink?"

She moved closer and lifted her arms to place her

palms flat on his chest, the feel of hard muscles meeting her fingertips. Tilting her head back, she held his eyes and breathed, "No...I want you to show me your bedroom."

His grin widened and he reached up to place his hand over one of hers, clutching her fingers as he led her down the short hall. The bedroom took up the entire back of the camper and most of the space was taken up with the bed. There were two nightstands on either side and just enough room around the bed for an adult to walk. Two lights were attached to the back wall and a shelf ran the back length of the camper.

Before she had a chance to investigate further, he lifted her under her arms and with an easy toss, she landed on her back in the middle of the bed. A girlie squeal was forced from her lips, but it died quickly as she watched him unbutton his shirt and toss it to the floor. Shirtless, he was a dream come true and she leaned up on her elbows to enjoy the rest of the show.

He unbuckled his belt and slid it slowly through the loops in his jeans. When the leather was free, he snapped it between his hands and her sex clenched. He bent to untie his boots before toeing them off. The sound of his zipper moving over his impressive cock had her squeezing her legs together in anticipation. His gaze dropped to her legs and he grinned. Dropping his jeans and boxers, he stood at the base of the bed, fisting his cock.

She bolted upward and crossed her arms at the base of her shirt but his words halted her movements.

"You don't move, baby," he ordered, his eyes dilated with lust. "That particular present is for me to unwrap."

She bit her bottom lip as she grinned, resting her weight on her palms, flat on the bed. "Okay...I'm yours to unwrap."

Hunter bent to grab her ankles and pulled her forward a few inches. Slipping her shoes off, he tossed them to the floor before putting a knee on the mattress. He made quick work of her jeans, sliding them down her legs, before staring appreciatively at her satin panties. Bending to kiss her skin just above them, he then slowly drew them down her legs as well.

Having unclothed her from the waist down, he kissed her calves, nibbling up her leg almost to her apex before moving to the other leg. The scent of her arousal was evident, and he sucked in a quick breath, tamping down his desire so that he could make the evening last.

She flopped back and groaned. "I wanted to keep watching you but my arms are so tingly they can't hold me up."

He lifted his head and stared at her for a moment, appreciating her honesty. *No artifice...with her, she plays no games.* Dropping his head, he continued his kissing assault on her legs, moving upward. Hearing her breath hitch as he neared her sex, he lifted himself higher on the mattress and placed his lips on her tummy.

Nuzzling the bottom of her shirt, he slipped his hands to the hem and began to shove it upward. When it caught on the underside of her breasts, he knelt beside her and lifted her to sit.

"Lift," he ordered, and she dutifully raised her arms over her head. He pulled the shirt off and tossed it to the side. His fingers skimmed over the mounds of her breasts threatening to spill out of the soft satin. He watched as she sucked in a quick breath and moved to unhook the delicate material, allowing it to drop to the side as well.

He stared at her lush curves, his cock twitching at the sight. *Made for me...fuckin' made for me.*

With a hand to her chest, he pushed her gently back onto the mattress and slid off the end, shifting his large body to place her legs over his shoulders as he kissed her thighs again. Only, this time, he licked her folds before latching onto her clit.

"Oh, my God," she cried, her hands clenching the bedspread.

She lifted her head just long enough to catch his eyes and he mumbled against her sex, "My present. Greatest gift ever."

An hour later, Belle lay with her head on Hunter's chest, her fingers moving gently through the hair there. Their legs were tangled and his arms were wrapped tightly around her body. She had experienced her first mouth and hands only orgasm, then another one when he powered into her body, rocking her hard as she met him thrust for thrust.

Now, their heartbeats had slowed and their breathing had returned to normal. His hand drifted over her shoulder, down her back to her ass, and up again. Warm and sated, she sighed in contentment.

"Whatcha thinkin', babe?" his voice rumbled from deep in his chest.

"I like your camper," she said. She felt his hand still on her back, his fingers twitching for a few seconds until they relaxed and began their trail again.

"Aint' no place special, but it means a lot to hear you say that."

She lifted up on his chest, her gaze on his face. "Anywhere you live is special, Hunter. Or, it should be."

"Yeah, but you talk about a real home as your dream. I mean, you've got a sweet home, Belle...one you've put time, effort, and money into to make it a nice place to live. And yet, you still want your own home." He smiled, adding, "Two stories, a front porch with a swing and a back deck where the bay breeze can keep you cool."

Her eyes widened in surprise. "You remembered?"

"I remember everything you've ever told me."

Sucking in her breath, she pressed her lips together. "That's sweet...so sweet."

"I think those words stayed with me, especially, 'cause hearing your dream made me look around and think that I'd like to have more one day too."

"A real home?"

"And real roots."

She cocked her head to the side, wondering where he would like to put down roots, but was afraid to ask.

As though reading her mind, he closed the gap between their faces and took her lips. The kiss was thorough, but he pulled back before it flamed too brightly. "Never found a place I'd like to call home until Baytown, babe. Never found a woman I'd like to be with until you."

Grinning, she lay her head back down on his shoulder, her fingers splayed on his chest. As the moonlight crept through the blinds and onto them, she felt sleep begin to claim her. Closing her eyes, she murmured, "I never found a man worth falling for, until you."

Her voice in the night settled over Hunter, filling him with hope.

15

Belle entered the pawn shop, hearing the buzzer sound in the back, alerting the owner that a customer had arrived. A thin man walked toward her and called out his greeting.

"What can I do ya for?"

"I was wondering if you had any motorcycle helmets...um, that could fit my head?"

His gaze moved from the top of her head and down her body before drifting back up. "Maybe." Jerking his head to the far wall, he said, "If so, they'd be over there."

She walked where he indicated and stared at the few helmets on the shelf. Two of them appeared to be well worn, but a blue one caught her attention. Picking it up, she checked the inside for cleanliness before sliding it on her head.

It fit snugger than the one Hunter let her use. He had mentioned getting a helmet for her, but she wanted to surprise him. Fastening the straps, she moved to the back of the store where a mirror was on the wall. A grin slipped over her lips as she stared at her reflection and imagined his face when she appeared for their next ride with her own helmet.

The thought of another ride did more than send sexy tingles throughout her body. And the idea of riding forever with him... Blinking, she shook her head to rid those premature thoughts. The heavy helmet stayed firmly in place, even with her head shaking, and she pulled her mind back to the task at hand.

"You got what I need?"

Jerking around, she realized the owner was not talking to her. Turning back to the mirror, she heard a gruff male voice. "You fuckin' know I do. I always fuckin' have what you need. Question is, can you pay?"

The voice had a threatening tone to it but, still behind tall shelves, she was hidden from their view. Curious, she thought about peeking around the aisle, but fear slid along her spine.

"That's all I'm getting?" the man growled.

"Take it or leave it. It's engraved so I gotta be careful."

She quietly unfastened the helmet and hesitated, waiting until the transaction at the counter was completed. Hoping the coast was clear, she walked around the tall shelf, seeing the man behind the counter, his attention on whatever was in his hand.

Walking up, she glanced at the object as he placed it on the shelf behind him. It looked like a gold pocket watch. Curiosity warred with her need to not appear suspicious. She plastered a smile on her face and announced, "Um…I need to think about it a little more."

"Sure," the clerk grumbled. His phone rang, drawing his attention away from her. "I gotta go to the back for a second to take this call." Without waiting for a response, he walked toward the back of the store, his phone at his ear.

Taking advantage of the moment, she skirted around the counter and looked at the watch. Picking it up, she gasped, reading, **_Your loving wife forever, Bea._**

Dropping the watch, she darted to the front door but the parking lot was empty. Uncertain what to do, she startled as the clerk's voice called from the back.

"You still looking?"

Sucking in a shaky breath, she nodded and turned to walk back. Her eyes continually moved to the watch behind him. _Should I buy it so I can make sure it goes to Mr. Rosenberg's relative? Should I call the police?_ Hesitating, she looked over, seeing him staring at her. With a nervous goodbye, she hurried out of the store. Sitting in the parking lot, she called Hunter.

"Hey, babe—"

"I need your advice because I don't know what to do," she rushed.

"What? Where are you? What's happening?" His words were just as rushed as hers, alerting her to his level of concern.

"I'm fine, I'm fine," she assured. "I just don't know what to do about something."

"Go ahead, Belle."

"I stopped at the pawn shop up on Rte. 13 to look for…uh…oh, I was going to buy…something and saw a pocket watch. When the clerk wasn't looking, I peeked at it. Hunter," her voice squeaked, "it was Mr. Rosenberg's watch."

"Are you sure? How do you know?"

"I snuck a look at it when the owner went to the back and and I recognized the same inscription." She waited for a few seconds but he remained silent. "Hunter? What should I do? Call the police? I didn't see the man who brought it in."

"Man? How—"

"He came in while I was there. I was in the back but could hear him talking about it, and he wasn't happy that he did not get more money for it."

"Does the clerk know you heard them and looked at it?"

"No, I…don't think so…I was careful, but I don't know what to do. Should I call Mitch?"

"No, babe, he's the chief for Baytown only. You're in North Heron County. That's Colt's jurisdiction."

"Oh," she muttered, irritated she had not thought of that herself. She heard him sigh heavily and waited to see what he would suggest.

"Look, Belle, I don't want you into this." She started to protest, but he continued, "Pawn shops can often carry stolen items and if someone finds out you're calling the cops, then you could be a target of someone's anger. Let me handle it."

"Okay," she said slowly, "but what are you going to do?"

"Don't know at the moment, but I'll figure it out. But, whatever I do, I want you out of it. Please, baby, tell me you'll let me handle it."

Huffing, she leaned back against the headrest in her car. "Okay," she assured.

"And I gotta ask, what the hell were you doing in a pawn shop?"

"I told you…I was looking for something."

"Belle?"

His lowered voice gave her the indication that he would keep pestering her until she gave in. Huffing, she replied, "I was looking for a motorcycle helmet. It was going to be a surprise."

"Oh, babe. You don't want to buy a used one. You never know if it was damaged in a wreck or something. We'll get you a new one." He added, "Please…we'll go together and then I can be sure my precious cargo is perfectly fitted and safe."

Precious cargo. She smiled, loving the compliment. "Okay," she agreed, her breath leaving her lungs in a rush.

Disconnecting after promising to see each other later, she started her car and pulled onto the road. Her mind turned over what she had seen and heard, but without seeing the man who brought the watch in, she had no way to determine who it was. *Plus, it could have been a female who took it and gave it to a male to pawn. So many people could have had their hands on it…there were people in and out of Mr. Rosenberg's room all day.*

Just as she pulled into her driveway, she realized she

had not thought about telling Mr. Weldon. *Of course, he would want to know!*

Walking into the employee lounge, Hunter heaved a sigh of relief that the room was empty. Scrubbing a hand over his face, he moved to his locker, his hand hesitating for a second before opening the door. At first glance, it appeared undisturbed, but as he pulled out his spare shirt, he felt something in the pocket. Looking around again to assure himself he was alone, he pulled out a small packet and once opened, spied ten, small, white pills inside with a note.

You'll find out what to do.

Shoving the packets into his pants pocket, he grabbed his helmet and walked out the back door toward the employee parking lot. Just as he swung his leg over his bike, his phone vibrated. As much as he wanted to talk to Belle, he felt up to his ears in his own situation and had no idea what to do about the stolen pocket watch at the moment. Looking at the caller ID, he saw it was not her. Answering with, "Simmons," he waited.

"You get it?"

Recognizing Lionel's voice, he affirmed, "Yeah."

"Good. You got a neighbor who's expecting it. Dade Blade."

"You gotta be shittin' me. Man's got a name like Dade Blade. Either his parents were high when they named him or he's a dumb fuck who has no idea how to fly under the radar."

A chuckle met his ear and Lionel said, "Just get the shit to him."

"And what do I get outta this?"

"A chance to score some more yourself. You do this and don't fuck it up, there'll be more like last time coming your way. Or have you forgotten what I did for you straight up, before you'd ever done anything for me? Trust, my man, goes both ways."

His jaw ticked. "I didn't forget. How hot is this?"

"Best way to stay cool is to have it move along…no one person holding the merchandise."

"Who's here on my end?"

"You're too new to the chain to know that, Simmons. Just get it to Dade each time and he'll make sure you get paid."

With that, he rang off and closed his eyes, his fingers digging into his thigh.

Hunter roared past Belle's house, hoping she was not home to notice that he did not stop. The packet of stolen drugs in his pocket felt as though they were burning a hole in him. Keeping his eyes forward, he drove past his camper and pulled into Dade's short drive next to his old mobile home. Not quite the dump he first assumed it would be, he walked past a kid's bicycle to the front door and knocked.

A thin woman opened the door, a baby on her hip.

"Yeah?" she asked, her voice sounding blasé at the sight of a large, strange man on her stoop.

Stepping back to the ground to appear less intimidating, he asked, "Dade?"

Pursing her lips, she jerked her head toward the left. "He's out back. Go around." With that, she closed the door.

Following her direction, he walked around the building, finding a thin man in a ball cap sitting in a lawn chair, rolling a cigarette. He looked up, his eyes narrowing for a few seconds until a slow grin spread across his face. "New guy? Friend of Lionel's?"

At his silent nod, Dade added, "Hell, a fuckin' neighbor. How convenient is that?"

"You wanna cut the shit and get to it?" he growled.

Dade's eyes narrowed for an instant before his face broke into a grin. "I like a man who knows what he wants." He held his hand out.

Reaching into his pocket, he pulled out the plastic packet and dropped it into Dade's hand. He observed as Dade opened and counted the contents.

Without any acknowledgment, Dade stood and walked the few steps to the back door of his house. Within a moment, he returned and handed him an envelope. "Your pay. Keep doing what you're doing and it'll go up."

Sucking in a breath, he turned to leave when Dade said, "Lionel says you visit the Pain Center. They takin' care of you?"

Staring back, he remained silent.

Dade chuckled, saying, "Yeah...they got shit there

but, most times, want therapy to do the job. You got pain, you come to see me. I'll take care of you."

Ignoring the comments, he turned and walked around to the front and climbed onto his bike, the familiar roar of the engine calming his raging blood. Sucking in a deep breath through his nose, he let it out as he jerked out of the driveway.

16

Belle sat in the stands of the town's baseball field, just over the railroad tracks near the pharmacy and diner. Katelyn and Ginny were on the sidelines, along with some of the men from the American Legion, helping to coach the children. Tori, Jade, and Jillian sat with her, cheering on the children playing.

On the field, she paid very little attention to the game as long as Hunter was near first base, coaching. The younger children had already had their game and now the older kids were playing. Even from the stands, she could see several of the teenage boys gravitating toward him. She was unable to keep her grin from spreading wide, as she recognized some hero worship in their eyes when he talked to them. Looking unassuming, but powerful, in his AL t-shirt and cargo shorts. *Gorgeous...*

"Looks like someone's got it bad," Tori smiled, looking at her.

Realizing she spoke out loud, she laughed while

blushing a bright pink. "I honestly had no idea how good he would be at coaching but he looks so natural out there with the kids."

Nodding, Jillian replied, "I know that for Grant, working with the youth teams for the America Legion has meant a lot to him."

Tori added, "I think for Mitch, Grant, Ginny, and Lance...because of being police officers, they feel like they're always seen as just that...police officers. But, coaching gives them a chance to meet the kids, teens, and their parents on a different level. Less intimidating."

"And influential," Jade said. "Lance feels like he has a chance to make a real difference."

She silently wondered about Hunter's motivations. Would some of the kids who lived near them see him in a different light...not just the big man on a motorcycle, but someone who could help them if they needed it?

"Hey, Belle, looks like Hunter wants you," Madelyn said, bumping her shoulder.

She jolted from her reverie and looked back to the field, observing Hunter moving toward the sidelines and staring her way. Standing, she carefully made her way down the stands and walked toward him. As she neared, she noticed his eyes dropped over her from head to toe and warmed at the appreciative smile on his face.

Reaching him, she instinctively placed her palms on his chest as his hands reached for her shoulders. "Hey, sweetheart, what is it?"

"You see Brittany today?"

Confusion crossed her face as she tried to remember. "Uh...just out on the field a little while ago. Why?"

"She's wearing a big T-shirt, which isn't unusual, but when she pushed her sleeves up earlier, I got a look at some bruises on her upper arms. As soon as I saw them, she dropped the sleeves back into place. I didn't approach because she seemed skittish, but I wondered if she would talk to you about where she got them."

"Oh, my God," she exclaimed, eyes wide, her head jerking around to look for Brittany. She dropped her hands and began to turn away, when his fingers squeezed slightly on her shoulders bringing her attention back to him.

"Gotta be cool, babe. Don't scare her away when you talk to her. Just let her know that she can talk to you... just like always. You're good with her...keep that communication open."

She nodded, but he was not finished.

"She got a boyfriend?"

Jerking her head back, she said, "No...she's too young—"

"Belle," he interrupted. "You gotta know not every girl waits..."

Pinching her lips together, she nodded. "I know, but to be honest, I'm more afraid it might be her mom."

Now, Hunter's lips tightened. "Okay, stay cool, but see if you can talk to her. Last I saw, she was hanging over to the side," he said, jerking his chin toward the other side of the stands.

Nodding, she said, "I'll go now." Hesitating, she looked up and asked, "Will I see you at Finn's?"

A smile slipped over his lips. "Wherever you are... that's where I'll be."

Hating to part, she concentrated on finding Brittany. Searching for just a few minutes, she found her sitting alone on the far side of the town stands. "Hey girl, I wondered where you were."

Brittany lifted her hand to shield her eyes as she looked up at her, a smile on her face. "Hi, Belle."

She plopped down on the seat next to the young girl and was glad for the sunglasses she wore, allowing her to visually search Brittany's arms without appearing to do so. With her large T-shirt sleeves hanging to her elbows, there were no bruises visible.

"So, how are you doing? I haven't seen you in a couple of days."

A shrug was the reply.

"I thought maybe you could come by this afternoon. We could spend some time together, if your mom won't mind."

"Not like she'd even notice," Brittany said, her voice as sullen as her words.

"How about after lunch? You come by and we'll hang for a while." She watched the flare of interest spark in her eyes. Shoulder bumping her, she prodded, "Come on...you know you want to."

A tiny smile curved the pretty teenager's lips and she nodded. "Yeah, sure." Seeing the game breaking up, she said, "I gotta go but I'll come by in a little while."

"Good, sweetie. Looking forward to it." She watched as Brittany walked away, observing the thin lines of the young teenager's body. Calling out, "I'll have something for us to eat," earned her another smile and a wave.

Blowing out her breath, she wondered how bad Brittany's home life was and if there was anything she could do about it.

Hunter walked into Finn's after helping put away the sports equipment and making sure all the children had been picked up or had rides to their homes. For the first time since arriving in Baytown, he truly felt like he belonged and he knew that a big part of that was the woman he wanted to lay eyes on.

Not disappointed, he watched as she walked toward him, her pastel flowered sundress swinging about her hips with a bright yellow ribbon holding back her hair. His smile stumbled as he observed uncertainty in her eyes. Determined to remove that specter, he stalked forward, clasping her body to his and leaning down to claim her with a kiss. Managing to keep it chaste, he nonetheless felt the softness of her lips straight to his cock. Leaning back before the evidence of his ardor was visible to everyone, he tucked her underneath his arm and escorted her toward the back where their friends were gathering.

He noticed the smiles sent their way but as he glanced down, saw Belle's face pink with a heated blush. "You okay?"

Her eyes darted up to his and she offered a tremulous smile. Standing on her toes, she whispered, "Yeah…

just feels weird to be the one that they're all speculating about. I've done it plenty with them, but to be on the receiving end...it's a little unnerving."

He squeezed her shoulder and said, "Are you happy? With me?"

"Of course!" she gushed.

Grinning, he said, "Then soak it in, babe. You're so giving to everyone else, it's time you were the center of their attention. Anyway, they're all looking at me, wondering why you let me hang around you."

She playfully slapped his chest and rolled her eyes. "I know for a fact, they're happy we're together."

Pleased with her words, he settled into a booth, gently pulling her down with him. Ginny, Grant, Mitch, and Tori were sitting across, with Jade and Lance next to them. Madelyn and Zac were at a table that had been pushed right next to the booth. Jillian was helping Katelyn, while Brogan and Aiden ran the bar. Colt and a few of his deputies came in and hung with the group as well.

After a few minutes of small talk and digging into the food that came their way, Hunter turned to her and asked, "What did you find out about Brittany?"

Her face fell, and she replied, "Nothing yet, but she's going to come over this afternoon for some girl time. I'm hoping to find out more then."

"What's the latest?" Ginny asked. "I used to take her home from the games but now that she's older, she says she prefers to walk. I'm never sure if that's true or if she's anxious about a cop driving her home."

Belle looked at the others and said, "Brittany comes

over a lot...I think she sees a kindred spirit in me, and I suppose, it's true."

"Something you need to report?" Mitch's firm voice carried across the table.

Looking first at Hunter before sliding her eyes back to Mitch's, she said, "Brittany's mom is not the best."

Mitch's lips pinched tightly and he nodded. "She's had some trouble with us, but mostly public intoxication and a few minor altercations in the neighborhood."

"I think Brittany likes to come over because I feed her and we can just talk."

"Her mom could afford food if she didn't keep losing jobs because of showing up high to work," Grant stated.

"Oh, my God," Jade cried. "That's horrible."

"I'd like to see the back section of the mobile home park cleaned up, but since it sits on the county-town line, it's a fucked-up place to monitor. We technically don't have jurisdiction, although the County Board of Supervisors, along with Colt's Sheriff Department, have given us leave to patrol there. But, what we find, we have to call it into his office."

"That's insane," she said, shaking her head. "I never thought about it like that. No wonder some of the houses back there are unkempt and have questionable renters and owners. Although I do hear the park owner is systematically stopping leases of those who rent, saying that he's going to shut it down until he can renovate, start over, and keep it clean."

Colt's eyes were on Hunter as he said, "Guess you hear a lot from where you're at, don't you?"

Keeping his voice even, Hunter responded, "Some. Gets a little loud, but I've heard worse."

Nodding, Colt continued to stare, adding, "Be good if you let me or Mitch know of anything specific."

Mitch's gaze moved silently between the two men, finally settling onto Hunter.

"Keep my nose outta other people's business," Hunter replied. "But, I got no problem giving you a call when it's needed."

The others' attention was diverted when Jillian and Katelyn brought more food and Colt waved goodbye, heading toward the door. Her gaze shifted nervously toward Hunter, feeling the tension radiating off him.

Giving her another shoulder squeeze, he turned to the food, avoiding Mitch's penetrating gaze.

Belle threw open the door and greeted Brittany with a huge smile. "Come on in, sweetie. Follow me, I'm in the back."

The teen stepped into her house and moved into the bedroom, where she had clothes out all over the bed. "What on earth are you doing?"

"I'm going through some of my clothes and before I give any away, I wanted to see what might fit you."

Brittany's eyes grew wide and her smile brightened her face. "Wow...I've never seen so many clothes."

"Oh, honey, I always feel like I have very few compared to most of my friends who need work clothes. Since I wear scrubs every day, my other clothes don't have to be so plentiful."

Brittany bent over the bed, her fingers gently trailing over a light blue sundress with yellow daisies over the skirt. "Why are you getting rid of some of these?"

Laughing, she stood with hands on her hips, and said, "You know what, Brittany? Most women worry constantly about their looks. They feel too skinny, too chubby, not enough boobs and ass, too much boobs and ass. Hair not right, makeup not right. Lordy, honey, it's a wonder any of us get out of bed each day! And that was me. I matured early and was always self-conscious. I like to eat and, while I take care of myself, I know these curves are here to stay. So, it's time to get rid of a few things that are too snug and I no longer want to keep hanging in my closet just waiting to see if those ten pounds are going to magically disappear."

Brittany's eyes drifted over her body as she talked and her grin widened. "You're so pretty."

"Thank you, sweetie. So are you, but I know what it's like to not have clothes that fit very well, and so I thought I'd like to see if any of these work for you." Looking down at her bed, she said, "There are four sundresses and two skirts for you to try, as well as two pairs of jeans, two pair of shorts, and about six shirts. The bathroom is through there, so get started."

She sat on the bed while Brittany picked up a handful of clothing items and headed into the bathroom. Coming out a few minutes later, Brittany's face was beaming.

"One of the pairs of jeans was too big, but these are great. And this shirt is fabulous!"

She met her smile, noting the jeans fit well and the peach colored top with three-quarter sleeves and gathered bodice was perfect. "That is super flattering on you," she enthused. "The color is wonderful for your tanned skin."

Brittany headed back in, this time coming out

twirling, the blue daisy sundress swirling about her legs. It was just a tad large, but overall looked adorable on her. Her eyes landed on the bruises on the teen's upper arms, but she chose not to ruin the moment by mentioning them. She stood and walked over to her and pinched the sides of the bodice slightly. "I can do a quick stitch up the sides to make this fit better and it would be perfect."

Brittany ran her hands down the skirt of the dress and said, "I feel like a princess. I've never had anything so pretty in my life."

"Then I'm thrilled they're going to you," she enthused. "Now, go on and try on the other things."

By the end of the next hour, Brittany had her arms full of most of the clothes. Together, they walked into the living room and she instructed her to lay them on the sofa while she got them something to drink.

Settling a few minutes later, she noticed Brittany's gaze often drifted to the clothes and her brow would lower as though deep in thought.

"What's wrong, sweetie?"

"I was just wondering if you'd mind if I left the clothes here. I could come to get them before school if I was going to wear something that day."

Understanding flooded her and her heart ached. "Your mom, right?"

Nodding, her face drooping, Bethany said, "She'd either take them for herself or to sell, or just get pissed that I had something so pretty."

Her voice soft and full of understanding, she said, "Of course, you can keep them here." Silence moved between them and she continued, "My mom was usually drunk and always had men over. Growing up in that was really hard. I had my grandmother's house to escape to, but no other real friends. Then, when Grannie moved to the nursing home, I would try to get there, but unless I took the bus, it was hard."

Brittany's eyes held hers as she nodded slowly. "I got some friends here. Margo and Judy both live down the street from you. Their parents let me stay over when things get too loud and crazy at our house." She sat for a moment, staring out the window. "It's weird. It's like the park is divided into two parts. This, which is really nice, and the very back, which is awful."

"I know, sweetie. The explanation is kind of complicated, with the land being both in the city and in the county. I know that doesn't make a lot of sense to you right now, but just know that the owner is working to get it all cleaned up."

Nodding, Brittany said, "Some of the trailers back where Mom and I live are now empty. The owner had two of the nasty ones hauled away last week."

"That's good...it'll take a little bit, but he's working on it."

"But, Miss Belle, what happens when Mom gets kicked out? Where will I go?"

Blinking, she realized she had not considered that possibility when desiring the back area to be cleaned up. She opened and closed her mouth a couple of times but had no answer. They sipped their iced tea in silence for a few minutes before she finally asked, "Please, tell me about the bruises on your arms."

Brittany shrugged her thin shoulders and said, "It's no big thing."

Keeping her voice soft, she replied, "Okay...maybe so, but I'd still like to know." She leaned forward, placing her hand on the young girl's arm and added, "I had my grandmother to keep an eye out for me. If it wasn't for her, I don't know what would have happened. I'd like to be that person for you."

Brittany's eyes grew moist, but no tears fell and she wondered when the last time she had cried was. Waiting patiently, she leaned back in her chair.

"Mom had some men over...partying as always. I usually just stay locked in my room and was trying to get some homework done. It was too noisy so I called Judy and she said I could come over." Sighing, she said, "If they had just been in Mom's bedroom, it woulda been okay. But when I walked to the front door, one of the men grabbed my arms and tried to drag me into his lap."

She gasped, outraged, but seeing Brittany's eyes jump to hers, she tapped down her anger so that the story would continue.

Brittany rushed to say, "He didn't hurt me. I mean, he grabbed me hard, but I kicked out at his leg and he let me go. I rushed out and went to Judy's. I spent the night there. I haven't been back home since."

"Honey, we need to make sure you're safe. We could talk to the police—"

"No!" Brittany shouted, her face contorting. "That'd make it worse."

She opened her mouth, but Brittany got there first.

"Don't you see? Sometimes Mom can hold down a job for a few months and during those times, we actually have some food in the house. I know she's a junkie and I'm not stupid, Belle. But, I'm in the tenth grade now and only have three more years to go until I graduate. Mr. Pullen at the grocery, said I could start working there in a few weeks and then I'll have money to save."

"Honey, if your mom's activities place you in danger—"

"But they don't. She's just got men over and they leave me alone. She's too out of it to bother me most of the time. If the cops arrest her, they'll place me in some home. I can ride my bike to the grocery but if I go somewhere else, I might not be able to have my job."

She pinched her lips together, not liking the scenarios presented—Brittany staying or Brittany going.

"Look…he grabbed me and I bruise easy. He caught me off guard, that won't happen again. I know to stay away. I usually go out my window," she confessed. "That's what I'll make sure to do from now on."

Sucking in a deep breath, she let it out slowly, her mind working furiously over the options. "Brittany, sweetie, what if one of the men try to—"

"I lock my door. In fact, I added an extra lock to my door. Mom hasn't even noticed. So, if someone tried, I can get out the window."

They remained quiet for a moment before Brittany leaned over, her eyes full of emotion and pleaded, "Please, Miss Belle. Don't call the cops. Not now. I promise, if it gets too bad, I'll let you know."

Sighing heavily, she agreed. "Okay, but with a couple of conditions. You stay safe and call me anytime anything happens. If you need a place to stay, you come here. And you have to understand, if I ever feel like the situation is worsening, I will call the police."

Her breath leaving her lungs in a whoosh, Brittany cried, "Oh, thank you, thank you. And I promise to let you know what is happening."

Lying in bed that evening, once more both sated and satisfied, Belle related Brittany's tale to Hunter, including her agreement.

"Did I do the right thing?" she asked, worry in her eyes.

He sighed, his arms around her, loving the feel of her head on his chest. He dipped his chin to stare at her face while his fingers skimmed down her arm and back again. "Hell if I know, babe. I know that as a kid who was getting the shit beat outta me by my dad, I felt powerless until I finally got big enough to put a whoopin' on him and got him to back off. I didn't have anyone to go to. Just knew to get outta his way. You had your grandmother and she has you but, babe, you gotta think about how you felt as a girl. For me, it sucked to feel Dad's fists but I never had to worry about being violated."

Her lips tightened and she nodded. "I know. That's what worries me about her. What if she can't get away? What if someone gets to her when she's not aware?"

Leaning up, balancing her arms on his chest, she cried, "I think I need to call Mitch...or Ginny."

"Did she describe him?"

"She just said he comes to see her mom fairly regularly. Her mom calls him Jim...or Jimbo...something like that."

He knew who she was referring to and just nodded. "I'll take a look into it, babe. I'll do it so there won't be any blow-back on Brittany."

He waited to see if she would agree or argue against his suggestion, but she just plopped her head back to his chest and let out a sigh of relief. He wondered if she would feel relief if she knew what he planned on doing.

The night was dark with clouds covering the stars and the moon. The owner had replaced the street lights in the back part of the park, but a few of them had been broken already, probably by miscreants who preferred to work under cover of darkness.

Hunter had Jimbo down on the ground, his knee in the man's back. With a hand on the back of Jimbo's neck, forcing his face into the dirt, he growled, "Saw some bruises on Trudy's daughter. I coach her and, even though she didn't say dick, I know who her mom scores her shit from. And brother, you just found yourself outta business in this neighborhood."

Jimbo tried to squirm and wiggle, but the pressure on his back and neck was too much. "I...I...Dade..."

"Dade's got a new man in town and it ain't you. I see

you around this neighborhood again, I'll put a world of hurt on your ass and you won't like the results." Pressing down harder, he said, "You get me?"

"Yeah, yeah, man."

He loosened his hold on Jimbo, who stood and spit dirt out of his mouth. Jimbo wiped his mouth with the back of his hand, his eyes glaring. Wisely deciding to back down from the furious, mammoth of a man he was, he said, "Trudy's worthless anyway. Scrawny bitch's only worth was a blowjob and she wasn't no good at that either."

Stepping closer, he said, "You stay away from her and her daughter."

His head bobbed up and down. "Sure, sure. I've got enough business...I don't need this fuckin' place." A slow smile crossed his lips and he added, "You want her daughter for yourself?"

Hunter's fist landed in his face, the satisfying crunch of a broken nose reaching his ears. Leaning over, he roared, "Get the fuck outta here."

Jimbo picked himself up and, wiping the blood from his nose, staggered toward the street. Just then, headlights came toward them and he inwardly cursed as a patrol car pulled into sight. Stopping, Mitch stepped from the vehicle, his sharp gaze moving between a bleeding Jimbo and him.

"Gentlemen. Having a problem?"

"No, no," Jimbo said. "I just tripped and landed on the concrete. This man was nice enough to help me up. I'll just be on my way." He turned and hastened out of sight, leaving him alone with Mitch.

Mitch stepped closer, his assessing gaze not wavering. "Hunter...something I need to know about?"

"No, Chief Evans," he addressed him officially. "I was taking out the trash. Helped Jimbo and was just on my way back home."

Mitch said nothing for a moment, both of them unyielding in their stares.

"I've gotten to know Belle really well over the past few years," Mitch said. "She and Tori are close friends and I think she's one of the nicest women I've ever met."

"I'd agree," he replied.

"I'd hate to see her get hurt."

"So would I."

"Damnit, Hunter," Mitch cursed. "Zac was thrilled when you moved here and I've enjoyed having you in the American Legion and being part of this community. But you share very little of yourself, and that's fine," he added, throwing up his hands. "But, seeing you around this part of this neighborhood, at night, in the dark, with someone like Jimbo...it makes me concerned."

"I'm not giving you a reason to be concerned, Chief."

Blowing out a breath, Mitch nodded. "All right, but it's gotta be said. Just because you're a friend of most of the BPD, that won't help you if you're breaking the law."

"Understood," he replied, then, watched as Mitch moved back to his SUV.

Walking back to his camper, he cursed, "What a fuckin' mess." Scrubbing his hand over his face, he thought, *I've got to put a stop to this if I ever want a normal future...one with Belle.*

A few fitful hours later, he rose with the sun and

stared out of the camper window over the sink at the sun rising above the trees in the distance. Belle's words echoed in his mind... *I try to observe each sunrise to remind me that a new day is God's gift to us. A new chance for life to be wonderful.*

18

"Mr. Weldon, when you have a moment, I'd like to speak to you in private," Belle asked, coming upon her boss in the hall.

Dressed, as always, in a fresh suit paired with a crisp shirt, bright tie, and a flower in the lapel, he turned with a smile on his face and beamed at her. "Of course, of course. If you have a moment now, we can certainly speak in my office."

They walked down the hall, both greeting the residents who were sitting in wheelchairs watching the news or at a table working on a jigsaw puzzle. A few were paired off, talking quietly as they waited for the dining hall to serve lunch.

Moving into Careway's office area, they smiled at his receptionist and walked into his office. "Please, have a seat," he invited, his hand swooping out to indicate one of the plush seats in front of his desk. "May I offer you some coffee, since I'm sure you haven't taken a break yet," he said, lifting one eyebrow and winking in her direction.

She met his smile with a tremulous one of her own, but declined. He stared at her for a moment before settling into the leather chair behind his desk.

"You appear nervous, Belle. Please...what's on your mind?"

Sucking in a fortifying breath, she let it out slowly before relating to him what she saw at the pawn shop, including that she told Hunter as well, who wanted to keep her safe.

"So, you see, I can't possibly identify the person who may have taken it, but I just know it was Mr. Rosenberg's pocket watch. I feel horrible thinking that someone here stole it, but there can be no other explanation."

He had remained silent during her recitation, his eyes narrowing at times and wide at others. He leaned back in his seat, the leather creaking with the movement, and with his elbows resting on the arms of the chair, he steepled his fingers in front of him. "I see..." he said with deliberation.

Surprised that he did not immediately jump up and demand they report the alleged theft to the Sheriff, she waited to see what he would say.

"I have a hard time believing that anyone on our staff would steal from a deceased member of our family —and that is what our residents are, you know. We're their family, we care for them, we provide for them. But, from what you're telling me, someone has violated that trust."

She nodded slightly, clasping her hands in front of her, waiting to see what else he wanted to do.

"I agree with Mr. Simmons that going directly to the Sheriff would not be the best thing since you are unable to identify the person who took the watch to the pawn shop—"

"But, wouldn't the police be able to make the shop owner describe who sold it to him?"

With a benevolent chuckle, he said, "I'm afraid those tactics might just be useful in the movies, my dear."

Pinching her lips together, she felt foolish. "Oh, I see."

"We need to handle the situation with care. We certainly don't want the news to get out about this because we don't want our residents or their families to lose trust in us. Careway Nursing Home has an excellent reputation, and we stay at full capacity all the time due to that reputation. But, we can certainly make our own investigation here to make sure it does not happen again. I will personally oversee a policy change and will inform the staff when that's completed."

Standing, he walked around the desk and leaned over, taking her hand in his. "Belle, having you as part of our staff for these years has been such a pleasure and a true gift to all of us. I hope you will continue to make Careway your home."

She stood as he gently assisted her from the chair and nodded. "I don't plan on going anywhere else. I've always been happy here."

"Excellent!" he enthused, his smile firmly back in place. "And when you graduate? And have your RN degree?" His face fell as he said, "As you know, we only have one RN staff position here, Linda's, but I assure you that while your job position won't change from what it is now, there will certainly be a raise for you."

At that news, she returned his smile, glad for the opportunity to be able to save more for her future house fund. "Thank you...that would be wonderful."

He escorted her out of his office and as she walked through the door, he reminded her, "I promise to look into the situation. We certainly don't want to lose the trust of our residents."

She nodded before moving past his receptionist and into the hall. Sighing deeply, she had a sinking feeling that he was not going to do anything for fear of Careway's reputation. *So, maybe I should do something...but what can I do?*

Hunter roared into his short driveway at the end of the day and spied Zac leaned against his truck, parked next to his camper. Pulling off his helmet, he walked over to shake his hand.

Zac grinned, saying, "Good to see you, man."

"You wanna come in, have a beer?"

"Be great."

Unlocking the camper, he led him in and nodded toward the table while he opened the small refrigerator and grabbed two beers, popping the tops off. Handing one to Zac, he settled into the opposite seat and leaned back. "You off work today?"

Nodding, Zac said, "Yeah...don't get many of those, but Maddie had the day off, so I decided to take it off as well. We took a drive over to Virginia Beach." At his raised eyebrow, he laughed, adding, "She wanted to do some furniture shopping. Not my thing, but we stopped for a good lunch. That, plus spending the day with my girl, totally worth it."

"Good for you, man," he grinned, taking a long drink.

"How's Baytown living so far? I know we see each other, but I feel like we haven't had a lot of time to spend together."

Shrugging, he replied, "Can't complain. Baytown's everything you said it would be. Welcoming, laid back. Hell, got a job, got my camper—"

"Got a girl," Zac quipped.

Chuckling, he dropped his chin and stared at the beer bottle for a moment. "Yeah...got a girl."

"I was shocked you and Belle hooked up," Zac began.

He shot him a look and opened his mouth, but Zac threw his hands up in defense and continued. "Hey, nothing wrong with it, just didn't see it coming. She's quiet...sweet as hell, but quiet. A few guys have asked her out over the years that I've known her but never knew one that made it past the first couple of dates. When you showed interest, I figured she'd do the same."

Sighing, he replied "Sure as fuck glad she didn't, but maybe she should have."

"Why?"

"She's everything you say she is...probably the nicest

person I've ever met in my life and if anyone deserves everything her heart desires, it's her."

"And you think you're not the man to give that to her?" Zac inquired, his hard stare beaming across the table.

Shrugging, he held Zac's gaze. "Isn't that why you're here? To warn me off."

"What the fuck, Hunter?" Zac growled, leaning forward.

"Sorry...Jesus," he sighed heavily again. "Never been in a relationship. Never stayed in one place for very long after I got away from home."

Zac sat back, his eyes assessing. "Your camper. That's why you live in a camper. You can pick up and take off, move somewhere different when you feel like it. No roots."

Nodding, he agreed, but said nothing.

Zac prodded, "And now? You want to move on again?"

His gaze shot back up to Zac's and he bit out, "No! Fuck no!" Slamming the bottle back onto the table surface after finishing the beer, he said, "For the first time in my life, I want to stay somewhere. I want to put down roots and do it with someone."

Zac's lips curved upward and asked, "So what's the problem?"

"There are things going on in my life...things I can't talk about but I'm working on them. I hate holding back anything from Belle, but I've got no choice until I can get everything straight."

"You think she won't understand?"

With a shake of his head, he said, "I don't know. And that scares the shit outta me."

Zac finished his beer and stood, tossing the empty bottle in the trash can by the counter. He turned back and said, "The Belle I know is probably the most under-standing person I've ever met. Non-judgmental... caring...big-hearted. She's carried her own secrets, her own past around like an albatross and it's been fucking beautiful to watch her let it go and just live her life with her goals. Since you've been in town, I've seen you do the same, so from my perspective...you two are perfect together."

Standing, he tossed his empty bottle as well and stepped outside with Zac. "Thanks man, that means a lot."

Zac's affable grin firmly in place, he clapped him on the shoulder. "So, advice friend? Get your shit together, whatever it is, and keep the girl." With that, he ambled out to his truck and climbed inside. With a wave, he backed out of his driveway.

He stood outside for a few minutes, smelling the fresh air of living just a mile from the bay. He looked at his motorcycle before turning to look at his camper. His phone vibrated in his pocket and, pulling it out, he grinned.

"Hey, babe—"

"I passed! I passed all my classes! I'm done!"

Chuckling at her exuberance, he said, "Belle, that's great! Great news."

"I get to go pick up my cap and gown next week and I'll be all ready for graduation!"

He listened to the excitement in her voice and an idea began to form in his head. "Babe, tomorrow's Friday...how about we celebrate this weekend?"

"Sure! What are we going to do?"

Grinning as he stared back at his camper, he said, "Just leave that to me. I'll see if I can take half a day off tomorrow to make the arrangements."

Her voice softened as she said, "Hunter, you don't have to do anything extravagant. Just being with you is celebration enough."

"Proud you think so, but this is something I want to do for you. I promise to keep it simple, but it'll be something I really want to do, okay?"

"Okay," she agreed. "See you later."

Disconnecting, he looked down at his phone and placed a call.

19

Belle waited anxiously for Hunter to arrive, looking out her front window, listening for the sound of his motorcycle. She was wearing a light green sundress, the hem skimming her knees and the ruched bodice tight across her breasts, and was modestly covered with a white, knit bolero sweater on top.

A dark blue SUV pulled into her driveway and she moved closer to the window to see who was driving. Surprised when Hunter alighted, she ran to the door and threw it open.

"Where's your motorcycle?" she called out.

He grinned as he met her on the stoop. Placing his hand on her waist, he bent to kiss her, hot and wet, but keeping it short. "Rented an SUV for the weekend. Wanted to cart you around in something that allowed you to wear your dresses."

She beamed her smile up at him, squeezing his hand. "I'll go get my bag." He had called earlier and told her to pack a bag for the weekend but would not give her any details. Returning to the front door, he took her bag, checked the door to make sure it locked, and escorted her to the SUV.

Once in, she turned to him and said, "Do you mind if we stop by Jillian's first? She said she had something for me to pick up and when I told her we were going out of town for the weekend, she asked if we could pick it up before we left."

"No problem," he replied easily, turning onto Main Street. Parking in front of Jillian's Coffee Shop & Galleria, he assisted her down and walked in with her.

Once inside, the barista waved and said, "Jillian's upstairs. She said to go on up."

Looking over her shoulder, she explained, "I'll just be a minute, Hunter."

He stared into the glass pastry counter, nodding. "I'll get some things for us to have tomorrow morning."

Excitedly wondering where he was taking her, she grinned and walked up the stairs. Rounding the banister at the top, she saw Jillian standing near the back windows.

"Surprise!" came screams from all around the room. "Happy graduation!"

Stumbling backward in shock, her hand at her throat, she watched as the room came alive, people jumping up from behind displays and tables. "Oh, oh..." she sputtered, jumping once more when large hands landed on her shoulders, steadying her. Whipping her head around, she looked up into Hunter's grinning face.

"Congratulations, babe."

"Oh, my God," she gasped, as the well-wishers

surged forward. Unable to stop the flow, she burst into tears. Hunter immediately turned her toward him, wrapping his arms around her body, pulling her close.

"Baby, what's wrong?" Hunter asked, bending to whisper in her ear, suddenly doubting the wisdom of the surprise graduation party.

She shook her head, breathing deeply to gain control over her emotions. Finally, she leaned back and choked out, "No...nobody's ever given me a...graduation party. Mama never even remembered I graduated from high school, she was so stoned." She planted her face in his shirt again, grasping his arms.

He held the back of her head and whispered softly against her hair. "Shhh, baby, it's okay. Well, not okay that your mom didn't do anything, but sweetheart, you've done all this on your own and now have friends who want to let you know they're proud of you."

Belle nodded and gratefully took the proffered tissue that someone produced, wiping her nose and her eyes. Turning in his arms, still tucked in his embrace with her back to his front, she faced the gathering, seeing the concerned expressions on everyone's faces.

Blinking rapidly through her smile, she said, "I'm fine, honest I am. Just overwhelmed at this."

Jillian, Tori, Madelyn, Katelyn, and Jade rushed forward, pulling her from Hunter's arms, which he only allowed after assuring himself she was good. Moving backward a few steps, he watched as she was swept along, greeted by others on her way to a table laden with food.

A hand clapped him on the shoulder and he turned,

seeing Zac and Jason next to him. Accepting a beer from Zac, he smiled at Jason who just grinned and with a chin lift in Belle's direction, said, "You did a good thing here. She deserves this."

Nodding, he agreed. He was stunned at the number of people who had come to celebrate. Mitch, Grant, Zac, Brogan, and Aiden, the original Baytown Boys were in attendance, but also Gareth, Jason, Callan, and Lance. Mitch's parents, Ed and Nancy Evans, as well as Jillian's parents, Steve and Claire Evans, were offering their congratulations. Marcia and Toby Wilder, Grant's parents, and the MacFarlane clan, Corrine and Eric as well as the grandfather, Finn stood to the side talking, waiting for their chance with Belle. A few other ladies from the American Legion Auxiliary had provided some of the food and were currently hugging her.

As Belle made her way around the room to chat with everyone, Finn took her firmly by the shoulders. "Knew Ruthanne, your grandmother. Thought the world of her. I know she'd be bustin' her buttons right now with pride over what you've done."

Tears flowed fresh as she embraced the older man and then found herself handed over to Hunter once more. As he held her close, blinking up at him, she said, "This is ridiculous. I keep crying."

"You wear your heart on your sleeve, baby, so go ahead and let it out."

She pulled herself together quicker this time and smiled as she peered up at him. Mouthing 'Thank you', she moved to the food table with him in tow.

Claire Evans stopped her with a hand on her arm.

Jillian's mom pulled her into a hug and said, "I never thanked you properly for how wonderful you were when my mother was in Careway. You were a blessing to all of us."

Returning the hug, she smiled and lifted her shoulders slightly. "It was my pleasure...honestly."

As the gathering finally filled their plates with food and stood around in small groups talking, someone clinked on a glass to gain everyone's attention.

Jillian, wearing her signature bright colors, stood on a chair with Grant protectively keeping his hands on her hips, and said, "I regret that I did not know Belle in high school...sometimes we look back at childhood through the eyes of an adult and wonder what we could have done differently...should have done differently. But I cannot begin to express how glad I am that I made her acquaintance when my grandmother was at Careway Nursing Home." Smiling down at her, she continued, "That was the beginning of a wonderful friendship and I am honored to have you in my life. So, here's to hard work, perseverance, dedication, and one of the biggest hearts I know—Belle Gunn."

The cheers and shouts had her bursting into tears again and as her eyes searched out Hunter's, he made his way through the crowd to engulf her in his embrace once more.

Belle giggled as the SUV bumped along, the blindfold keeping her from seeing where they were going.

"Where are you taking me?" They hit another pothole and she bounced in the seat.

"Heading to a five-star resort, babe. Only the best for you," Hunter replied, grinning as she giggled again. Uncertain if it was the wine she had at her successful graduation party or the bouncing potholes, he was glad to see her tears had ended and she was having a good time.

He pulled to a stop and cut the engine. "Stay put. I'll be around."

He walked around the hood of the SUV and opened her door. Reaching in, he put his hands on her waist and she squealed as he lifted her out.

"I'm too heavy," she said, grabbing his shoulders.

"Told you not to say that. To me, you've got the perfect body." Holding her in his arms, he carried her forward. "Don't want you to twist an ankle in those shoes," he explained.

Belle huffed in pretend annoyance, but as he set her feet on the ground, she felt it shift under her feet. "Are we at the beach?" she asked, feeling the breeze blow against her face.

He did not answer but, instead, settled her next to his body with one arm banded around her waist and gently untied the blindfold. She blinked several times, focusing her eyes against the evening sun. She stared out onto an unfamiliar beach, definitely not the Baytown beach. The waves were higher, the dunes and seagrass taller, and as she turned her head to look up at him, she spied his camper set up nearby.

"What? Oh, my God!" she gasped, grabbing his

forearm harder. Looking up at his grinning face, she said, "What on earth? Where are we?"

Chuckling, he replied, "One of the men in the American Legion has some beach rights here on the ocean side of the Eastern Shore. He said I could set my camper up here sometime for a weekend, if I wanted. Never had a reason, but this seemed perfect."

Leaning down, Hunter placed his lips near her ear and said, "And the best part?" He felt her shiver as he swept his arm out toward the water, "From here, we can watch the sunrise over the water."

Her face crumpled and she twisted to bury it in his shirt again. Now, more used to her emotions, he wrapped her up and said, "Oh, baby. Don't cry."

"This is the nicest thing anyone has ever done for me...this whole evening...the absolute nicest."

Able to pull herself together, she bent and slipped off her high-heeled sandals before linking fingers and walking toward the camper. He explained that they would not have air conditioning, but with the ocean breeze they should be comfortable.

"I've also filled the tanks with water. Enough for a shower each, the kitchen sink, and the toilet."

"It's amazing," she enthused, stepping inside the camper.

He walked back to the SUV to get her bags and moved past her to place them on the bed. Turning around, he said, "Wanna take a walk?"

"Absolutely!" Changing into shorts and a T-shirt, she once more linked hands with him and they headed down the beach.

She began stooping and he watched as she picked up what appeared to be small pieces of glass. As her collection grew, she shoved it into her shorts pockets and continued to collect.

"What is that?" he inquired, staring into her open palm.

"Sea glass."

He offered a silent, lifted brow question and she explained. "When the ships toss out glass bottles, they break into little pieces and are tumbled by the water and sand, taking off the sharp edges, leaving little shards of pretty glass. You might have seen some of the artwork at Jillian's place earlier. Lance is an artist on the side, and he makes creations from the sea glass."

He shook his head in amazement, "I had no idea."

She sighed, saying, "I had a little collection from the few times I would go to the town beach, but my mom threw them away, saying it was a waste. Since I've got my own house now, I gather some, but don't have a lot of room. But, when I finally get my dream home, I'll fill jars and jars and have them sitting around everywhere!"

His heart squeezed at the thought of what all she had endured, and her positive outlook on life. They continued down the beach, both collecting sea glass, before turning and making their way back.

"Yes!" Belle cried, her fingers digging in his shoulders as her heels pressed against his ass. For the first time in her life, she had experienced hotdogs cooked over a camp-fire, sitting underneath the stars on a blanket spread over the sand, and finally crawling into bed, making love with the sound of the surf in the background.

Hunter lifted his chest up, balancing his weight on his forearms, cupping her face with his hands as he powered into her tight channel. "Jesus, babe, you feel so fuckin' amazing," he growled out, surprised he was able to make somewhat of a coherent sentence.

He took her lips, plunging his tongue in, tangling with hers in time to the thrusts of his cock. Kissing along her jawline, he nipped at her wildly beating pulse point on his way to her breasts. Sucking deeply, he rolled her nipple with his tongue, before letting it go with a pop and kissing his way over to the other.

She squirmed underneath him, crying out, "More… deeper," and he pulled out and with a deft move, flipped her over on her stomach before she had a chance to protest. Sitting back on his heels, he grabbed her ass and pulled her up.

The sight of her sweetheart derriere had him dig his fingers into her lush flesh as he bent to place a kiss on her ass cheeks before driving into her from behind. Knowing this position was a first for her, he broke out in a sweat trying to control his movements.

"Oh. My. God," she cried, figuring out the rhythm and rocking back against him as he thrust forward.

He held on to her hips with one hand and the other moved forward to palm her heavy breasts, tweaking her nipples as they moved together. "You close?" he groaned, wanting her to come before he did, but knowing he was barely hanging on.

"Yes, yes," she replied, each word forced out on an exhale.

He slid his hand from her breast, over her tummy, and fingered her clit. With a pinch on the swollen nub, he felt her inner muscles grab his cock just as she cried out his name. She had never said his name during sex before and it slammed through him as the sweetest and sexiest thing he had ever heard. Before he had time to process that further, his own orgasm hit and he lost all thought other than the tightening of his balls and pouring himself out into her body. Neck straining, teeth clenched, a roar came from the depths of his chest.

He continued to hold on to one of her hips as she collapsed onto the mattress and it was all he could to do keep from squishing her as he fell on top of her, rolling partially to the side. They laid there, speechless, the only sound their raspy breaths.

Finally, their breathing slowed, as well as their heartbeats, and in unison they rolled to each other. Neither of them spoke for several minutes as the sound of the waves crashing in the background floated on the breeze through the screen windows.

Holding each other's gazes, they laid tangled together. Reaching up, Belle cupped his face, her fingers tracing his jawline and said, "I love you."

As soon as the words left her mouth, she blinked, surprised that they had spilled out. Opening her mouth again, he placed his finger over her lips.

"Oh, no," Hunter warned softly. "You don't get to

take those words back. No way. Not when I feel the same way about you." Seeing her eyes widened, he grinned, moving his hand so that he now cupped her jaw as well. "I love you, too, Belle."

A tear slid down her cheek, landing on the pillow. "No one, other than my grandmother, ever told me they loved me," she said, her voice hitching.

His heart melted at her words and he kissed her gently before pulling her closer to him. Resting her head against his heart, he confided, "Only time those words were ever spoken were by my mom before she left us."

She leaned back, just enough to see past his jaw and into his eyes. "Oh, Hunter...I'm so sorry."

"Loved my mom, but swear to God, the older I got, the angrier I got with her. How could she have left me there with him?"

Shaking her head, she whispered, "I don't know. Any more than how my mom could do what she did to me."

"I used to wonder if I was fucked up because of my parents," he confessed.

Nodding, she said, "I wondered that too, but my grandmother always told me that I was not my mom. Just like you're not like your parents."

With one arm pressing her back and the other one cupping her jaw, he let her in. "I love you, babe. With all my heart."

He leaned down to snag the sheet. Jerking it to cover them, he tucked her in again, wondering if sleep would come. A few minutes later, he took her weight and soon followed her into slumber.

Early the next morning, they dressed in T-shirts and shorts, and with cups of coffee in their hands, left the camper and walked to the beach. Sitting on the blanket, they watched as the sun rose in the sky, painting it with colors of ever-lightening shades of blue.

Belle's face glowed in the sunlight, taking his breath away. She turned to him, her smile beaming, and said, "This has been the most amazing thing I've ever seen."

"The sunrise?"

She shook her head slightly and corrected, "You and me together...at sunrise...on the beach."

He wrapped his arm around her and they embraced as the sun continued to rise in the sky, sharing a kiss as gentle as the dawn.

"How's it feeling?"

Hunter watched Dr. Caldwell walking over and standing next to the physical therapist who had been massaging his leg.

Nodding, he said, "Better…surprisingly better."

"Good, good. These exercises will strengthen the area that was affected by the scar tissue. As they stretch, you will find less pain. Are you sleeping at night without any pain medicine?"

Holding back a grin as he thought of his nights with Belle, where he fell into a peaceful sleep after exhausting himself making love, he kept his expression neutral as he simply answered, "Yeah. I'm sleeping fine."

"Good, good. Well, Phil will keep seeing you here for another few weeks and then we'll discharge you from physical therapy and have you on a consultation basis. You can always come back as needed."

Shaking Dr. Caldwell's hand, he continued his exercises with Phil. He found out his therapist had been in the Navy also, many years before. The barrel-chested man with a grey, high and tight haircut worked him hard, but as they talked, he found the time always passed quickly.

As he stood at the reception desk, making his next appointment, he heard the front door open and recognized Lionel's greeting to the receptionist. Keeping his head down, he took his appointment card and turned to leave. Catching his eye, he grimaced as Lionel shot him a smile.

Ignoring him, he walked outside, only to find Lionel had parked his delivery van next to his motorcycle. He swung his leg over and settled into the seat, hoping he would take a long time in the clinic, but his luck did not hold out. Before he had a chance to leave, Lionel came out, walking straight toward him.

"How dumb are you?" he asked. "The last thing we need is to be seen together."

"And here I was, wondering how dumb you are."

Growling, he reached down to start his motor, but Lionel was not finished.

"Heard you got some attention the other night."

Staring at him with a hard glare, he said nothing.

"Mr. Uptight himself, Police Chief Mitch Evans?"

"None of your concern. I had some fuckin' trash to take out. Made my statement to the trash and it's done."

"Yeah, well you gettin' on the radar of the town police isn't smart."

"Don't tell me how to run my life—" he bit out.

"And you just remember who's fuckin' in charge."

Fighting back his response, he kept quiet, his jaw

ticking with anger, watching with unease as a slow smile crossed Lionel's face.

"Hate to think that pretty nurse you're banging would have a problem—"

He moved faster than the weasel had a chance to react and cut his words off. Off his motorcycle, with his hand at Lionel's throat, he pushed him back against the truck as Lionel clawed and grasped. As Lionel's face turned red, he leaned in close.

"You don't look at her. You don't talk to her. You don't talk about her to anyone. I hear you even fuckin' breathe in her direction, *you* will stop breathin' free. You got me, asshole?"

Still struggling to get loose, Lionel gasped, "Yeah, yeah."

Letting him go, he watched as Lionel slumped against the truck, his hand at his own throat as he sucked in air. He lifted his eyes to Hunter's but said nothing.

Moving back to his motorcycle, he roared out onto the street, his mind racing. *This has got to end. I've got to end this now.*

Belle walked down the hall of Careway, escorting a nervous Mr. Rasky to the activity room. "You'll be fine," she assured, smiling down at the man who was slicking his hair back with his hand.

"Is my face okay?" he asked. "That new aide doesn't give as good a shave as the one who left."

"Yes, yes, you look wonderful. Ms. Betina will be impressed, I'm sure."

"Hmph, who says I'm doing this for some woman?"

"Oh, I've seen the looks the two of you have given to each other. Anyway, she asked if you would sit next to her during Bingo today, so that's kind of like a date."

"Women don't ask men for dates," he continued to grumble.

"They do nowadays," she assured. "And admit it, you wanted to sit next to her."

Just then Hunter walked around the corner and Mr. Rasky called out to him. "Mr. Simmons." Gaining his attention, he asked, "Do you think a woman should ask a man out?"

His eyebrows rose as his gaze darted between the older man and her smiling face.

She leaned forward and whispered, "Ms. Betina asked him to sit with her during Bingo. Mr. Rasky is going, but feels the need to grumble about it."

"I do not," the older man continued to grouse. "I just don't want her to think I'm easy."

Her giggle rang out in the hall and Hunter grinned. "Well, sir, I'd have to say that if a nice, pretty woman like Ms. Betina expressed an interest, then you should take her up on it."

Mr. Rasky cast his sharp eyes between her and Hunter and said, "Don't think you two are sneaky. I've seen the looks you've given each other too."

She blushed and Hunter laughed. "And if she asked me out, I'd definitely say yes."

Leaning back in his wheelchair, Mr. Rasky allowed a

small smile to play about his lips. "Well, good. Shows you got sense, boy." Looking up at her, he said, "I'll find my own way into Bingo. I don't need a chaperone." With that, he continued wheeling himself down the hall.

She turned to Hunter, but her smile died as she observed the expression on his face. "What's wrong? Is it your leg? You had an appointment this morning...did the physical therapist work you too hard?"

Hunter both loved and hated the concern she was showing. "No, no, it's good."

Just then, his radio sounded and she reached out to touch his arm. "I'll see you later, okay?"

"Count on it, babe." He watched her walk down the hall and sucked in a deep breath, letting it out slowly. Checking his radio, he headed to Mr. Weldon's office.

An hour later, he wiped his brow as the sun beat down on him. Standing on the roof, he ascertained that a professional roofer would need to be called to patch a possible leak. The only section of the roof that had shade was near the back, where a few taller trees cast a shadow over the edge. Walking there, he sat on an upturned bucket and pulled out a bottle of water from the pocket of his cargo pants. Guzzling the tepid drink, he sighed heavily, his mind on Lionel's threat.

Hearing the sound of a truck, he glanced over the side and watched as the man in question drove his pharmaceutical van to the back door. His anger peaked again, but as the back door opened, he watched with interest at the person who came out and began to talk to him. Stunned at the blatant audacity, he continued to observe as Lionel reached under the seat of his van and pulled out a packet, handing it to the Careway employee.

He recognized the same type of packet that had been placed in his locker and realized he was looking at the person dealing the drugs from the nursing home. Swiping the sweat from his brow, he pulled back out of sight and considered what to do with that information.

Near the end of his day, he walked into the staff lounge and opened his locker. There, tucked in his jacket pocket, was the packet. Handling it carefully, he slid his jacket on, and walked out. Seeing Belle moving toward him, a smile on her face, he halted, forcing a matching smile to greet her.

"Hey, sweetie," she said. "Well, I can report that Mr. Rasky and Ms. Betina had a rousing competition of Bingo followed by sharing their afternoon snack together."

"That's great," he replied, feigning enthusiasm.

Her brow lowered as she tilted her head. "What's wrong? Are you hurting?"

Giving his head a quick shake, he replied, "No, no. Everything's fine. Listen, I've got somewhere I need to be tonight and I won't be able to come over."

"Oh," she said, disappointment evident as the corners of her mouth turned down slightly.

"I...well, it's important...and, I...well, I just need you to know that I love you. No matter what, I love you."

She placed her hands on his arms, peering up into his eyes. "I love you, too. Are you sure you're alright?"

"Yeah...just gotta deal with something. I...it's important that no matter what, you know I love you."

Hearing him repeat himself sent alarm bells off in her head, but Belle swallowed hard and nodded. "Okay...I'll see you tomorrow?"

"Sure...yeah." Bending to kiss her, he stood quickly and walked out of the building, leaving her standing alone.

The sun had just barely set, casting the neighborhood in long shadows while still being light enough to enjoy the walk. Belle, feeling restless, had walked over to visit with Ms. Sanders. Waving goodbye, she was not ready to go home and decided to walk toward Hunter's camper, just in case he had returned from whatever task he needed to accomplish.

She hoped he would come over to see her, no matter how late the hour, but he seemed rather sure that he would just see her the next day.

As she neared his camper, she spied his motorcycle, but noted all the lights were out on the inside of his home. Sucking in her lips, she wondered if she should stop. Making her way to the door, she lifted her hand and knocked but there was no sound from inside.

Wondering if he was also out walking, she continued down the road, past the playground that was now empty and silent. Heading to the swings, she sat on one and began pushing out with her legs. Not swinging high, she nonetheless felt the sense of flying that she had so enjoyed as a child. The mobile home park did not have a playground when she was little, but she always played on the swings during school recess. It was something she enjoyed but it was also a solo endeavor. No need for pretending she was not being ignored by the other children.

Sighing, she dragged her feet in the dirt to slow down and stood up from the swing. Casting a last look toward the back side of the park, wondering about Brittany, she almost turned to head back home when she glimpsed Hunter outside one of the run-down mobile homes, talking with a man known in the neighborhood as a troublemaker. *This was who he needed to meet with?*

Her legs took over her common sense and she skirted around the back side of the playground and along a parallel street for a block. The shadows had increased and she realized her precarious position, cursing herself for her stupidity.

"This is what you get," she heard Hunter's voice. "And, I'm telling you, he doesn't learn his lesson and threatens me again, I'm not going to be happy."

The sound of his voice was unlike anything she had ever heard from him before. Hard. Cold. Angry...*no... filled with rage.*

"No worries, no worries. I got it, man. You just keep doing what you're doing and I'll make sure it's all right."

She did not recognize that voice but assumed it was the man who lived there. Now scared, she silently hurried back the way she came and rushed toward her house. Making it to his camper, she stopped, standing outside, pressed against his door, wondering what to do.

As rational thought returned, she realized she

wanted to talk to him...needed to talk to him. She did not have to wait long before Hunter walked around the corner, stopping dead in his tracks as he saw her standing by his door.

"Belle?"

"Why were you talking to him?"

She watched as his face grew hard and a muscle in his jaw ticked.

"Don't deny it, I saw you."

"What the fuck were you doing out in the dark walking back there?" he cursed, taking a step forward, stopping when she threw up her hand.

"Don't deflect, Hunter. Please tell me you don't know what kind of man he is." She watched as he placed his hands on his hips and dropped his chin to stare at his boots.

"Tell me. Be honest, Hunter. Tell me you don't know he's bad news."

He remained silent and she shook her head slowly, her heart aching. "Then tell me what you're doing."

"Belle, there's stuff I can't talk about. Won't talk about. I told you I'm working through some things."

Standing up straighter, her voice barely a whisper, she said, "Are those things the reason Mitch and Colt have been a little unfriendly with you lately? Are you doing something they don't like?"

"Babe, don't ask questions you know I won't answer."

"Why not?"

"Because I'm trying to keep you safe," he said, his

face full of anguish as he stepped closer. "But I can't do that if you stick your nose where it doesn't belong."

Rearing back as though slapped, she sucked in a quick breath. "Fine. Consider my nose...unstuck!" She moved forward, skirting around him but his hand slashed out to latch gently onto hers.

"Belle, babe. Please...try to understand—"

"No, Hunter," she cried, pulling her arm from his. "You know. You know what I was raised with. I'm not about to be with someone who's involved with drugs. It almost ruined my life once...it killed my mom...and I will not let it around me again." She turned to walk away, then stopped and looked over her shoulder, swallowing audibly. "I only want the best for you. Please get clean and get help."

He stayed silent, watching her walk away before he stepped into his camper, his body tense. Taking a beer from the refrigerator he took several long swigs before he stood rooted to the spot for a moment. Whirling, he threw it to the side in the confined space with all his strength, the bottle shattering on the cabinet, beer spraying out. Raging, he put his fist through one of the cabinets. Staring down at his bloody knuckles, his heart pounded. *Fuckin' hell...how could things get so fucked up?*

Sitting on the bedroom bench, staring at the clouds marring the sunrise, Belle sighed. Clouds had never bothered her before. In fact, her grandmother had taught her to appreciate each new day regardless of the weather. But today, the clouds and impending rain matched her mood. Dreary.

Wincing, she remembered a time when she asked her grandmother about her mom's addiction.

"Belle, she's my daughter and I love her. I accept that she's got problems, but I won't let her drag me into them until she's ready to face up to what she needs to do. And I won't let her drag you into them either. But, my love for her never changes. And she knows that—I've told her over and over...I'm here for her. Not to be taken advantage of, but to love her unconditionally."

Hanging her head, her heart ached, not only with what Hunter was facing, but also with her words to him last night. *God, I was so judgmental. So scared to even take a chance.* With one last look out the window, she jumped up and quickly dressed. It was her day off, but she suddenly had the desire to talk to him. To tell him that she would stand beside him.

She drove down the road to Careway, her foot pressing the accelerator harder than usual. *If he has an addiction problem, then I should help.* Wrestling with herself, she also realized that unless he wanted help, it would never work. *But, I've got to try.*

Turning into the parking lot, her foot hit the brake, jolting her body as she viewed the scene in front of her. Flashing lights from state police and sheriff cars covered the front of Careway. Terrified of what had happened to the residents, she pressed on the accelerator and hurried into a parking spot as close as she could get. A crowd of people had begun to gather, some employees and a few onlookers.

Jumping from her vehicle, she jogged toward the front where she saw Colt and Mitch standing nearby with a few people wearing State Police uniforms. Pushing her way through, she recognized Mr. Weldon walking out with Hunter right behind him, seeming to be escorted by State Police officers. Linda, crying, was following them…in handcuffs.

Heart pounding, she stared at Hunter, who had not seen her Coming closer, she observed the hard set of his jaw, anger pouring from him. *Oh, God…Oh, God. He's being arrested.* Her chest quivered as she gasped, trying to take in air. He stopped in front of Colt and Mitch, his back to her, and she heard him speak, "I'd say I was sorry, but you know how it is. I had no choice."

Mitch asked, "And Belle? How does she fit into this?"

"She doesn't. She's clear. I've checked her out, just like the others. She's clear."

Mitch's eyes shot behind Hunter and his face fell. "Fuck," he breathed.

Hunter jerked around, his eyes landing on her, surprise in his face. "Shit, babe."

Her gaze was snagged on something shiny and as she dropped her eyes, she saw a badge clipped to his belt. Stunned, her eyes jumped back to his, her eyebrows hitting her hairline. "You...you're..."

"Belle, why are you here today?" he asked, his harsh voice laced with surprise as his brows lifted.

Chest heaving, not caring who was around listening, she said, "Because...I...came to talk to you. I hated how we parted last night...what I said. I wanted to convince you to get some help...but, this..." Her voice trailed off as she watched Mr. Weldon talk to one of the policemen.

"The publicity! It will ruin us! Please..."

His words slid into the background, her attention snagged by Linda being placed in the back of a sheriff car. As though the world she knew had floated away, she turned her gaze back to Hunter, the ramifications hitting her and she stumbled backward. "Oh, my God. You said you cleared me. You were investigating me—"

"That's not how it was...not after our first meeting. You know that," he clipped, stepping closer.

"I don't know anything," she said, dragging her hands through her hair at the sides of her head. Her fingers caught on the ribbon she wore like a headband and the yellow strip of material fell away, fluttering to the ground, unheeded by her. Gasping as her stomach clenched, she cried, "Oh, my God. I shared with you. About my mom, her addiction, my childhood. My horrible, fucking childhood. The poor, dirty kid with ill-fitting hand-me-down clothes that nobody wanted to play with. My mom, when she wasn't turning tricks, taking our food money and spending it on drugs. I thought you understood…but the whole time, you were wondering if I was doing the same."

"Belle, listen to me," he growled, "That's not true. I knew you were innocent before I ever went out with you the first time. There was never a question of you being involved."

Swallowing deeply, her eyes darted around, realizing they had an audience and she had just exposed her hellish background to Colt, Mitch, and Mr. Weldon. Not willing to see who else might have their eyes and ears on her, she turned and ran, pushing through the crowd near the front of the building just as rain began to splatter on the pavement.

"Belle!" Hunter shouted, taking a step toward her only to find his arms grabbed by Mitch and Colt.

"Stay cool," Mitch warned. "You've got an audience and you're not finished with your work here. You may have been working undercover for the State Police, but your supervisor will not be happy if you fuck up the case because of personal involvement."

"Fuckin' hell," he cursed, shaking his arms loose from them as he watched Belle climb into her car and screech out of the parking lot.

"You'll get your chance to make it right, man," Mitch assured. "But first, you gotta finish the case."

Looking down at his boots, with his hands on his hips, a yellow ribbon caught his eye. Bending, he scooped it up, fingering the soft satin. Stuffing it into his pocket, he stared longingly down the now empty street.

Hunter, sitting in Mitch's office with two other State Police officers, Colt and two of his deputies, and Grant and Ginny, finished his report while discussing the case with the others.

"The Virginia State Police were working with the Maryland State Police for a couple of years on this case. We knew some of the lower members but did not have the whole picture until me and a couple of others went under-cover at several facilities in the two-state area," he said.

"We also knew it revolved around at least two drivers for Matrix, and we were able to identify Lionel fairly early as one of the deliverers. Careway was a lot harder to figure out, until they made me part of their chain. Even then, it was a complete stroke of dumb luck that I was able to spot Linda with Lionel. Since she's the one who normally handles the drug deliveries, it was not unusual that she would be talking to him."

"So, how'd you get her?" Colt asked.

"I was up on the fuckin' roof, doing maintenance and spied them from above. I saw her get a packet from him and an hour later that same packet was in my locker."

"Their whole scheme seems simplistic," Mitch groused. "Matrix drivers make some duplicate deliveries to certain places who have someone who takes them. Those people then get them to the next one in the chain, who deliver them to low-level distributors like Dade."

Nodding, he agreed. "Absolutely simple in execution as long as you have people you can trust."

"How'd you get them to trust you?" Ginny asked.

"Met up with Lionel at the Pain Management Center. I needed them anyway, which made for a good cover, because it was legit. I got a name of a common acquaintance of his from the other undercover officer on the job. Made the connection with him and got him to think I needed pills and the center wouldn't give them to me. He found I worked at Careway and I had an automatic in with him."

"And Linda? A Registered Nurse?" Grant asked. "What the fuck was her deal?"

"Money. Pure, simple money was her motivation. Once she made a delivery the first time, she was in their hooks."

Mitch added, "I'm glad to get them all shut down, but especially with Dade out of the Baytown area. Colt and I are going to work with the owner to get the rest of the park cleaned up."

While the congratulations flowed, his mouth was fixed in a tight line, unable to get Belle's face from his mind. Finally, the State Police officers left, as well as the deputies.

He assumed the others would leave, but found Colt, Mitch, Grant, and Ginny still seated at the table. Scrubbing his hand over his face, he said, "Please tell me this isn't going to be discussing what I think you want to discuss."

Before anyone had a chance to speak, Zac came bolting into the room, an open expression of incredulity on his face. "State Police? What the fuck, Hunter? State Police? Jesus, man, how the hell did that happen?"

Sucking in a heavy breath, he said, "Can we put off show and tell until after I talk to Belle?"

Zac lifted his eyebrow and said, "Sorry, Hunter. You may find that hard to do. I just got off the phone with Madelyn and the women are all over at Katelyn's house, surrounding a very upset Belle. No way you're gonna get near her now. And, depending on what all they talk about, you might not get around her for days."

Leaning heavily in his seat, he said, "Shit..."

Colt stared hard at him and said, "Damn, you were good. I can usually spot undercover but had no idea you weren't who you said you were."

Mitch nodded his agreement.

Staring at the table, he decided to give them the abbreviated version, saving the full story for the one person who deserved it—*Belle*. "Most of what you know is true. Was a mechanic from a no-where town in Tennessee. Joined the Navy out of high school, doing maintenance on a ship. Got out after four years, tried going home but found that it was just as no-where as it always was. Moved to Norfolk. Figured I could get a job somewhere and it was my second home when in the Navy. Got a job as a maintenance worker for the State Police Headquarters in Richmond. After a year of watching them, a friend talked me into getting my associates degree. Did it and got into the police academy. After two more years, I started doing some undercover work…seemed my maintenance abilities made it easy for me to get into places without suspicion."

He looked up at Zac, and continued, "You had been inviting me to come to live here. When we were trying to bust a prescription drug ring, it all came together. I moved to Baytown, got on with the nursing home, and my Navy injury allowed me to get in with the Pain Center to make contact with someone in Matrix."

Throwing his hand out, he said, "That's it. That's my story in a nutshell."

The entire gathering sat stunned into silence until Mitch finally asked, "What about Belle?"

"Jesus, man, this isn't middle school—"

"Cut the shit, Hunter. We know you care for her, that's not what this is about," Grant butted in.

"Then what is it about?" he bit out, his frustration pouring off him.

"You know her, her insecurities, her past—" Grant continued.

"Maybe, just maybe, you feel guilty because way back in the day, you didn't treat her as good as you should have," he accused, shooting a glare at him. "I don't care if you guys are her friends now, I'm not fuckin' talkin' about her behind her back."

Ginny waded into the middle of the testosterone. "I wasn't here back then, when you all were in high school." Her words had the men's eyes jump to her. "But, I got to know Belle when I came to town. She's part of Jillian's posse and they all took me in and made me welcome into their group. Sure, she's shy, doesn't give away a lot about herself but she's intimated some about her upbringing. I think, for the most part, she's a strong woman who has overcome a shitty childhood."

Shrugging, she stared at him and added, "You had a job to do and you did it. Maybe you should have held off on the relationship until your cover was complete, but you didn't. I think she'll be able to deal once she comes to grips with the new turn of events."

The men stayed quiet and he sighed heavily. "We clicked. I haven't had a lot of close *anythings* in my life… she got close. We both did."

Zac walked over and clapped his hand on his shoulder. "Can't say the news about you working for the State Police didn't shock the shit outta me. I know we lost touch when I was still in the Navy and you were back here, so when we finally got in touch last year, I just made the assumption that you were still working maintenance."

"Never meant to lie to you—"

"Hey, no worries. You know I don't care if you're a cop or in maintenance. I'm just glad you're here."

"Are you here?" Mitch asked, once more drawing everyone's attention back to Hunter.

The silence was deafening.

"Oh, fuck, man…you're leaving now that the case is

over," Grant moaned. "That's what all the concern about Belle is. I thought it was a shock to her and she felt like she'd been lied to. But, now that the case is over, you'll be leaving."

He stared at the others in the room, the noose tightening around his neck. Swallowing hard, he said, "I'll have to go back to Richmond to complete the rest of this investigation."

"So, you are leaving her..." Zac said, plopping down in his chair again.

Standing, he pulled himself up to his impressive height. "I'm talking about this with her, and only her."

As the others opened their mouths, Ginny jumped in. "He's right. That's where this conversation needs to be."

With a curt nod, he walked out of the room, noticing Colt's eyes staying on him longer than the others. Not giving that any thought, he headed to his vehicle, wondering how to convince Belle that his feelings about her were true when so much of what she thought about him was not.

22

"I feel foolish," Belle said, her swollen eyes still puffy in spite of Jade's cold compress. She had driven around after leaving Careway, not wanting to go home. Home would remind her of Hunter and that was the last thing she wanted in her face right now. Calling Jillian had instigated the immediate phone tree of friends so, now, she was ensconced in Katelyn's house, surrounded by Tori, Jillian, Madelyn, and Jade. "I mean, there I was, going to talk to him about what I thought was an addiction and, instead, I found him making arrests! I should be glad, right? I mean, I'm glad that he isn't into drugs! But the secrecy, the withholding...it feels like I don't even know him."

She turned her gaze to the others, observing their expressions of concern.

Jillian groused, "I know I'm married to a cop, but he's never been undercover. I have no idea what that would be like...to not know..."

"I thought Lance was just an artist and when I found

out he had been a cop, I was stunned," Jade said. "But, then, we were still learning about each other." Sighing, she added, "Sometimes I wish he were just an artist and not a cop...I would worry less."

"Mitch had to be careful with me," Tori said, drawing her attention to her. Leaning back against the sofa cushions, nursing Eddie, she said, "Remember? He was investigating a murder that took place at my house. He was involved with me and yet, for a little bit, I was under suspicion."

She sighed heavily, nodding. "I forgot about that."

"Oh, my goodness," Madelyn rushed, her eyes wide as she stared at Tori. "I wasn't here then. How on earth did you deal with it?"

Chuckling ruefully, Tori replied, "Not very well. I was upset and we had to back away from each other for a little bit until I was cleared." Her eyes landed on her and she smiled softly. "Honey, what do you feel for Hunter?"

"I love him," she confessed, swallowing back the tears. "I just feel so vulnerable. I told him everything about my childhood." Pressing her lips together, she looked down at her clasped hands in her lap. "Things I've never told anyone. He knows exactly who I am, better than anyone, in fact. But what if he isn't who he showed himself to be?"

The gathering sat quietly for a few minutes while she continued to grapple with the words in her heart.

"It was hard, growing up with a mother addicted to drugs and alcohol...doing whatever she needed to do to stay supplied. She hid nothing from me, so I saw it all...

the drugs, her passed out drunk...the men. I hated it...
sometimes, hated her. But, with my Grannie's help, I
knew Mom's way was something I could avoid. It was
hard in high school, when the boys looked at me like I
put out when I didn't. Girls looked down their noses at
me because of the way I dressed. I just knew that I had
to work hard to pull myself up out of the muck my
mom raised me in."

She glanced around, shocked to see tears in the eyes
of each of her friends. Blowing out a breath, she
continued, "You know I love each of you. From the first
time I walked into your shop, Jillian, and you welcomed
me, I felt friendship. Real friendship. And with each
addition to our group here, I have still felt that love. I
watched with utter happiness as you all found the man
of your dreams and hoped that, one day, I might find
mine too."

Katelyn swiped a tear and shook her head. "I'm so
sorry you had those experiences."

Tori leaned over to pat her arm, jiggling Eddie
slightly. "You're the bravest person I know."

Snorting, she said, "I don't feel very brave. I just
walked away from a man I love because he kept something from me and I feel betrayed. And now I'm questioning everything because of it."

Jillian laid her hand on her arm, warm and comforting. "That makes sense, Belle. Hunter is a lying, conniv-
ing, untruthful—"

"No!" she said suddenly, sitting up straighter.
Shaking her head, she looked Jillian in the eyes.
"Hunter's a good man who did what he needed to do to

take down the ones involved. I mean, Linda? My head nurse was peddling drugs? What the hell?"

The others blinked at her cursing but could not hold back their grins as she vehemently defended Hunter. Jillian winked at Katelyn, watching as her words appeared to spark something in Belle.

Standing, Belle began to pace the room, stepping over their feet as she rambled. "Hunter has taken everything I've ever told him and made it better. You know what he said when I told him about my childhood? He said everything bad about it was someone else, it wasn't *me*. That I was surrounded by darkness but I was always the light. And yeah, he didn't tell me about his work, but he told me all about how he grew up. He shared his hurts, the things he wishes had been different. It wasn't easy for him, but he did it. And the way he is with the kids? You should have seen how worried he was about Brittany when she showed up with bruises. He's so protective, and loyal, and kind, and sweet—" She paused abruptly and sucked in a quick breath. "Oh, my God. I really am being foolish, not just feeling foolish. The reality is that he had a job to do and it was a necessary job. I'm being selfish sitting here feeling sorry for myself when I didn't get the man of my dreams the way I would have liked. It has nothing to do with who he is and who we are together, and everything to do with the situation this puts us in."

She looked at her friends, grinning widely back at her. Cocking her head to the side, she realized how much she had been defending Hunter. "I said some terrible things to him," she confessed.

"Honey, with all that was happening this morning, I think it's understandable," Madelyn stated.

"This morning!" She stared down at Madelyn before allowing her eyes to drift over the others. "Poor Mr. Weldon..." Blinking, she gasped, "Oh, my God, Mr. Weldon! Here I've been feeling sorry for myself and he's having to deal with the aftermath of this mess without his head nurse."

Whirling around, she spied her purse on the floor, next to her shoes, and ran over. Slipping into her shoes, she said, "I've got to go. I need to get to Careway and see what needs to be done. There're residents who'll be confused. The aides need direction. The medications need to be looked at and possibly reordered."

The women jumped up and surrounded her, their arms wound around each other. Katelyn said, "I feel like we didn't do much for you—"

"Oh, no," she gushed. "Just giving me a place to be myself...let me blow off some steam...that's what I needed."

"Honey, you just suffered through an emotional time," Jade said, her green eyes piercing hers. "Are you sure you should go to work?"

Blowing out a breath, she said, "If there was anything my grandmother taught me, it's that no matter how bad things are, some hard work will push it to the background. That's what I need. Some hard work."

With a final hug, she hurried out the door and to her car.

"Belle!"

She turned, looking at the aide who was hurrying her way. "Yes?"

"I don't know what to do," Sarah said, her face as harried as Belle felt. "Mr. Rasky says he won't talk to anyone but you. I tried to explain that things were a little topsy-turvy today and you were busy, but—"

"It's okay," she said, her smile covering up her fatigue. "I'll talk to him."

Hurrying down the hall, she was waylaid by Mr. Weldon, popping out of his office, his usual unflappable appearance now ruffled. "Oh, Belle. I need you for a moment."

"Sir, I'll be there just as soon as I speak to Mr. Rasky." Turning into the resident's room, she spied the older man sitting in his wheelchair by the window. "I understand you need me," she said, walking over to him.

"Been a strange morning."

"Yes, but we have everything under control," she assured.

He lifted his eyes to her and cocked his head to the side. "Saw our maintenance man, Mr. Simmons, out there with the police."

"Yes, it seems that he was—"

"Undercover." He grinned and added, "I watch detective shows on TV. I know all about undercover cops." His smile slowly faded as he said, "I liked him. Going to miss having him around here."

"I'm sure Mr. Weldon will be hiring a replacement soon."

"Won't be the same. Will it?"

She stared at his intelligent eyes and she felt the shock of his words to her core. Tempted to deny it, she knew that would be foolish and easily discerned. "No... it won't be the same."

She rested her hand on his shoulder and he reached up to pat it. "Hearts are funny things, Ms. Belle. Never know when they'll break apart and never know what'll put them back together." With that, he suddenly said, "Well, time for Bingo. I'll talk to you later."

She watched him roll out of his room and shook her head to clear the fog from her mind. Remembering Mr. Weldon, she hurried back to his office.

Knocking on the doorframe, she waited until he looked up, his tense smile and wave greeting her. Entering, she took the seat he motioned toward and he immediately launched into his concerns.

"Oh, my dear, what a nightmare! I've been on the phone with a PR firm that will assist in my drafting a letter to the residents, and their families, about what has occurred and how we plan on assuring them that they are safe. I know this mess will hit the news and when it does, I want to have things in place."

Nodding, she waited for him to continue, not that he was giving her a chance to speak.

"And Linda!" he exclaimed. "Who would have thought? Besides my secretary, she was my right-hand person. She seemed so caring...so truly into caring for our residents. I don't know how she could have done this...such a mess!"

"Mr. Weldon, do we know what happened? Was she taking drugs from our patients? I mean, I never came up short on the drugs here for any patients I was giving them to."

His eyes widened and his mouth opened and closed several times. "I hadn't thought of that," he cried. "I just thought she was getting them from the delivery driver, but, oh, my God...what if she actually took them from the residents?" Slapping his forehead with his palm, he moaned, "That's what they meant." Seeing her tilted head, he explained, "The police officer told me that we needed to check all medications. They'll need the information for their case. In all the excitement, I forgot we needed to take care of that."

His voice rose with each word and she could see his face reddening to the point of concern. "Mr. Weldon, shhhh," she tried to calm him. "We don't know the facts yet and let's not borrow trouble. We can easily check to see that all residents have the medications they need and you can order what is needed. I can pull together some of the nurses and aides and we can work on it this afternoon."

Wiping his sweaty brow, he nodded emphatically. "Yes, yes, you're right. So stupid of me to lose my head. I'm normally so calm, but this has completely undone me."

His tie was loosened and his suit jacket was slung haphazardly over the back of his chair, something she had never seen.

"May I get you a glass of water, Mr. Weldon?" she asked. Rising from her seat, she considered taking her stethoscope from about her neck and checking his heart rate.

"No, no, my dear. I'm fine...just discombobulated." He appeared to calm before speaking again. "Belle, please don't think that this is a rushed decision, but the timing of your graduation is fortuitous. Will you consent to be the head nurse here at Careway? I cannot think of anyone more suited for the position."

Eyes wide, she stammered, "Oh...I hadn't even thought about...uh...what we would need...I..."

"Please say 'yes', oh, please," he begged. "I'm sure you think this is just coming from desperation and I'd be a liar if I tried to deny I'm desperate, but you're more than qualified and we would be so honored for you to step into the position."

Blowing out a slow breath, she nodded. "I agree, on one condition." She caught his wide-eyed stare. "I'd like it to be on a conditional basis to begin with. If you find that I'm not suitable or if I find the job does not allow me to have continued presence with the residents, we can go back to how it is now, and you can look for another head nurse."

"Yes, yes," he nodded emphatically, "but I'm sure that won't be the case. You're perfect for the job."

"And first thing, Mr. Weldon," she added, gaining his attention once more. "I will initially institute a new procedure for how we intake the drugs from the pharmaceutical companies. As soon as you ascertain from Matrix how they will deliver, there will be two of us who check in the drugs and add them to the cabinet. No more just having one person do the job. This will create a checks and balance system."

Clapping his hands, with the first smile of the day on

his face, Mr. Weldon exclaimed, "Oh, yes…a wonderful idea!"

She left his office, after being told her new duties would begin immediately…and the raise to go with it. Stopping at the end of the hall, she leaned her head back against the taupe-painted wall and dropped her chin. Staring at her feet for a moment, she realized this was the very spot where she crashed into Hunter, landing on the floor underneath his ladder.

Sighing heavily, she stood quickly, moving back down the hall, refusing to give in to any more emotions…*I have a job to do!*

23

Hunter sat in the outdoor chair, his forearms resting on his knees as he fingered the yellow ribbon that had been in Belle's hair early that morning. He had been sitting there for a couple of hours. Waiting. Wondering. Worrying. The evening was just on the cusp of night and the sound of children playing had faded into the background, replaced with the chirping of crickets.

Finally, a car came down the street and as he lifted his head, he saw the headlights turning onto the short driveway. He watched as Belle alighted from her car and began walking toward her front door.

She had not seen him yet and the closer she got, the harder it was for him not to jump up and rush to her, wanting to hold her once again. "Belle," he called out as she neared.

Jumping, she squealed, her eyes darting to him sitting in one of her lawn chairs. He was in the illumination of the front light, but she kept her hand at her throat for a moment, just staring.

He stood, shoving the ribbon into his pockets and peered at her. Her skin was pale, and her eyes appeared tired, partially due to the dark shadows underneath. Her normally neat hair was falling out of her bun, and her scrubs were slightly wrinkled.

"This was supposed to be your day off," he said, wincing as he stated the obvious. "I thought you were with your friends, but when I called Jillian, she said you went back to Careway."

"Yes. Well, the head nurse was taken out of the nursing home in handcuffs, the residents were upset, the aides had no idea what to do, and Mr. Weldon nearly broke down with the business implications. Someone had to step in and handle what needed to be handled." Without giving him a chance to respond, she threw her hand up and continued, "And, no, I'm not saying Linda shouldn't have been arrested or marched out in handcuffs. Quite frankly, I'm so pissed at her, there's more chance of her being harmed by me before she ever reaches a trial."

Her words were spoken without rancor but he heard the underlying frustration. His lips twitched, and he said, "I have a hard time believing you could commit bodily harm to anyone, Belle."

She had been speaking to his chest but lifted her gaze and he felt the heat of her glare.

"Don't doubt me, Hunter. What she did is so despicable, it makes me furious."

"Then I guess it's a good thing she's behind bars tonight."

Her shoulders slumped and his fingers itched to take

her in his arms. Standing a few feet away from her felt like they were miles apart.

Sighing, she ran her hands through her hair and said, "Why are you here?"

"I wanted to talk—"

"And we should. There's a lot to say and you have a lot of explaining to do. But, Hunter, I'm exhausted. I've got nothing left in me right now and another long day tomorrow at work. I—"

"Please...I'm begging you..."

She held his gaze for a moment and he was unsure if she was going to acquiesce. Finally, heaving a sigh, she nodded and moved to sit in one of the lawn chairs, making it obvious she was not going to invite him inside. He was frustrated, but would take whatever he could take.

He sat back down in the other chair and, rubbing his hands together, suddenly wondered what to say. He had spent the past few hours practicing what he would say and now was afraid of stepping on a verbal landmine.

"Hunter," she said, her shoulders still sagging, "just talk. Whatever it is you feel like you need to say, just say it."

He held her gaze, praying she would understand. "Everything I told you about growing up was true. My mom leaving, my dad's rages and how he took them out on me. He'd end up in jail for a night sometimes when he'd go on a drunken bender and pick a fight in a bar. The only thing I ever knew about the police was sometimes I wished they'd show up and haul my dad away and other times I was scared that they actually would."

Scrubbing his hand over the back of his neck, he continued, "I understood what you said about not having many friends growing up. Other families didn't want their kids coming to my house to play and that was just as well, since our place was kind of crappy after Mom left. But, then, they didn't much want me to go over to their houses either. If it hadn't been for the old mechanic who let me hang around his shop and then taught me what he knew, I'd probably be in the same boat as my dad...a drunk...a mean drunk."

She looked like she wanted to say something, but clamped her mouth shut, allowing him full rein to talk.

"I thought about staying in the Navy for a career. Hell, I had no home to go back to. There was nothing in Tennessee for me. But, after the accident, I knew I would have to get out. I ended up in Norfolk, staying with an old Navy buddy who got out earlier than I did. I needed a place of my own, though, and found an ad for a campground that was renting out campers. Got one, stayed there, and loved it. Small...just me...didn't have to worry about much rent. Worked maintenance for a couple of places...temporary jobs mostly. Then I heard that there were state jobs for veterans. I got hired as a maintenance technician for the headquarters building of the State Police in Richmond."

At this, he watched her eyes light with interest despite her fatigue. Nodding, he said, "I did a lot of what I do at Careway...building maintenance." Chuckling, he said, "It was not lost on me that my dad would have turned over in his grave if he knew I was working for the police. Guess in my own way, it was a bit of a *fuck you* to him."

Her face softened and he knew it was probably an asshole move on his part to play on her sympathies, but he simply did not want any more secrets between them.

"I got to know some of the officers and have to admit that, after my formative years of fearing them, I had a chance to admire and respect them. One, in particular, would talk to me and he encouraged me to get my Associates Degree. I'd never thought of college but after being in the military, I knew I could get money to further my education. I had no other plans...and have to admit that working in maintenance the rest of my life was not exactly what I wanted to do, so I did it. Took two years, then I went to police academy school."

Her eyebrows hit her hairline at that and she shook her head slowly. "Wow...that's impressive."

"No more impressive than you earning your Nursing Aide certificate, then going to college for your LPN, and now your RN."

She sucked in her lips, her eyes darting between his but did not respond. He took that as a positive and continued.

"After a couple of years, my supervisor came to me and I was asked to go undercover. They needed someone on the inside of a company that they thought was dealing drugs and, with my maintenance background, it was easy to get me in. It took a while, but with no one suspecting me, I was able to get the evidence needed."

"That's wonderful, Hunter," she said, her voice soft but sincere.

"You think you don't know me but, Belle, you do. I'm the same man you've been spending time with for the past month. Yes, I work for the State Police, but when I was working maintenance at Careway, that was me also. I'm still the same man you know."

"I know."

He jerked at those two words, surprised to hear her say that after what went down that morning. "You do?" he asked, tentatively.

She shook her head, "You've been honest with me about everything except what you really did for a living, right?" Catching his eyes and holding them intently, she questioned. "This is it. No more secrets, right? You've told me everything?"

"Absolutely. That is the only thing I couldn't be up front about."

She looked deeply into his eyes for a minute, assessing him. Finally, she breathed out, "I believe you. And I'm sorry I reacted the way I did this morning. You caught me off guard."

"You have nothing to be sorry for. That's all on me. It was never meant to come out like that."

Neither spoke for a minute but, finally, he said, "I had an apartment in Richmond, but I never cared much for it. I decided that I preferred the camper. So, when I knew I was coming here, I bought one and let my lease on the apartment expire."

"How does Zac fit into all this? Baytown? Was it just a coincidence?"

"Zac got hold of me through Facebook, if you can believe that. I never used it until I went undercover the first time. I was told that it would make me look more realistic. So, I had my maintenance job listed and added a few non-police friends. Next thing I know, Zac contacts me. I always liked him and we started talking. He told me about the American Legion here and I gotta say, it sounded nice. Baytown was a great place for him to come home to, compared to my hometown that didn't exactly roll out the red carpet for Dan Simmons' son returning from the Navy." A rueful snort escaped, as he added, "Sins of the father and all that."

Her face melted in sympathy and he continued to press his story, glad for every moment she allowed him to share.

"I was intrigued and, other than my job, I sure as hell wasn't established with friends in Richmond. But kept putting him off. Then, this undercover assignment landed at my feet. A drug sting operation with someone on the inside. With Careway and the Pain Center both being part of Matrix Pharmaceutical's line, and Careway advertising for a maintenance person...it was perfect."

"Perfect," she repeated, her voice barely above a whisper as her eyes searched his.

"Yeah, perfect," he said, leaning forward. "Perfect for a lot of reasons. I finally got out to Baytown. Reconnected with Zac, and Jason, which was a nice surprise. Got in with the American Legion. Met you."

She crossed her arms protectively, and asked, "Would you have done all that if it hadn't been part of the job? I mean, that could have just as easily been all for your cover. Make it look good. Be part of the community."

Slashing his hand through his hair, he bit out, "No! No, Belle. That was for me. All me." Flopping back in his seat, he said, "I'd never been part of a community before in my life outside of work. The Navy? Yes. My fellow police officers? Yes. But friends...real friends? No. Not until I came here. So everything I experienced here in Baytown was real. I never expected it, but I sure as hell wanted to live this kind of life. And part of that life that I never expected, was meeting you."

Sucking in a deep breath through her nose before letting it out slowly, she remained quiet, her eyes still searching his face.

"I've never met anyone so nice...so pure...so fuckin' sweet, in my life. Never. For two months, I watched you, at work, in town, with our friends. I just wanted to be near you, to feel like your sunshine could warm me the way you shine it on everyone. Belle, I need you to know that playing you never happened, it was the furthest thing from my mind."

She swallowed deeply, dropping her eyes to her hands twisting together in her lap.

"I never expected you to have anything to do with the drug dealing. Logically, you had no access to the Matrix driver, you did not handle the deliveries, and you sure as hell did not take meetings with Dade. You were clean and I knew that early on. But because I had to even think about it, because it was part of my job to be thorough, I never planned on approaching you, even though in any other circumstance I would have. Then, one day you just landed at my feet and when I realized you were hurt, all I wanted to do was care for you and that was it—I couldn't stay objective anymore."

He threw his hands out to the side, palms up toward her and said, "Once I had you close, I wanted to keep you close...keep you safe." Sighing, he continued, "I reached for the sun, knowing I could get burned, but it would be worth it."

Her gaze shot back to him and she asked, "What about me? What about me getting burned?"

"I..."

"How was this supposed to go, Hunter? You were eventually going to catch the people responsible. You were eventually going to have to come out in the open. You were going to have to stop pretending to be a maintenance worker at a nursing home. You were going to have to admit that, at least initially, I was a suspect. You were going to have to admit to being a police officer." Her voice continued to rise, "I mean, really? How did you see this ending when I live here, my life is here, and you live, where? Wherever they tell you to go?"

"I don't know," he responded. "But I know what we have, you know what we have...what we feel. I love you. That's real and it hasn't changed."

The air between them was charged with electricity, each vibrating with emotions. Placing her hands on the arms of her chair, she stood slowly and he matched her movements. She turned and walked a few feet away and he hated the distance. She looked at him and wrapped her arms around her waist, as though holding herself upright.

"I love you too, but how does it solve the problem?"

"Are you wishing you hadn't gotten involved with me, that I had stayed away or that you knew what you were getting yourself into? You know I couldn't share what I was doing."

Her face winced with the harsh sound of his words. "I don't know, Hunter. I wish I could say yes, no matter what I would have jumped in, but you said it yourself—you stayed away because you knew this would get messy. And now both of our hearts are involved and it is messy…and it hurts." She pierced him with her clear-eyed stare and softly asked, "What about now, Hunter? Where do you go? Where will you report to work tomorrow?"

His heart plummeted, understanding her implication. Sighing, he said, "You know I won't be back at Careway. I have to report to headquarters tomorrow… there will be more work I need to do to finalize the case against the ones arrested."

Nodding slowly, she said, "Yes. That's what I thought."

"This doesn't have to be the end of us," he pleaded, his heart aching. "Lots of couples do long-distance…"

Her lips curved in a sad smile, her chest heaving with a sigh. "I fell in love with a man who lived near me, in a simple camper, who understood that I wanted a place by the beach. A man that showed me I didn't have to depend on myself all the time, he would be there for me. What happens the next time you have to go under-cover, Hunter? Where will you be then?"

Unable to give her an answer, he sighed and shook his head slowly.

She stepped up to the front door, her hand shaking as the key turned. Twisting her head to look at him again, she added, "I understand why you did what you did, and I promise you, I'm not angry about it. But I don't see how this can work. You know me now. You know what I want...what I need. Someone to be there for me... And you can't do that. You have a job to do two hours away and I have one as well, that's here. Both important with many other people dependent on us." A tear slid down her cheek as she said, "I wish you well, Hunter...you'll always have a part of my heart, but I don't see how we can move forward. Goodbye."

He stood, his heart aching as he watched her door shut firmly and heard the lock click into place.

24

"Nurse Gunn!"

Belle walked into the room of Carlotta Martinez and smiled broadly at the scowling woman. "What can I do for you, Mrs. Martinez?"

"You can help me find my necklace."

She observed the older woman as her arthritic hands rummaged through an old jewelry box.

"My Charlie gave it to me on our first anniversary and I wanted my granddaughter to have it for her wedding day."

After gaining a description, she searched the jewelry box to no avail and then widened her search to Mrs. Martinez's drawers.

"It's rose gold with two C's entwined around a heart."

Unable to locate the necklace, a sliver of unease began crawling along her spine. "When did you have it last?"

"I wore it on my anniversary last month. Charlie might not be here any longer but I still remember him and wore it to honor him."

"Are you sure?"

"Of course, I'm sure," the older woman snapped. "My daughter made a comment about it when she saw my picture."

"I'll have the housekeepers look for it as well, Mrs. Martinez."

Hurrying down the hall, she stopped by Mr. Weldon's secretary, greeting her before saying, "Please let him know as soon as he has a chance, he and I need to meet. There're some things we need to go over."

"You can go on in, Belle," Roberta agreed. "He just got in from meeting with the PR company."

Settling in the chair indicated, she observed Mr. Weldon, seeing the deeper creases next to his eyes, knowing they were no longer just laugh lines. Hesitating for a few seconds, she plunged ahead, "I know you're just coming up from the Linda fiasco, but we never got back to talking about the item stolen from Mr. Rosenberg that ended up in the pawn shop. You said you would speak to the police and I wanted to know if they found anything."

She watched two spots of pink appear on his cheeks and he dropped his eyes, but replied in the affirmative.

"Yes, yes, of course I reported it. They said they would check on it, but to be honest, I haven't thought about it with everything else going on."

"Oh...okay. I just hate to think that we have an

ongoing problem with thefts. Now, Mrs. Martinez is missing a necklace."

"The last thing we need," he said, his voice clipped, "is another scandal. And as far as she goes, her memory is not very good."

"I agree, but—"

"How is everything else going?" he asked.

"Fine," she answered, uncomfortable with the change in subject. "The residents appear to be resettled after the events of the past couple of weeks."

"Good, good, that's what we need." His smile was now wide and beaming toward her. "You've had a great deal to do with that and I appreciate your dedication more than you can know."

She nodded, then observed as he glanced at his watch. Taking the cue, she stood and walked back down the hall to her small office. Taking over for Linda, she had an office of her own, connected to the nurses' station. Sitting at her desk, she rubbed her head, willing the burgeoning headache to abate.

The last few weeks had proven to be difficult, but not impossible. The gossip from the staff centering around Linda had finally eased and they had rallied around Belle in her new position. Mr. Weldon and she had worked with the state's Department of Health, to devise new policies for the receiving of pharmaceuticals. Matrix Pharmaceuticals was also creating new policies for their drivers and customers. She knew he was facing scrutiny from the families of the residents, but life seemed to be returning to normal at Careway.

She loved working on the changes, but still made

sure she spent time on the floor with the residents every day. Deciding she needed a break, she headed out the side door to the courtyard. A smooth walkway offered the residents a chance to move easily between the flower beds, tables set up with umbrellas, and the small water fountain. Several crepe myrtle trees provided shade and a brick, outdoor grill gave the chef a chance to have a few barbeques during the warmer weather.

She was pleased to see that the courtyard was empty and she strolled past the flowers, choosing to sit on a bench underneath a tree by the fountain. Closing her eyes, she allowed the sunshine to warm her, easing her headache.

"Surprised to find you taking a break."

Opening her eyes at the voice, she smiled at the man in the wheelchair, rolling toward her.

"Mr. Rasky, how are you?"

He stopped his chair in the shade, putting on the brakes. "I'm an old man, how do you think I am?"

A giggle slipped out as she caught his grin.

His eyes never left her face as he said, "But I think the important question is, how are you?"

"I'm fine." She caught his raised eyebrow and she hastened to add, "I admit the job change has taken some getting used to and, certainly, the reason for the change was unexpected—"

"Not to me," he quipped.

She jolted slightly at his words and her eyes widened. "I'm sorry?"

"Linda was nice enough, but she never looked me in the eye when she talked to me. Always thought that was odd. I don't trust someone who doesn't look me in the eye."

She opened her mouth to speak, then, snapped it closed, uncertain what to say as her mind cast back to Linda's behavior prior to her arrest. After a moment, she said, "Yes, well...uh...I just thought she was an excellent nurse...I guess that shows how much I know about someone's character."

"I'll tell you something I said to Mr. Simmons one time—once you get an idea about someone, it's hard to let it go."

She dropped her chin and sighed heavily, before peering at him in the eyes again. "Why do I get the feeling you're not just talking about Linda?"

He settled his wise gaze on her and added, "I'm a good judge of character and I thought he was just the type of man you needed in your life."

"He...we just...well, he's gone now."

"Must have been a disappointment to find out that he was an undercover cop."

Blinking, she stammered, "No, uh...not a disappointment. Just...surprised."

"Some surprises are good," he quipped. "Keeps life interesting. Takes us out of the ordinary. Gets us thinking...dreaming...hoping."

The weight on her chest, just as heavy, pressed in. "Yes, but Mr. Rasky, some surprises kill our dreams."

"Maybe," he replied, flipping the locks off his wheelchair before wheeling backward. "But, then again, new dreams can always take their place. You just have to be willing to give them a try." With that, he deftly turned his chair and wheeled away.

She stared at his back, wondering if she had refused to consider the idea of a new dream.

———

Belle walked into the Baytown Police Station and smiled at the indomitable receptionist. "Hello, Mrs. Score," she greeted.

"Why, Belle, hello! I haven't seen you in forever. How are you?"

Giving the requisite response that hid her heart, she said, "Fine, just fine."

"Whatcha need?"

"I was wondering how to find out if a police report had been filed."

Before Mable had a chance to respond, Mitch walked from the back, his gaze landing on her.

"A report?" he asked, walking closer. "Come to my office, Belle."

His concern was warming and she appreciated his interest. She followed him into his office, only slightly bigger than hers and even messier. She remembered when his father had been the Police Chief and even further back, his grandfather.

Taking the chair he indicated, she said, "It's just that I discovered a theft from one of our residents and the director was going to report it to the police, but...um..." Her voice trailed off as she realized that she was implying Mr. Weldon had not done his duty.

"Was it at the nursing home?" Seeing her nod, Mitch explained, "That would have gone through Colt and the Sheriff Department, since the nursing home is not in the town limits of Baytown."

Blushing furiously, she said, "Oh, how stupid of me. Of course." Jumping up, she blurted, "I'm so sorry."

"It's fine, Belle. Please, sit. I haven't seen you in a while, so please..."

She slid back into her chair, the heat of blush still on her face. "I don't know why I never thought about the location of Careway."

Chuckling, he said, "It's easy to forget. Plus, Colt works with us on a lot of cases, so it makes it even easier for others to blur the lines."

They sat in silence for a moment before he asked, "How is Careway? I heard you were now the head nurse. Congratulations."

"Thank you...and things are okay. We've had to work closely with the Department of Health to make sure that none of the patients' health was compromised with Linda's actions. They weren't, but as you can imagine, all *i's needed to be dotted and t's crossed* in the reports."

"I'm sure it hasn't been easy."

She nodded politely and smiled again, "It's better."

"And you?"

Her eyes widened but before she could think of a response, he continued, "About you and Hunter...I know it hasn't been easy."

Heart pounding, she swallowed deeply. Having poured her heart out to the girls, including his wife, Tori, she was sure he must know the depths of her hurt.

Before she stopped herself, she blurted, "To be honest, it hasn't. I'm really proud of him but, well…kind of feel like I was blindsided by it all. And now, he has his life in Richmond and I have mine here."

He appeared to want to say more, but instead, just nodded. "Well, you should go talk to Colt about your concerns with the nursing home."

Standing, she clasped his outstretched hand and thanked him. Walking out, she looked over her shoulder as he called out, "Sometimes lives change, Belle. You never know."

Tilting her head, she simply nodded before passing Mable and walking back into the sunshine.

Sitting in Colt's office, she recognized the similarities to Mitch's, but it was significantly bigger. In fact, the entire Sheriff's Office was larger, considering the size of North Heron County compared to little Baytown.

Colt was tall—probably as tall as Hunter, but had lean muscles, instead of Hunter's bulk. Inwardly grimacing, she wondered if she were now going to compare every man to Hunter, and find them lacking.

"Ms. Gunn?"

Startled out of her musings, she blurted, "Sorry, Sheriff Hudson. My mind is…everywhere. And, please, call me Belle."

Colt smiled, his outward demeanor of an easy-going cowboy in place, but she was sure that image was a mistake to anyone who crossed him. She explained what she had found at the pawn shop and her subsequent confusing conversations with Mr. Weldon.

He tilted his head and turned to his computer. After several clicks, he shook his head. "Belle, there hasn't been a report filed about anything to do with Careway, Mr. Rosenberg, or a missing pocket watch."

Blowing out her breath, she leaned back in her chair. "But why...why..."

"Would you like me to look into it?" he asked. "I can drop by the pawn shop and nose around."

"I don't know," she replied, honestly. "I mean, I don't know what the protocol is. Maybe Mr. Weldon has just been so overwhelmed that he forgot and then didn't want me to know he's forgotten."

"Has there been anything else missing?"

"Well, yesterday, another resident seems to be missing a necklace. To be honest, when I left here I was going to go to the pawn shop and just see if it happened to be there."

"No, don't," he warned. "Let us do the checking." Taking down the description of Mrs. Martinez's necklace, he said, "I'll have one of my deputies go take a look."

"I would feel better if Mr. Weldon was doing this himself, but I know he's so busy."

He nodded noncommittally, but assured her that he would check into it. Thanking him, she stood and walked to the door, when he called out, "Have you heard from Hunter?"

She looked over her shoulder, wondering how long everyone was going to be asking her about him, and shook her head. "No." His expression was intense but as she stared, he just nodded.

"I'll let you know what I find."

Walking out, she pondered the meaning behind his question…and the look he gave her.

25

Belle sat in her car outside Mitch and Tori's beach cabin, uncertain that she wanted to go inside. She knew all of her friends would be there, but dreaded the uncomfortable silences as they danced around the subject of Hunter and passed shared glances between each other, unaware that she noticed.

Pressing her lips tightly together, she dropped her head to the steering wheel for a moment, steeling her nerves. *I've lived through worse.* She knew the thought was true but in the three weeks since Hunter had left, she had cried rivers, her heart aching. Nights had been hard, but sunrises were worse. Now when she peered out on the dawn, she wondered what the new day would bring, no longer excited about the possibilities. Finally, she bolted from the car, angry that she was allowing the situation to keep her from having fun.

Walking out onto the back deck, she surveyed the activities, so familiar to her. Callan, Ginny, and Brogan playing volleyball with a few of the Coast Guard servicemen. Tori, Katelyn, and Jillian setting up the food while Mitch, Colt, and Grant manned the grill. Aiden was flirting with a woman Belle did not recognize and assumed she was a vacation fling. Jade and Lance were around the fire pit with Zac and Madelyn.

The scene was exactly like the many times she had come to the beach parties single. All normal...and yet, not so, now that she was alone again. *Why did being single not bother me before Hunter?* With no answer to that question, she threw a quick smile at her friends before deciding to take a walk along the beach. With her shoes in her hand, she wandered past the volleyball game and down to the water.

Hunter stepped out onto the deck, his gaze scanning the gathering, quickly assessing who was there and who was missing. Belle was the only one he did not see. Moving to the grill, he greeted some of the others just before Zac spotted him.

Hustling over, Zac called out, "Good to see you, man. Didn't expect to see you here today."

The other men welcomed him as well, but he noticed the women's smiles aimed at him did not reach their eyes.

"Still got my camper here and had some vacation time accrued, so I wanted to come back. I know we've got an AL meeting and another youth game coming up."

"Good," Mitch replied. "The kids will be glad to see you."

He accepted the beer Zac handed to him and stayed on the deck, noticing that no one mentioned Belle. The women had moved to the tables, huddling around and he had no doubt he was being discussed.

Turning to Zac, he asked quietly, "How is she?"

Zac rubbed his chin and sighed. "Don't know what to tell you, Hunter. I haven't seen her in weeks until today. I will let you know that she's down on the beach somewhere. Madelyn says Belle hasn't been around town much and hasn't gone out with the girls at all. Seems she's been buried at work ever since...well, you know."

His gaze shot toward the beach, scanning, until he spied her in the distance, her blue sundress fluttering in the breeze. Her long hair was braided, tied with a blue ribbon.

He turned to step off the deck, but his arm was caught by Zac's hand. He tilted his head to the side, the unasked question heavy in the air.

"Look, man, I have no idea what's going on between the two of you, but she's hurtin'. She tries to hide it but it shows."

"Don't plan on making it worse," he said, his voice rough.

"Your plans and what actually happens might be two different things."

The retort died on his lips as he sucked in a quick breath.

Zac continued, "So, is Baytown your vacation town now?" Throwing up his hands, he quickly added, "Hey, if it is, that's fine. Lots of part-time residents here and

I'll be glad to see you whenever you can make it back." He hesitated, then, continued, "It's just that I have no idea where that'll leave you and Belle."

Shaking his head slowly, he said, "I don't know either, but standing here won't help. There's only one person I need to be talking about this with and she's down on the beach." Standing to his full height, fortifying himself, he said, "I'll see you later."

He stepped off the deck, ignoring the pointed looks being shot his way from Belle's girlfriends and the sympathetic expressions from the guys.

He walked through the sand, the sight of her warming him as much as the sun. Her back was to him as she wandered slowly down the beach, her eyes on the shore. Occasionally she would stoop and pick up what he assumed was sea glass. Not wanting to startle her, he called her name out softly.

She turned, lifting her hand to her forehead to shield her eyes as they searched the source of her name. He noted the instant she first recognized him. Sucking in a sharp inhale, she stood rooted to the spot.

Her breathing became shallow, the closer he came. As he stopped directly in front of her, she tilted her head back to hold his gaze.

"Breathe, Belle," he whispered. She let her breath out in a whoosh and he smiled.

Swallowing deeply, she clasped her hands tightly in front of her and tilted her head ever so slightly. "Hello, Hunter."

"Hello, Belle."

Her gaze drifted behind him and she licked her lips.

He twisted his head around and noticed most of their friends back at the cabin, all eyes on them. "Shit...never been much for an audience."

"Are you back for a visit with Zac or Jason?" Almost as an afterthought, she nodded, and said, "Or the AL game?"

"Yeah...sort of. I had some vacation days accrued and decided to take them. My camper is still here."

"Yes, I noticed."

His gaze jumped to hers, glad she had been aware that he planned on maintaining a presence in the area.

They stood, awkward in their silence, and she finally said, "Well, I should be getting back. I have...uh...work to do today."

"Work? On a Saturday?"

"Yes...uh...I work lots of...weekends now."

Pink heat spotted her cheeks and he knew she was lying. Sighing, he said, "Belle, please don't go. If my presence makes you uncomfortable, I'll leave. The last thing I want to do is make you uncomfortable."

"No, no," she rushed, her hand reaching out to his arm before snatching it back. "I just popped by to say hello to everyone and then I needed to go."

"Belle..."

Dropping her chin to her chest, staring at her toes, she sighed. A rueful chuckle slipped out and she confessed, "You know I'm not a very good liar."

He stepped closer until he was just a foot away from her, desiring to be close without crowding. "I don't want you to ever have to lie to me."

She lifted her head, holding his gaze. "The truth?"

He nodded.

"It's hard. I've taken Brittany home a couple of times and drove past your camper, so I know it's still there and have been wondering if you were selling it. And wondering how it would be to see someone else in it. Or, if one day, it would be gone, and having to accept that you'd taken it away. I go to work, expecting to see you down the hall or in a room, but have to remind myself that you'll never be there again." Her gaze swept over his shoulder to their friends, now gathering at the food tables, and added, "And even here, I'm reminded of what we had and what I lost."

"I'm sorry, Belle. I never meant for you to be hurt. And," he gained her attention again, "you're not the only one hurting."

She stared for a moment and then slowly nodded. "I see that now. At first, I only felt my pain, because you walked in knowing how this would end and I didn't. But, I know this was not easy on you either."

They stood, holding each other's gazes before he lifted his hand and tucked a wind-blown wisp of hair behind her ear.

"How's work going?" he asked, truly wanting to know, besides desperately wanting to keep their conversation going.

"Pretty crazy," she replied. "Mr. Weldon asked me to take over as head nurse, plus we've had tons of meetings with the Department of Health, residents, family members, and that's on top of instituting new policies and just day to day taking care of everything, including hiring a new maintenance worker."

"How'd that go?" He bit back his jealousy, knowing he had no right to express it.

"He seems okay. A little old, but he had been maintenance for a company in Virginia Beach and retired early. Decided he didn't like retirement, so when he moved here, he was looking for something to do."

Silence moved between them and she cast her gaze back to the bay before asking, "And you? How're things in Richmond?"

Shrugging, he said, "The case is moving forward. The involved drivers for Matrix Pharmaceuticals are in jail, as well as Linda and a couple of others that worked in health facilities in the northern part of the Eastern Shore."

She reached out again, this time placing her hand on his arm, her expression earnest. "That's amazing, Hunter. I always thought you were a talented maintenance worker and, obviously, you're good at whatever you do."

Her hand burned warm on his arm and he fought to keep from covering it with his own. "So, are you going to leave? Before getting something to eat?" he asked, holding his breath as he awaited her answer.

She glanced to the side again, at their friends who had settled around the fire pit with plates piled high. Sighing, she nodded. "I'm sorry, Hunter. I'm not trying to be a bitch, but the idea of sitting with everyone acting awkward around us just isn't what I feel like I can handle."

His face fell and he nodded sadly. "I'm the one who's

sorry, Belle. Can I walk you to your car? I'm not in the mood to socialize either."

Nodding, she agreed and they fell into step as they walked toward the driveway near the cabin. She glanced over at Jillian and gave a little wave, receiving one in return.

Stopping at her car, he said, "Listen, I'm going to be in town for the week and if you need anything, just let me know. Or, if you want to talk...well, I'll be at the camper."

She offered a little smile and said, "Okay. Thanks." Opening her car door, she turned her face up to his. "I'm glad we talked, Hunter. I...well, we...well, I'm just glad."

He closed her door and watched as she backed out of the parking spot and drove down the road, staring until she was no longer in sight.

He felt a hand on his shoulder and twisted his head, seeing Zac and Colt standing behind him.

"You okay," Zac asked.

"Not really...but hopefully, in time."

"She know?"

"Nope. And I'm not telling her. At least, not now." With a chin lift, he climbed onto his motorcycle and roared down the lane, his mind full of what he wanted and how to make it come true.

26

Sunrise had found Belle sitting at her window looking out, her mind whirling, unable to keep Hunter from her thoughts. Seeing him yesterday at the beach had shaken her more than she expected. His hair, a little longer, had her fingers itching to run through it. His T-shirt, straining at the arms and across the chest, had her imagining him without it, so she could trace his tats covering the muscles. His eyes, so blue, pierced hers.

Blowing out her breath, she had closed her eyes, letting the sun warm her face, but the only sight in her mind was his face.

At work, she had moved through the motions but had found herself irritated with Mr. Weldon, knowing he had not called the Sheriff's Department over the thefts. Wondering if she should contact Colt to see if he had found anything, she had been diverted, answering a call from one of the nursing aides.

Now home, she stood at her stove, stirring tomato soup and considering whether or not she wanted a grilled cheese sandwich. Too tired to give it much thought, she just reached for the crackers instead.

A loud knocking on her front door jolted her out of her musings. Turning the stove off, she heard Brittany call out her name.

Hustling, she threw open the door, greeting, "Come on in for some soup—Oh, God, what's wrong?" Seeing Brittany's pale, tear-stained face, she reached out and grabbed her arm, drawing her into her house.

She pulled Brittany into a hug, but felt her body stiffen. Holding her at arm's length, her heart pounded as she attempted to ascertain what was happening. "Sit down, sweetie, and tell me what I can do."

Brittany's breath hitched as she blurted, "I can't deal with it anymore."

Leading her to the sofa, she gently settled the girl and hustled back into the kitchen to grab a glass of water. Taking it to her, she watched as she drank a few sips before placing the glass on the coffee table.

Sitting next to her, she desired to wrap her arms around her again, but uncertainty held her back. "Can't deal with what, honey?"

Brittany's hands shook as they fiddled with the ripped threads at the knees of her jeans. She kept her eyes down as she shook her head slowly. "Just everything." Almost as an afterthought, her voice barely a whisper, "I hate her."

She took in Brittany's appearance, carefully observing how pale and thin she was. How her hands were shaking and her shoulders slumped. How her eyes were downcast, not seeming to take anything in. Fear slithered through her stomach and she had to force the words from her mouth. "What happened, Brittany? Please tell me, what happened? I promise..." she reached over and placed her hand on the smaller one and gave a squeeze, "you can tell me anything and I'll help you."

The silence was cold in the room, causing her stomach to clench in fear.

Taking a shuddering breath, Brittany said, "She's got some men over...partying as always. I was in my room, and she came in."

A shiver ran over the young girl's thin frame and she jumped up to grab an afghan from the back of a chair. Shaking it out, she placed it over Brittany's shoulders and wrapped it around the front of her, enveloping her in as warm a cocoon as she could. Sitting back down, she said, "Go on, honey...talk to me so I can know how to help you."

Her voice was barely above a whisper, as she said, "She said she didn't have no money." Her chin quivered. "I knew that 'cause we didn't have any food in the house. She shoots it all up."

Belle's heart stuttered and she tried to swallow past the lump in her throat.

"She said, if I'd let one of her *friends* come into my room and play for a while, he'd give her the money she needed."

Gasping, she jumped from the sofa, her heart pounding, and knelt at the terrified girl's feet. Getting close, she held her hands, rubbing them gently. "Oh, baby, baby..."

Brittany looked up, her wide eyes on her and rushed, "I said 'no'. I didn't care if she ended up dead on the floor from not having her fix...I said 'no'."

Nodding, her head, she said, "Okay. Okay. What...did..."

Brittany's hand snaked out from the blanket and she wiped her nose. "I heard her...she was mad. Told the man that he could do what he wanted anyway."

"No, oh no," she gasped.

"But I crawled out the window," Brittany said. "I got outta there."

Throwing her arms around her, she pulled her close, rocking her back and forth gently. "Oh, baby, I'm so sorry. You're safe...you're safe." Her mind raced as anger boiled throughout her body. She kissed the top of Brittany's head and moved to grab her phone from the coffee table. Without thinking, she dialed.

"Belle? Hey—"

"I need you. You've got to come now."

"What the fuck? Be there in two minutes."

The phone disconnected and she tossed it to the sofa, wrapping Brittany back in her arms. The young girl looked up and sniffed. "Who'd you call?"

Blinking, she realized she did not think beforehand...she simply called the first person who came to her mind. Swallowing deeply, refusing to overthink her decision, she said, "Someone who can help."

Hunter leaped out of the camper, his boots slamming

onto the asphalt as he ran toward Belle's house. Within a minute he was throwing open her door and rushing inside. Uncertain what would greet him, he stumbled to a halt at the sight of Brittany, engulfed in a blanket, her pale, wide-eyed face staring up at him with Belle's arms wrapped tightly around her.

Forcing his wildly beating heart to slow, he was not sure he trusted his voice, so he caught Belle's gaze and tilted his head slightly.

She looked at Brittany and said softly, "Sweetie, I'm going to talk to Hunter for a moment in the kitchen...okay?"

"I thought he was gone...thought he'd left."

"He's back for a little bit. He's a good guy and can help."

"I thought he broke your heart," Brittany whispered, her eyes darting between Belle and him.

"We're still friends," she rushed. "He just lives some-where else now, but..." her eyes darted up toward him, "we still care about each other."

He watched the conversation play out and jolted as he heard her words, his heart praying she was telling the truth. He gave a quick nod and watched her face closely, but it gave no other indication of her feelings, other than softening ever so slightly. As she turned her attention back to Brittany, so did he, his hands fisting at his side.

Brittany heaved a sigh and nodded. Belle squeezed her hands again and said, "You stay right here. I'll talk to Hunter and fix you a cup of hot chocolate." Standing, she walked past him toward the kitchen.

He followed, her kitchen still keeping them in sight of Brittany on the sofa. He watched silently as Belle moved to heat milk in the microwave and then squirt chocolate into the cup.

She stirred it and then walked back to Brittany and handed it to her. "Here, drink, honey, and I'll be right over there."

Brittany took the cup but then blurted, "I ain't going back—"

"No. I won't let you go back. Now, here, drink and let me talk to Hunter so he can help us."

Moving into the kitchen again, she stepped closer to him and stared up into his face. He fought the urge to pull her close, to take the worry from her eyes. Remaining quiet, he let her talk.

Keeping her voice low and even, she leaned forward and said, "Her mom's a junkie...parties a lot. Brittany keeps to herself, locked in her room when men are over."

His eyes narrowed, knowing the direction the story was heading, but forced his breathing to steady.

Her words, spoken softly, came out in a rush. "Her mom's out of money and wants Brittany to let the men in her room and if she does, they give her mom the drugs she wants." She leaned in and placed her hand on his arm, her eyes pleading, her voice catching in her throat. "Hunter, her mom is trying to pimp her daughter for drug money."

The feel of her hand on him shot through his body, which was welcome considering her words froze him deep inside. The desire to rage was tamped down, knowing Brittany was carefully watching. Nodding, he calmly said, "I'll take care of it."

Her fingers flexed on his arm. "But how?"

He leaned down closely and held her gaze. "Babe, you called me...why? Why me?"

"I...uh...I...I don't know...I just..."

"Why Belle? Why me?"

Her breath left her body in a whoosh as she admitted, "I knew you'd help. I knew I could trust you to take care of her. I just knew..."

Nodding, his lips curved ever so slightly. "Yeah. In here," he tapped his forefinger over her heart, "you knew. I'll always be here for you."

Standing straight, he walked to the door and said, "You two stay here and stay locked in."

Belle glanced between him and Brittany's wide eyes, and rushed to him, catching his arm as he was about to leave. "Hunter, what are you going to do?"

He turned and looked at her face, full of concern, and said, "Don't worry about me, sweetheart. I'm just going to take out some trash."

With that, he walked out the door, determination firmly planted on his face.

After placing a call, Hunter stalked straight to Brittany's house, immediately noting the difference between her mother's and Belle's houses. Garbage cans overflowing. Beer bottles and cans strewn on the ground in the vicinity of the garbage cans. Two men in lounge chairs in the front yard, one appearing high with a sloppy smile on his face and the other wasted, passed out.

He slowed as he stomped by, his finger out, pointing at them. "Stay," he ordered. "I know who you are, where you live, you move a muscle and I'll hunt you down. You do not want the shit-storm I'll rain down on you if I have to waste my time doing that."

The sloppy smile man's eyes widened as he slurred, "Damn man. Chill."

He walked over, towering above the man and growled, "You tell me to chill again and I'll ram my fist down your throat so far, I'll grab your worthless balls and pull them out your mouth."

He turned, not giving the man a chance to think of a response, and stalked to the front door, banging loudly. "State Police. Open up!"

He tried the door and, finding it unlocked, threw it open, calling out his warning once more. The sight of Brittany's mother on the floor, passed out, greeted him, her clothes hanging off her, a man scrambling up, trying to zip his pants.

"Don't move, asshole. Don't move a fuckin' muscle."

The man, heavyset, his beady, dark eyes glaring at him, said, "Who the fuck are you?"

A slow smile curved his lips. "Your nightmare, man. I'm your fuckin' nightmare."

Within ten minutes, Mitch and Grant pulled up, Ginny right behind them. Colt and four of his deputies, one a female, came a minute later. Zac, with a volunteer EMT, pulled up in the ambulance, parking in the front yard.

Taking Hunter's statement, Mitch nodded toward Ginny and said, "You go to Belle's to talk to Brittany."

Colt added, "I want Deputy Tina Blackwell to go as well." He nodded to his female deputy, who nodded in return and moved toward Ginny. "And I've called Annette Porter, a counselor from Child Protective Services to meet you there. She might already be at Belle's. If you need to wait on her before questioning Brittany, then do so."

Hunter turned and called out, "Let Belle stay with her when she gives her statement. She's the only one Brittany trusts right now."

"Got it," Ginny replied, as she and Tina walked to her patrol SUV.

A black car came swerving into the lane and Melvin

Smith, the park owner, jumped out, his face red with rage. He stalked up to Colt and Mitch, saying, "I want them out. All of them. Every last troublemaker. How can I make this happen?"

Colt said, "You got a clause in their lease that says you can terminate if their behavior is destructive or illegal?"

Blinking, Melvin nodded. "Yes, but until now, they never been bad enough for me to fight that battle."

"Well, today's your lucky day," Colt drawled. "The people in at least four of these residences are being arrested as we speak."

The ire in Melvin's face eased and he sucked in a deep breath. "Then they'll have their leases terminated immediately." He turned and looked at the gathering crowd of park residents standing in the area. Raising his voice, he called out, "And this serves as a warning. I'm already working with the County Board of Supervisors as well as the Baytown Town Council. New health and safety ordinances are being drawn up and if I find violators, you'll be evicted as well. I want this place to be a safe environment!"

He was met with applause from most of the gathering and a few guilty expressions on a few others. Turning back to the law enforcers, he nodded before moving back to his car.

Colt's deputies were hauling the handcuffed men from the trailer and front yard and Zac was inside treating Brittany's mom under a deputy's watchful eye before they could safely transport her to the hospital for drug treatment, since she would be under arrest at the same time.

Colt, Mitch, and Grant looked at the man being placed in the sheriff's SUV before swinging their gazes, in unison, back to Hunter.

Colt's lips twitched and he asked, "You wanna tell me how that guy got a black eye and busted nose?"

"He tripped," he replied. "Must be an uncoordinated fuck along with all the things you can charge him with."

Mitch and Grant, unable to hold back their grins, just shook their heads.

Colt said, "You gonna be a problem?"

His insides easing for the first time since getting Belle's call that evening, he shook his head. "Nah, just thorough." Sighing, he asked, "What's the protocol for Brittany?"

"Annette's the best. Great counselor. The county's got some good foster families, a few of them trained as therapeutic foster parents. She'll make sure Brittany is well placed and well cared for."

"Will Belle be able to see her, check up on her?"

"I'll let them know she's on the approved list."

Nodding, he glanced around. "You all have this, I'm outta here. I'll come into the station, talk to you tomorrow."

He watched Colt nod and, with his own goodbye to the others, he jogged back down the street, bypassing his camper and going directly to Belle's.

Hesitating at the door for a few seconds, he wondered if he should knock or let the women inside finish what they needed to do. Before he had a chance to ponder further, the door opened and he was greeted by Belle, relief evident on her face.

Throwing open the screen door for him, she whispered, "Come on in."

He stepped into her living room, seeing Brittany still sitting on the sofa with Belle's afghan around her shoulders. Ginny was sitting in a chair in front of her, while Tina was on the other side, still taking notes. Annette was on the sofa next to Ginny, speaking softly to her. He shot his gaze to the side, observing Belle motioning for him to follow her to the kitchen.

Her face scrunched in fear, she whispered, "They're just finishing up. She wasn't touched but her mother threatened to pimp her out to more than one man—"

He placed his hands on her shoulders and drew her close. Wrapping one hand behind her back and cupping the back of her head with the other, he held her against his chest. Leaning down, he whispered, "We got 'em. Colt and Mitch, they hauled them away. Throwing the book at 'em, sweetheart. She's got nothing to worry about with them."

She tilted her head back to stare into his face. Licking her lips, her voice still breathy, "Oh, God, thank you, thank you, Hunter. You've saved her—"

He shook his head, interrupting, "No, babe, you've got that wrong. You saved her."

"But—"

"No buts about it. You befriended her a long time ago, gave her a safe place to come, a safe place to talk. And tonight, you recognized that she needed intervention and you called me. Babe, it's all you. Because of you, that young girl can rest easy tonight and for a fuckin' long time after tonight."

He watched as a tear slid down her cheek and she sucked in a ragged breath. He lifted his thumb and gently wiped it away, bending down to kiss her forehead.

"Belle?"

He dropped his arms as Brittany called softly from the other side of the room. He hoped he offered a little strength back to her so that she could now do what she needed to do for Brittany.

Belle whirled around and rushed over, dropping to her knees in front of Brittany.

"Yeah, honey?"

"They want me to go live with someone else right now. I don't know what to do."

She glanced at Annette, who gave a nearly imperceptible nod. Turning her attention back to Brittany, she said, "You've been handling things on your own for a long time, and now it's time to let some others help you. Ms. Porter knows some really good families, Brittany. Much better than you or I had, and they can give you what your mom couldn't. Stability. Care. Even fun, sweetie."

"What'll happen to Mom?"

She opened her mouth, but snapped it shut quickly, realizing she had no idea what to tell her. Her gaze jumped to Ginny, who said, "Brittany, your mom needs help. She needs help with getting clean and she'll have to face responsibility for certain actions."

"Is she going to jail?" Brittany asked, more tears forming in her eyes.

"Right now, she's being transported to the hospital," Ginny continued. "Once she's better, there will be charges pending."

Sucking in her lips, Brittany looked back at her, "So, this foster thing. What do you think?"

Taking Brittany's hands in hers, she said, "I think you need a change. I think you need to let someone take care of you now. I think Ms. Porter will make sure that happens and put you with a family that knows how to love and has a lot of love to give."

"Can I still see you?"

Receiving a nod from Annette, she smiled a tearful smile, and said, "Every chance we can."

A few minutes later, after more hugs between them, she stood back and watched as Annette and Tina escorted her outside. Ginny hung back and offered her a hug, saying, "You did fabulous, Belle. I've known Brittany through the AL ball teams and even took her home a few times, but never had a cause to step in. I'm so thankful she had you."

By the time Ginny left and the door closed behind her, Hunter barely made it to her before she collapsed in his arms.

Hunter carried Belle to the sofa and sat with her on his

lap. Wrapping his arms around her again, he let her cry, knowing the tears were as much for Brittany as they were for her own childhood memories.

After a few minutes, she calmed to sniffles, her breath hitching several times. He leaned over and snagged some tissues from the end table and handed them to her. She cleaned her face and then looked at him, shaking her head slightly.

"I'm a mess," she said, but he hushed her.

"You're beautiful, as always."

She peered at him, his piercing blue eyes holding her gaze. Blushing, she started to push off him, but his arms clamped tighter.

"Belle, if you want off my lap, I'll let you go instantly, but you're right where I'd like you to be. Please let me take care of you."

All protestations left her mind as exhaustion claimed her, and she leaned against his chest. For several minutes, they sat, not speaking, letting the events of the evening settle over them. After a while, he glanced to the kitchen and said, "How about I fix us something to eat?"

"I had some soup heating," she replied, "but it's probably gross now."

Chuckling, he shifted her to the side and stood. "You relax and I'll rummage up something."

"I was thinking about grilled cheese sandwiches."

He smiled down at her and touched his finger to her nose. "Sounds good, babe. Hang on and I'll get 'em going."

She watched him in her kitchen, her heart aching at

the sight, remembering when she thought it was a sight she would always see. Sighing, she realized that she wanted him in her life...even if only as a friend who came by occasionally when he was in town.

Ten minutes later he walked to her and settled onto the sofa next to her, placing a plate in her lap. "Best grilled cheese you'll ever find," he claimed.

Unable to stop the giggle from slipping from her lips, he threw her a glare.

"Do you doubt my culinary skills?"

Taking a bite, she moaned in delight. "Well, considering I only had white bread and American cheese, I wasn't sure what you could accomplish, but I must be really hungry, because these are good."

They ate in companionable silence and she settled back into the cushions.

She glanced at his hand and reached out to touch his knuckles. "Your knuckles are roughed up. What happened?"

"I had a little talking to do with one of the men that was at Brittany's house."

"Talking?" she repeated.

"Yeah."

"Since when do you talk with your fists, Hunter?" she asked, her eyes wide.

"Don't usually...in fact, almost never."

"Almost never?"

"Belle, are you going to eat or just repeat everything I say?"

Setting her near-empty plate down, she turned to

him fully. He sighed and mimicked the gesture with his now-empty plate.

"My dad used his fists in ways that weren't good. I don't. But when faced with the cocky attitude of the man who was going to rape a fifteen-year-old girl just as payment to give her sorry-ass mom drugs? I decided that it was time to let him know just how much I didn't like that."

Her heart melted a little at his words and she lifted his hand to her lips and kissed his reddened knuckles. His smile beamed at her, warming her even more.

Taking a fortifying breath, she held his gaze, his face as familiar to her as her own. "Hunter...what are we doing? What are we going to do...about us?"

His chest heaved as he reached for her fingers, linking them with his. "I fucked up, Belle." He saw her head tilt in silent question and he continued, "I came here to do a job, but fell in love in the process. That wasn't the fuck up. That was the most wonderful thing that's ever happened to me in my life."

Seeing her rapt attention, he said, "My fuck up was that when it all blew up in our faces, I didn't stay and fight for you. I knew I had to go back to Richmond, to headquarters to wrap up the case. I wanted to keep seeing you but I understand that, at that moment, when you were dealing with all the new information about me, a long-distance relationship was asking a lot of you. But I should have worked harder to make you see that it could have worked."

Belle sucked in her lips, pressing them tightly before saying, "I think I was just so stunned and reacted rather selfishly. You were just doing your job and I should have never assumed I should be the most important thing in your life—"

"But you are," he rushed. "I love you, Belle. That never stopped just because I was on a case."

She stared, unspeaking, uncertain what to say.

"That's one of the reasons I came back for my vacation time. I wanted to see if you were finished with me or if there was something there."

"It's only been three weeks, Hunter. My heart is nowhere neared healed. So, yes, the love is still there. Honey, even if you had never come back, it would still be there."

He leaned forward and she met him halfway, their lips colliding. She grabbed his shoulders as he hauled her back over his lap. Their noses bumped as they twisted and turned their heads, both searching for maximum contact.

Their tongues clashed as they tangled, each flaming the fires even as they threatened to consume. Thrusting his tongue, the taste familiar and welcome, Hunter felt the blood rush to his cock but ignored its pressing against his zipper as Belle dug her fingers into the flesh of his shoulders, trying to pull him closer.

He finally pulled back and stared into her lust-filled eyes and kiss-swollen mouth. "We gotta stop, babe."

Moaning, she asked, "Why?"

"Because this is not about sex. This is about care, comfort. This is about me loving you so much I want to give you what you need, not necessarily what you want."

Licking her lips, she tried to force her breathing to slow as her chest heaved. "What do I need?"

"Rest. A chance to recuperate from the drama and trauma of the evening."

She nodded slowly, then said, "But I don't want to be alone."

"You're not alone, babe. I'm right here. I'm staying right here. We'll sleep in the same bed, curled around each other, but no sex. Not right now. We've got other things to talk about, but for tonight I just want to hold you and know that you're safe in my arms."

Belle's heart warmed with his declaration and she nodded, as the exhaustion of the day threatened to overcome her once more. "Okay," she whispered.

With a nod, he stood and linked their fingers, leading her into her bedroom. Hunter stripped to his boxers and waited until she emerged from the bathroom in pink drawstring pajama shorts and a matching camisole. She stood in the doorway for a moment, until he lifted his hand, then she moved quickly his way.

Crawling into bed, he turned her so that she was facing him, her head on his chest and his arm wrapped around her body. Tucking her in tightly, he waited until sleep claimed her before following her into slumber.

28

Waking, warmly wrapped in a cocoon, Belle slowly blinked her eyes open. The room was still dark, but just like every morning, her body knew when sunrise was near. Twisting her head, she saw the dark scruff of Hunter's square jaw, his blue eyes open, staring at her.

"Hey," she said, softly, her hand curling on his shoulder.

"Hey," he replied, his smile wide.

"I thought I might oversleep."

"Baby, you never oversleep," he replied on a grin.

She leaned forward, touching her lips to his. He groaned and slid his arms around her, cupping the back of her head to angle it so that he could slide his tongue in and gain maximum contact. After a moment, he pulled back, and reminded, "Babe, the sunrise."

She slid her hand from his shoulder to cup his jaw, her eyes pinned on him. "If I could wake up like this every morning, I'd never have to wait on the sunrise to know I had everything I could ever want."

His blue eyes darkened and he rolled on top of her and they welcomed the dawn in a new way, one that she realized, even if repeated, would remain her favorite sunrise christening ever.

Their early morning activities had taken time and caused Belle to hustle getting ready for work. "I wish I didn't have to go in today," she complained, pulling on her nursing scrubs.

Hunter kept his eyes on her, smiling as she ran a brush through her hair and twisted it back, securing it away from her face. She moved to the rack that held her ribbons and selected a deep green one to match her scrubs.

"I like those," he said, gaining her attention as she twisted to look at him over her shoulder. "Your ribbons. You always match them to your scrubs."

Her lips curved upward and she said, "My grandma gave me ribbons for my birthday and Christmas. She didn't have much money, but she always gave me ribbons to tie in my hair. It became habit...one I'm not willing to break."

Her face scrunched in thought and he asked, "What's goin' through your mind?"

"Mr. Weldon said that I can wear business clothes now that I'm the head nurse and don't have floor duties like I did. But, that's not what I want. For one thing, scrubs are the only work clothes I have and I sure can't afford to go buy a whole new wardrobe. Plus," she sighed, "he and I have a few things to work out before I worry about clothes."

"Things not okay at work?"

Lifting her shoulders, she said, "I really like Mr. Weldon, but since the whole mess with Linda blew up, he's been almost frantic trying to get things back on track and he's become forgetful. You know that watch that had been stolen from Mr. Rosenberg?"

He nodded, his eyes concerned. "Yeah. What about it?"

"Well, another resident, Mrs. Martinez, is missing something and when I mentioned it to Mr. Weldon, he assured me he would report it. Then I checked with Mitch and Colt and he hadn't reported either event."

"I don't want you worrying about that," he said. "You've got enough on your plate. I'll talk to Colt."

"I've already talked to him—"

"And I'll follow up." He stood and placed his hands on her shoulders and turned her body so that it was facing him. "We got shit to talk about but you've got to get to work so I'll have a chat with Colt."

"Talk about?"

Nodding, he said, "Yeah. About us, where we're going and what to do to make all this work."

"Oh…"

He observed her furrowed brow and smoothed it with his fingers. Bending, he kissed her hair and said, "Don't worry, babe. We'll talk tonight. It'll be good, I promise."

Hunter shook hands with Colt as he entered the Sherriff's Office. Taking the chair offered, he asked, "Everything okay here?"

Colt nodded, his dark, intelligent eyes piercing as he leaned back in his chair. "Got about five of them in the holding cells. Brittany's mom is detoxing at the hospital, but under arrest. Talked to the County Attorney this morning and she's ready to kick ass and take names."

Chuckling, he grinned. "Good. Get that section of the park cleaned up and it'll be a great place for families." Sobering for a moment, he sighed, saying, "Of course, people like Brittany's mom will always find a supplier."

"How the hell she could have offered her daughter as payment..."

They sat silent for a moment, the enormity of the situation and how it could have turned out so different, moving through them.

Finally, Colt asked, "All good with Belle?"

His eyes jumped to Colt's, but he saw a flash of humor there. "Hope so. Got a lot of shit swirling right now with her new duties, what happened at Careway, what happened with Brittany, and all that on top of our mess."

He noted Colt did not ask anything else, so he volunteered, "She knows we got more to talk about, but as of last night, things are a lot better."

"Good," he said, before asking, "Anything special bring you here today, besides all the shit from last night?"

"Told Belle I'd check with you about what she reported about the possible thefts from Careway."

"Yeah, went to the pawn shop. The owner wasn't real keen on talking but he was easily swayed when presented with the possibility of me parking a deputy outside his establishment."

"Can you tell me anything? 'Cause when she told me that she was afraid Weldon wasn't reporting, I got suspicious about him being involved."

"It was a young man who brought in the pocket watch and after a little more pressure, he admitted it was the same man who brought in the necklace. I did not talk to Belle about it, not wanting to involve her at this point in the investigation, but we're looking into it. There isn't an employee at Careway that fits the description, so we are assuming someone there is taking the items and handing them off to an accomplice who takes them to the pawn shop." Colt pierced him with a stare, again asking, "You suspect Weldon?"

Shaking his head, he said, "From what I saw of Weldon when I was working there he is an upstanding man who manages a tight, well-run home. I never got a feeling about him that he was involved in anything negative at all, but I gotta admit, I hate like hell that he did not report the last theft when it might have been in time for you to find out who was stealing."

"I will tell you that one of my detectives, Carson, thinks he's located the man and is looking at his friends to see who might work at Careway."

He cast his mind back to the employees, wondering who might be the thief.

Finishing her reports, Belle walked into the dining room at lunchtime. She smiled at the residents and other nurses. Weaving through the tables, she nodded toward Mr. Weldon who also moved around the tables, checking on the residents, joking with some, pouring water for others, and keeping conversations flowing.

She walked over to him and said, "Excuse me, Mr. Weldon. The reports that you needed were sent to your email."

His smile widened and he gushed, "Oh, Belle, thank you so much. You are a true gem."

"You just now figuring that out?" Mr. Rasky asked. "I could have told you that a couple of years ago!"

The others at the table laughed and Mr. Weldon nodded emphatically. "I knew it then, but know it even more now."

He turned toward her and whispered, "Do you know where Nola is? She should be in here assisting and I haven't seen her."

"No, but I'll go see if I can find her." With his nod, she walked out of the dining room and went in search of the errant nursing aide. Checking the employee lounge, she found it empty. Turning a corner, she caught sight of Nola coming from one of the resident's room, sticking something in her pocket.

Curious, as well as suspicious, she followed Nola as she walked down the hall, glad for her quiet, rubber-soled shoes. Reaching the next corner, she slowed and peeked around, seeing her at the back door. She watched as Nola pushed against the door bar before propping a small piece of wood in the frame to keep the door from locking behind her.

She hurried down the hall, stopping at the side of the door, peering out the window, spying Nola standing in the parking lot, staring down at what appeared to be a pearl necklace in her hand. Stunned, she realized Nola was the thief, but before she had a chance to think what to do, she watched as a black pickup truck pulled up to her and a man got out.

Gasping, she slipped outside and saw the driver hold out his hand and Nola dropping the pearls into it before standing on her toes and accepting a kiss from the young man. He slid his ball cap back from his forehead and grinned. "Looks good, Nola girl. I'll see you tonight."

Not wanting to lose him, she ran toward them, screaming, "Stop! Give that back!"

Nola whirled around, eyes huge, and screamed, "Shit, Frank, go! Go!"

Instead of leaving, his face hardened and he pulled out a gun, pointing it at her and firing, the sounds of Nola's screams filling the air.

29

Hunter stood and shook Colt's hand before walking to the door. "Thanks for everything, Colt—"

"Sheriff Hudson!" a deputy called out, rounding the corner. "Multiple calls came in of a shooting at Careway Nursing Home. Detective Carson is on the scene. The man he was tailing was making a pickup from a female employee and when approached by another employee, he shot her before taking off. We've got three units in pursuit and ambulance dispatched."

His heart dropped as Colt barked, "We got a name on who was shot?"

The deputy shook his head as he headed back toward the front of the office. Hunter began running down the hall, his phone in his hand, calling Belle. No answer.

"Hunter!" Colt called out behind him.

He turned around and saw Colt jogging toward him, his phone at his ear, speaking to someone.

"Yeah, yeah. Got it. I'll tell him."

Observing Colt's hard jaw, fear clawed at his throat, and he ordered, "Talk to me."

Colt's face fell as he said, "It was Belle. She caught someone named Nola Slidell handing off stolen jewelry to Frank Hensey, Nola's boyfriend. Instead of leaving, Frank pulled a gun and shot Belle. We're in pursuit of Frank and Nola's been arrested at the scene."

Lightheaded, his heart jolted. "Fuck! Oh, fuck. Where is she?"

"Zac's got her in the ambulance, taking her to the hospital."

As he started to dart out, Colt grabbed his arm. "You're riding with me. I'll get you there faster, I promise."

Barely aware of the sirens blaring, he sat, numb, as Colt raced down the highway toward the hospital. The scenery passed by without his noticing, his mind solely on the woman he knew would be fighting for her life at the end of the ride.

The surgical waiting room was packed but, with a number of the visitors wearing uniforms and badges, the staff said nothing about the overcrowding.

Colt stood with Mitch, whose arm was around Tori, taking her weight as she leaned into him. Gareth and Grant had their arms around their wives, as Jillian and Katelyn held hands. Jade looked up as Lance walked in, having just been relieved by another officer. Aiden stood with Ginny and Brogan. Callan stepped off the elevator, heading straight to Zac and Madelyn.

Hunter, alone, stood by a window staring out into the night. It had been hours since Belle had been brought in, a gunshot wound to the gut. He kept one hand in his pocket, his fingers twining around the yellow hair ribbon he still carried with him. He sucked in a ragged breath, his eyes lifting to the heavens. He had never been particularly religious, but he prayed nonetheless. For her life...for a second chance...for another sunrise with her.

Belle opened her eyes slowly, pressing her thumb on the patient-controlled analgesia pump, delivering the small, but needed, dose of morphine. Inhaling gently, she tried to ignore the pain as she turned her head to the side, seeing the sun barely peeking in through the blinds. The slim light gave evidence to a man sleeping in the chair by the window, his head reclining to the side in what must be a painfully uncomfortable position. She was awake yesterday, just long enough for her to whisper a plea for him to leave and sleep in a real bed, but Hunter stubbornly insisted he would not leave her side.

Four days. It had been four days since she stood outside of Careway, indignant at seeing Nola hand a stolen necklace and was giving it to a man. Four days since she had foolishly charged ahead to interrupt the deal. Four days since she had stared at the barrel of his gun pointed directly at her and heard the deafening sound of it being fired. Four days since she spent six hours in surgery as the doctors fought to save her life. She did not remember the first couple of days, yesterday being the first that she began to understand what was happening.

And now, she stared at the man in the chair, a heavy scruff covering his face and his hair standing on end as he had spent a great deal of time running his hand through it.

The pain medicine was easing through her system and she looked up as the door opened. One of the nurses walked over and checked her vital signs.

Bending near her, the nurse whispered, "Hey Belle. I'm Carol. I've been with you since the first day, but I'm sure you don't remember me."

"Nice to meet you," she whispered back, unsure if her gut would hurt with the effort of talking. "How am I?"

Carol grinned. "I know you're a nurse, so I'll give it to you straight and then have the doctor come in a talk to you as well. The bullet missed your major organs, so the blood loss and internal trauma, as well as the surgery, is what you'll be dealing with in your convalescence. Your vital signs are good and you're currently on IV antibiotics to fight against possible infection." She glanced to the PCA pump and said, "You've been on IV pain medication and now you can control it more yourself. The idea is to wean you off the morphine and to use it only when you need it."

Continuing to whisper, she asked, "How long will I be here?"

"I'd say at least four or five more days, but that'll depend on what the doctor says about your recovery and your plan for when you return home."

"I live alone—"

"I'll be with her to help care for her," Hunter said, sitting up in the chair, his blue eyes penetrating the fog surrounding her.

She opened her mouth to speak, but he got there first, standing to lean over her bed, his hand, strong and warm on her forehead, smoothing her hair back. "Four days, babe. Four sunrises sitting here wondering if I was ever going to have another sunrise with you. No way in hell will I squander one more sunrise."

She blinked, not feeling pain but having the urge to cry nonetheless. Staring at all that was him, she blinked again.

"I'll be there," he repeated.

As the pain medication did its magic, his hand cupping her face and his words in her ears helped her slip into another deep sleep.

———

"Hey, girl," the call from the door rang out.

Belle looked up as Tori, Jade, Jillian, Katelyn, Madelyn, and Ginny walked into her hospital room. Still hooked up to several machines, with a few drainage tubes connected to her abdomen, she knew she looked like shit, but was unable to keep the smile from her face.

She wanted to sit up, but moving the bed to a reclining position was the best she could do. Weakness from loss of blood kept her still most of the day and night.

They fanned out into the room, Katelyn immediately sliding into a nearby chair. Belle's hand wandered to her hair, once more realizing how horrible she must appear.

"Stop," Jillian said. "You look beautiful."

Snorting, then wincing, she said, "I'm sure I don't, but thanks all the same."

"Well, we came armed with some things to make you feel better," Tori said, her smile wide as she held up a few bags.

Curious, she grinned as she watched her friends pull out dry shampoo, a comb and brush, and several of her ribbons. Relaxing back into the pillow, she allowed them to pamper her as they sprayed and combed her hair before Jillian braided it, tying it off with a pink ribbon.

"Hunter said they're getting you up to walk some today," Madelyn said, her lifted brows indicating her surprise.

Nodding, she said, "At least to go to the bathroom." They were ready to take the catheter after reporting she had no more blood in her urine and as much as she dreaded the pain, she wanted to get out of bed, if just to pee. Keeping this tidbit to herself, she asked, "So what else is in those bags?"

Katelyn grinned as she leaned over and pulled out body wash and deodorant.

"Oh, my goodness," she cried, her smile widening.

Her gaze then dropped to Katelyn's smaller stomach and she gasped.

Katelyn grinned, saying, "Yep. Yesterday, we welcomed Gareth Finn Harrison into the family."

Her eyes filled with tears. "How are you—"

Katelyn rose from her chair gingerly and moved to the bed, grasping her hand. "Shhh. I'm fine, baby's fine. He's sleeping right now in my mom's arms and I can't wait for you to meet him. I wanted to come visit before I get discharged."

"I can't believe you all are here," she said, trying to keep the tears at bay.

"We're here to pamper you," Jade said, "so just lay back and let us do the work."

At first self-conscious, she soon closed her eyes and allowed her friends to give her a sponge bath on her arms and legs, before she slicked on the deodorant, loving the scent of both. "This makes me feel human again," she enthused, thanking them profusely, despite her weakness.

"Do you know when you'll be able to get out of here?" Ginny asked.

"Not only will I start getting up and walking this afternoon, but I'm also going to start on some solid food. Probably soft, easy stuff, but they want my digestive system working, so probably about two more days." She rolled her eyes and said, "I'm ready to be out of here, but know that it'll be a while before I'm back to normal."

"How are you and Hunter?" Jillian asked, her eyes mirroring the other women's, warm with concern.

Sucking in her lips, she inhaled deeply then winced at the pain. Panting for a few seconds to ease the discomfort, she observed their concern. "Sorry, when the pain meds are working I forget to move easy." Thinking for a moment about Jillian's question, she finally said, "He's been here every day. I don't know how since he's got a job to do in Richmond, but honestly, I haven't asked about that. He told the nurse that he would be taking care of me when I'm discharged. I know he said he had vacation to take when he first came back, but I don't know when that will be gone."

"Are you okay with that?" Jade asked softly.

She fiddled with the thin hospital blanket for a moment, deciding how much to confess, before lifting her gaze and staring at each one of them. All friends. All women that she had witnessed fall in love. All women that included her in their inner circle. A slow smile curved her lips and she said, "Just before this happened, we told each other that we still loved each other. But the morning that I got shot, he had stayed with me and said that after work we needed to talk. About what we were doing. That obviously never happened, so I have no idea what his thoughts are."

"You didn't see him in the waiting room," Jillian began.

Her anguished tone drew Belle's attention.

"He was a man haunted," Madelyn continued, sucking in a huge breath. "It gutted Zac to see him that way."

Her gaze drifted down again, her heart aching. She startled when Tori squeezed her hand.

"Don't try to figure it all out right now," Tori advised. "You need rest, you need to heal, you need—"

"To go to the bathroom on your own," Katelyn quipped, drawing laughter from them all.

"Oh, that hurts," she said between giggles. Glad that Katelyn had taken them away from the heavy topic of her and Hunter, she hugged them each as they stood to leave.

Hunter kept one hand on Belle's hip and the other around her shoulder, offering support, trying to keep from hurting her more. He observed the sheen of sweat on her pale face, her breath raspy, and her mouth tight with pain.

"I could fuckin' kill that asshole," he said under his breath, helping her shuffle to the bed. Twisting her body so that her back was to the mattress, he settled her, covering her legs with the blanket again.

After a few minutes of steadying her breathing, willing the pain to recede, Belle finally said, "Well, at least the good news is that I went to the bathroom." Grimacing, she added, "It should mortify me that you helped with that, but I don't think I have any modesty left."

Chuckling, he bent to kiss her forehead. "Babe, I'm so fuckin' glad you're breathing, there's nothing I won't help you with."

She watched him heft himself onto the mattress next to her and hold her gaze. "Hunter?"

"Right here, babe."

"We were supposed to talk...that day...you know."

"Yeah, I know."

"That was a week ago. I know you've got to get back to Richmond to work—"

"Don't worry about that."

She pinched her lips together, huffing. "But—"

Hunter reached down and took her hands in his, rubbing his thumbs over her soft skin. "Belle, babe. You need to heal and I'm gonna be here for that. Nothing else matters. We'll talk, but later. Right now, you concentrate on you and we'll deal with whatever comes when it comes." Bending closer, he asked, "Can you do that for me?"

He watched her nod slowly, her dark eyes holding his gaze, and he moved in, kissing her lightly. "I'll take you home when you get discharged tomorrow, yeah?"

"Yeah," she whispered, a slight smile curving her lips.

Kissing her once again, he met her smile.

30

TWO WEEKS LATER

Belle wandered out of her bedroom, her gait stronger every day. Stopping at the end of the hall, she stared at Hunter standing in her kitchen. Wrapping her arms around her waist, pressing slightly against her injury site, she could not help but gawk.

His hair was longer, starting to curl at the ends. His muscles strained against the tight cotton of his T-shirt. Her lip caught between her teeth as her gaze dropped lower, appreciating the way the cargo pants encased his ass.

He turned, his eyes widening for a second at seeing her standing in the hall, before he broke into a wide grin. "Good to see you up and about, babe. Hungry?"

"You're spoiling me, Hunter," she said as she walked into the kitchen. She strained to not limp, forcing her body to stretch out the tight muscles. Having seen his eyes darken often in the past couple of weeks when he looked at her, she so wanted to return to some normalcy.

"Hurtin'?"

She should have known he would be watching carefully. He had barely left her side since she was shot over three weeks ago. "Not much. I made it through the night with no ibuprofen. Little twinges as I first start moving in the morning, but still a helluva lot better."

The creases in his face relaxed and he walked over, his arms pulling her in for a hug. They stood for several minutes before he kissed the top of her head and stepped away.

"Breakfast is almost ready."

She settled at the table, looking askance at the amount of food he plated for her. She opened her mouth, but he jumped in.

"You gotta get some weight back on you, Belle. Not to mention, getting your strength back up."

"The doc says I'm doing fine," she said, telling him something he already knew considering he was right with her at the follow-up appointment. "I'm hoping to be able to go back to work next month."

He nodded as he moved to get her cup of coffee. She fiddled with her napkin, wondering how to bring up what she really wanted to ask.

"I can tell you got something on your mind, babe," he commented, setting her cup on the table and, with one hand on the back of her chair, leaning down to kiss her lightly on the lips. "Let's have it."

Sighing, she said, "Hunter, I've loved having you here, but what about work? I know you have to be at the end of your vacation time. In fact, I'm sure you've extended it."

He sat down next to her, his blue eyes intensely staring into hers, and said, "After breakfast, how about we take a little drive?"

She thought his request was a strange way to deflect her prodding, but simply nodded, thinking how much it would be nice to get out of her house and get some fresh air. Watching the smile curing his lips, she began eating, anxious for their excursion.

Hunter turned off the main road, just north of Baytown, and pressed on the brakes slowly so that he was able to maneuver the curves in the road without jiggling Belle in the passenger side. She was quiet, her eyes taking in the scenery as they approached the end of the lane.

She had asked him about the black SUV he was driving, and he had informed her that he had bought it. "Can't have you riding on the back of my motorcycle for a while, babe. Anyway, I needed something else."

Turning onto an oyster-shell drive, they wound through a grove of pine trees into a small clearing. He heard her gasp as she stared out the windshield and his heart pounded at what he was going to say.

Parking next to his camper, he squeezed her hand and climbed down from the driver's side before rounding the hood and opening her door. Carefully lifting her from the cab of his truck, he continued to carry her to his camper. Instead of going inside, he walked around the back where he had a small, wooden-plank deck with two lawn chairs.

Setting her feet on the solid wood, he assisted her into one of the chairs. Her eyes were wide as they stared at the bay over the sea-grass covered dune.

"You moved your camper," she stated unnecessarily. "I would ask why, but this is gorgeous."

He chuckled, saying, "I looked at a lotta land, but this is close to Baytown and was available, so…"

"You bought this property?" she asked, her voice raised in surprise, twisting around to look at him.

"Yeah."

Eyes wide with her mouth hanging open, she tucked a wind-blown strand of hair behind her ear, and asked, "But…your job? I don't understand."

"I was going to talk to you that day that you got shot, but well…afterward, I just wanted you to focus on getting better." He knelt so she was directly in front of him, his arms wrapped around her, holding her closely. "I quit the State Police—"

Another gasp left her lips as she gave a start, blinking at his words. "But—"

"I can't live and work in Richmond when my heart is here with you." A smile gentled his face and he continued, "So, I've been hired by the North Heron Sheriff's Department. I work for Colt now."

"You…you're staying?"

"Belle, I fell in love with you and there's nowhere else I'd rather be. So, I bought some land and brought my camper out here so that we can enjoy it when we get a chance as our house is being built."

Eyes now bugging out, she stammered, "H-house… our house?"

"Gonna give you your dream, babe. A real house, on our own piece of land. One with an upstairs and downstairs. One with a front porch that'll hold a swing, and a back deck, where the breeze off the bay can keep us cool."

Tears flowed freely as Belle peered into his face, his blue eyes holding her gaze. Leaning forward, she threw her arms around his neck, kissing him with all the joy she had inside.

31

SIX MONTHS LATER

The activity room in Careway was filled with wheel-chairs lined on either side, mixed with a multitude of guests sitting in white folding chairs. At the front of the room was a simple, wooden archway, draped with ivory sheers and flowers.

Hunter stood underneath the archway, his blue eyes pinned to the back of the room. To one side stood Zac, Jason, Mitch, Brogan, Aiden, and Grant. On the other side, already having walked down the middle aisle, were Jillian, Madelyn, Tori, Jade, Ginny, and Katelyn.

Most of their parents, as well as other members of the American Legion and Auxiliary, were sprinkled among the Careway residents.

He thought over the last six months and knew the decision to join the North Heron Sheriff's Department was the right move to make. He had finally settled into the new job and spent more time with friends. Baytown continued to be a place of welcome and the care they had shown Belle when she had been shot overwhelmed him. He closed his eyes for just a second at that thought. He had finally gotten to the place where he did not see her lying near death in the hospital bed constantly. But when his eyes strayed to the scar on her stomach, his heart still jolted.

Zac's elbow against his arm caused his eyes to jump open and the doors in the back opened again. His breath caught in his throat, but this time it was awe that held his attention. There, dressed in a simple ivory wedding gown, stood the most beautiful woman he had ever seen, escorted by a beaming Mr. Rasky, wheeling next to her. The unadorned, layered, silk dress fell to her knees, swirling as Belle walked toward him. Her long hair was pulled up in a swirl of curls and tendrils falling to frame her face, with ivory ribbons threaded amongst the tresses. Her eyes stayed pinned on him and he forced his knees to lock for fear he would drop to the floor in awe of her as she neared.

When she reached the front, he could see the nervousness in her eyes and stepped forward taking her hand from Mr. Rasky.

The minister said, "Mr. Rasky, I believe you would like to say something?"

Belle's eyes widened, just as surprised as he was. This had not been part of the rehearsal. He drew her closer to him, turning her slightly so they were both facing the older man.

Clearing his throat, Mr. Rasky said, "Didn't have any daughters, so I never got to do this. Shocked as hell when you asked me to give you away. But, then, it seemed right, 'cause if I had had a daughter, I would have wanted her to be just like you."

He felt Belle's shoulder begin to quiver and he wrapped his arm around her protectively.

"So, Belle, you can tell the impact you have on people when you have a gathering like this, all willing to call you their own. You got friends, you got family. Might not be the family you were born into, but you got family." He then turned his eyes toward him and said, "I knew when I first met you what kind of man you were, and I was not wrong. No one better for this woman. So, I'm pleased to give her to you."

At that, Belle bent, embracing Mr. Rasky, her eyes filled with tears. With a final pat on her back, he rolled back to sit next to Ms. Betina.

Saying their vows, the ceremony was soon over, and he leaned down to kiss his bride. Stopping just before his lips hit hers, he whispered, "From now on, every sunrise is yours." Before she had a chance to burst into tears, he stole her breath with a kiss.

Two Years Later

The high school auditorium was filled with parents and students. Graduation was a week away, but the Senior Awards Ceremony was taking place and Belle sat with

Hunter near the front. Multitudes of awards and scholarships earned were handed out.

Finally, the principal stood and said, "Each year, we have a senior give a speech and it is our honor to have the teachers and students choose the person they think exemplifies the Senior Class. This year, I am pleased that the student chosen has received a full scholarship to the university of her choice and has received many awards today. She is a teen volunteer at Careway Nursing Home and has donated numerous hours to the local battered women's shelter. It's my honor to present to you today, Miss Brittany Barton."

She and Hunter clapped heartedly, along with everyone else, as Brittany stepped up to the podium, nervously looking over the crowd. Brittany's eyes landed on Belle sitting in the front, and smiled, her beautiful face glowing.

"On this road we call life, there are many twists and turns, bumps and potholes, one-ways and detours, yields and stops. And sometimes as we travel this life road, we wonder where we're going and how we'll get there. If we're lucky, we have family in our lives that guide us, point us in the right direction, give us a helping hand over the bumps and holes, assist our decisions when we come to an intersection. For some of us though, our birth family is unable or incapable of filling that role in our lives. When that happens, we have to turn to others to point the way.

"I was fortunate that many years ago, I lived near such a person. Someone who took the time to get to know me. Someone who told me I was beautiful and smart and worthy. Took the time to make sure I had breakfast before school. Someone who drove me to the bus stop when I was afraid. Someone who gave me a safe place to hang out when things at home became too difficult. Someone who clothed me when they saw a need.

"Someone who taught me that each new day is a beginning and that the possibilities are endless. And, especially, one night when my world crashed, someone who took my hand and did not let go, helping me onto another road that was paved with goodness."

Belle's breath caught in her throat and Hunter's arm snaked around her shoulders, pulling her toward his strength. She pressed her fingers to her lips in a futile attempt to keep the tears from falling.

"There are other people I have met on my life's road who have offered assistance as well. Teachers, my wonderful foster parents, a dear social worker, friends. But, I will always cherish the one person who reached out to me first, taking the hand of a scared little girl and showing her the way to a better life. She taught me to dream, and to work as hard as I could to make that dream come true. Her grandmother gave her that advice and now I pass it on to you.

"You can be what you want, but it all starts with a dream. So, I encourage you to find the people in your life who can help you on your journey. For me, Belle, you will always have my eternal gratitude and the only way I can return the gift is to let you know that I will pass it on to someone else and help them through their life."

The audience erupted into cheers, but Belle only heard the beating of her heart and the feel of Hunter's arm holding her tight.

One Year Later

Hunter rolled over, not surprised to find that the other side of the bed was empty. He lifted his head and viewed Belle sitting on the deep cushion of the window seat, tucked underneath the large bay window in their bedroom. Her face was turned to the side as she watched the sun rise.

His smile broadened, staring at the serene expression on her face as she held their baby boy. She was whispering, and he did not have to hear her words clearly to know that she was telling him about the new day dawning and the possibilities that it could bring.

He leaned his head up, propped on his hand with his elbow on the pillow, and stared, unsure he could take the idea of more possibilities. That Dan Simmons' son had made a good life for himself. That such beauty was his. A family was his. This house on the beach was his. He had a good job and good friends.

She turned her head and noticed him staring at her. A smile curved the corners of her lips and she glanced down at the now-sleeping bundle in her arms before looking back up and mouthing, "I love you."

"Love you too, babe," he whispered. His gaze drifted to the window behind her and he watched the sky turn shades of lighter blue, creating a halo behind her head. Tossing back the covers, he rose from the bed and padded over to her, looking down at their sleeping son. "I'll put him back down," he whispered again and gently lifted the baby from her arms. He bent to take her lips in a soft kiss before turning and walking out of the room toward the nursery.

Belle's eyes followed Hunter until he was out of sight, but the glory of her man carrying their son almost seared her eyes, so she turned back to stare out the window. As the sun rose over her house, setting on their piece of land, having an upstairs and a downstairs, a front porch with a swing, and a back deck, where the breeze off the bay kept them cool, she smiled.

"I dreamed, Grannie. I dreamed, and I worked hard. And now," she whispered, turning her head toward Hunter as he walked back into the room, "I have it all."

Standing, she moved back to the bed and they climbed in together, making the most of their time before the sun rose higher.

For the next Baytown Boys
Hear My Heart

He was ready to give up the party life.

After years of no commitments with the vacationing

women who visited his family's pub, Aiden MacFarlane yearned for more out of life.

But for single mom, Lia Smith, the last thing she was interested in was the town's Peter Pan.

First impressions were not favorable… for either of them, but eventually see what lies beneath the surface.

Her job is to find out who might be stealing money from the town and knows her investigation will ruffle feathers. As Aiden falls for Lia and her adorable daughter, he takes on the role of protector when she is threatened.

Will Aiden be able to save them before someone takes away his chance to truly live life to the fullest?

Please take the time to leave a review of this book. Feel free to contact me, especially if you enjoyed my book. I love to hear from readers!

Facebook

Email

Website

Jaxon

Jayden

Asher

Zeke

Cas

Lighthouse Security Investigations

Mace

Rank

Walker

Drew

Blake

Tate

Hope City (romantic suspense series co-developed

with Kris Michaels

Brock book 1

Sean book 2

Carter book 3

Brody book 4

Kyle book 5

Ryker book 6

Rory book 7

Killian book 8

Saints Protection & Investigations

(an elite group, assigned to the cases no one else wants…or
can solve)

Serial Love

Healing Love

Revealing Love

Seeing Love

Honor Love

Sacrifice Love

Protecting Love

Remember Love

Discover Love

Surviving Love

Celebrating Love

Follow the exciting spin-off series:

Alvarez Security (military romantic suspense)

Gabe

Tony

Vinny

Jobe

SEALs

Thin Ice (Sleeper SEAL)

SEAL Together (Silver SEAL)

Letters From Home (military romance)

Class of Love

Freedom of Love

Bond of Love

The Love's Series (detectives)

Love's Taming

Love's Tempting

Love's Trusting

The Fairfield Series (small town detectives)

Emma's Home

Laurie's Time

Carol's Image

Fireworks Over Fairfield

Please take the time to leave a review of this book. Feel free to contact me, especially if you enjoyed my book. I love to hear from readers!

Facebook

Email

Website

Made in the USA
Las Vegas, NV
10 February 2022

43560911R00194